THE
FIRST
COVENANT

DARK UNIVERSE SERIES #2

ALEX SHEPPARD

My girls—brawn and brains, and everything else.

THE
FIRST
COVENANT

Introduction to Dark Universe

Picking up the second or third book in a series always gets me debating — should I re-read the previous book(s) or should I jump into the new one and try to recall things as I go? While writing this book, I've wondered how to best relieve my readers of a similar dilemma.

After much thought, I settled on a super short re-cap. There's also a glossary — a detailed compilation of people, places, and other terms present in The Last Stryker — to refer to as needed.

If you remember most events in The Last Stryker, simply skip to the first chapter: Somenvaar.

<u>The Story So Far</u>

Ten years have passed since the Locusta-Vanga War. The invasion by the deadly Locustans had pushed the galaxy to the brink of extinction. It took a lot of valor and sacrifice to drive the Locustans away and finally the galaxy has settled back into a peaceful cadence.

The *Endeavor*, a battleship-turned-freighter commanded by Terenze Milos, the hero of the Locusta-Vanga War and former member of the Confederate Space Command stumbles on a debris field in a remote star system. They find a lone surviving space-fighter and the crew hauls it in.

A few days later, Ramya Kiroff, the seventeen-year-old heir of House Kiroff runs away from her educational institute, the CAWStrat, to avoid being forced into a marriage of convenience by her influential father, Trysten Kiroff.

While running away from CAWStrat and the clutches of her iron-fisted father, Ramya comes across a mugging in a deserted alleyway of the nearest spaceport. She chases off the thugs beating a man who turns out to be someone from the *Endeavor*. Hiding her true identity, she offers to work in lieu of a spot on the ship and becomes an apprentice to the ship's medic, Sosa.

Ramya discovers the *Endeavor's* crew is on its way to meet the leader of the Confederate Space Command to hand over a craft—a space fighter they call a Stryker—salvaged from a debris field. The man Ramya saved is actually the Stryker's pilot, Habardein.

Habardein recognizes Ramya as Trysten Kiroff's daughter. He tells her that the Kiroffs had a factory in Sector 22 where they were secretly building the Strykers. However, something went wrong during the trials and of the five Strykers, four attacked the GSO space fleet protecting the area, destroyed them, and vanished. He chalks this up to a call from the Locustans. He warns of an impending Locustan invasion before falling back into a coma.

Captain Milos suspects Trysten Kiroff was experimenting with alien technology of the Locustans. He is worried because Locustans had deadly ways of proliferating their genetics, which the Confederacy didn't quite understand yet tinkered with. He wants to hand the Stryker to Confederate Space Command as soon as possible.

On their way to meeting with Admiral Kanaa of Space Command at Alameda, a GSO ship intercepts the *Endeavor*. Lieutenant Gael Arlington of the GSO, who is evidently in the employ of Trysten Kiroff, commands it. Ramya also recognizes Gael as the man she danced with at the last gala at CAWStrat.

Trysten Kiroff demands Captain Milos hand him the Stryker and not to Admiral Kanaa. When the captain refuses, Lieutenant Arlington tries to board the *Endeavor* and take the Stryker by force. However, the *Endeavor* escapes.

Captain Milos rushes to meet the Admiral but in a roundabout way to give Trysten Kiroff the slip. In the meantime, the Stryker that had not allowed anyone inside it so far allows Ramya access after detecting her Kiroff genetics. Inside the craft, Ramya meets Dakrhaeth, the AI of the Stryker, a Locustan entity known as the Viriskshi. Dakrhaeth warns her that the four missing Strykers are intent on weakening the galaxy from within while the Locustan forces prepare for the second invasion. He pleads her to not give the Stryker away to Admiral Kanaa and warns that the admiral will not spare the *Endeavor* or its crew when they try to hand the Stryker to her.

Captain Milos changes his plan to meet the admiral at Alameda. Instead, he decides to drop the Stryker off at the adjoining star system of Totori and then inform the admiral of its location. However, Admiral Kanaa is already waiting with a powerful fleet when the *Endeavor* reaches Totori. Captain Milos tries to convince the admiral of the real threat — the impending second invasion by the Locustans.

Admiral Kanaa ignores the captain's warning and orders her fleet to attack the *Endeavor*. The captain orders Ramya to take off in the Stryker and save the Endeavor from the fleet's attack. Piloting the Stryker, Ramya, with the help of Dakrhaeth and Commander Ross, fights the massive Drednots of the admiral's fleet and wins.

However, during the battle, the Stryker is separated from the *Endeavor*. Ross believes the captain will land the battered *Endeavor* on a nearby habitable planet; the most viable possibility is a Mwandan sanctuary on Morris II. Ramya steers the Stryker toward Morris II, a planet in the Kashiyap system.

SOMENVAAR

The Kiroff castle Somenvaar, the centerpiece of the family's expansive holdings along the Batacan Coast, was a sight that made every spectator hold their breath. With a shimmery white façade crafted with the rarest sandstone quarried from a planet two systems beyond, and the spires and turrets that rose from its sculpted midsection, the castle could easily belong in a fairytale. Popular fantasies often swirl and grow with abandon around powerful people and their fanciful abodes, and Somenvaar, the unofficial power center in the galaxy, was nothing short of a living legend.

The summer morning was glorious and young, only an hour or two away from turning into a sweltering day. Trysten Kiroff stood in his office—a massive room with a semicircular glass wall that soared twenty feet above him—and stared out at the deep blue waters of the Berianic Seas. Although his blue-gray eyes reflected the gentle waves that crashed along the golden shorelines, he felt nothing but anger roiling within him. If he could, he'd smash up a few things to let that anger ease a bit. No one would stand in his way. He was king of his keep; he could do as he pleased. But Trysten Kiroff knew better. Uncontrolled anger was the most useless thing in the universe. On the other hand, he could tame it, feed it, and use it, and there was nothing more powerful. He had wielded anger with absolute precision before, but this time was different.

Trysten's mouth stretched to lines as he pondered the setbacks he'd been handed in the past few weeks. First, the utter destruction of the GSO fleet and his factory in Sector 22. Then the missing Strykers. The worst was Milos, that grizzled, old buffoon, refusing to give up the one Stryker they'd tracked down.

Failures, one after the other. Trysten flinched at the thought. He was not used to failing. Teeth gritted, he reminded himself of the basics of power play he'd learned over the years. He couldn't let his frustration show, or his fear.

The universe—brutal and envious—was always watching. One crack and they'd descend like a pack of vultures on a prone carcass. They'd take away everything he'd built over the years.

Intent on subduing his frenzied thoughts, Trysten walked up and down along the glass wall scrutinizing the manicured gardens that lay between the sandy shore and the castle. Not a leaf out of place. Somenvaar, at least, was perfect, flawless. Or was it?

Trysten hated to admit it, but something was missing. Life . . . Somenvaar was missing a soul. This place, his home, was an empty shell. A beautiful, impeccable, but empty shell. He half turned to look at the life-sized portrait of his wife who was never present. Her liquid brown gaze was distant even in the picture and her petite nose tilted up as if in contempt. Lady Sonya, the famous socialite, spent most of her time galaxy trotting with her elite coterie of friends. Somenvaar didn't interest her, never had.

Trysten, however, liked to spend most of his time at the castle and that fondness was growing with every passing year. He often wondered why. Was it because he liked spending time with his rapidly aging mother, or was he getting too old to run around anymore as if he were in his twenties.

Neither! Trysten swiftly and expertly banished the sentimental thoughts that were threatening to encroach on his mind. He liked being at Somenvaar simply because it suited him. The first benefit was the appearance. His reluctance to travel outside his abode added to the air of mysticism around him. It kept him unreachable, a specter of boundless authority and infinite power. A myth was a good thing to have.

Besides, he didn't need to run around—a waste of valuable lieres and time—like his predecessors to keep on top of things. With technological advances, he was no less connected to any business aspect. For the most part, the Confederacy's vast communication network across the galaxies sufficed, but Trysten had also built his private networks to manage his business affairs, reserving traveling out of Somenvaar for the most important matters.

A gentle buzz sounded behind him and his brows furrowed. With a heavy, frustrated sigh, he turned and walked over to large desk that stood at the center of the room. A sizeable flashing button imbedded into the wooden desk was screaming for attention. Etched on the transparent surface was the word "Access." One of his men—had to be Wultoph—was outside, requesting permission to enter.

Trysten's grimaced as his finger hovered over the access button. Wultoph was not supposed to be here now, and it was likely that he hadn't brought good news. A week ago, five Strykers from Trysten's secret research center had gone rogue, destroyed an entire GSO fleet, and disappeared from the face of the galaxy. Since then, all Trysten and his men had been doing was trying to find the missing Strykers. With little luck.

The buzz sounded again, louder this time. "All right, all right," Trysten seethed under his breath. Part of him wanted to wish the man away, but he knew there was no wishing away the disaster at Sector 22. Whatever news—likely bad—Wultoph had brought had to be heard. There was no point in delaying the inevitable. Besides, he was Lord Paramount, not a weakling.

Trysten slammed his palm onto the button. The dark-grained panels between two massive bookcases on the opposite wall glided apart. Wultoph Aristide, wiry and anxious, rushed in, taking care to keep his gaze stuck to the floorboards. He stopped near the desk and quickly bowed.

"There's news," Wultoph said in a tight whispery voice, his gaze scooting across the shiny surface of the moshon-wood table. "There was a sighting of the *Endeavor*."

Trysten stiffened. *About time.* Two days ago, Trysten's agents had tracked down one of the five missing Strykers. A beat-up old freighter, the *Endeavor*, run by Terenze Milos, an ex-captain of the

Confederacy fleet, had picked it up from Sector 22. Trysten had asked Milos to return the Stryker back to him. Nicely too. But Milos, true to his honor-bound form, refused. He was going to deliver the Stryker to the Confederate Space Command and no one else. Trysten's men had had Milos cornered, but the old fool escaped, Stryker and all.

A moment of silence and then Trysten let the words leave his throat growling. "Where?"

Wultoph looked up, his startled brown eyes momentarily meeting Trysten's before they drooped again. "At Totori. They destroyed a Drednot."

Trysten let out a long sigh before waving distractedly at a chair across from him. "Sit, Wultoph," he said. Wultoph rushed to pull a chair. After he had sunk into it rather noisily, Trysten spoke again. "Now, explain."

"Admiral Kanaa met them at Totori. She had four Drednots with her. There was an encounter, and one Drednot was decimated."

Trysten pulled his chair and slowly lowered himself into its smooth yet firm embrace. None of it made much sense. He absentmindedly tapped the red folder on the desk.

"Why would they fight the Confederacy?" he said after a while. He didn't expect Wultoph to answer; speaking out loud was just a way to help his mind connect the dots. "Milos wanted to hand the Stryker over to the Confederacy. That's why he fought us."

Wultoph leaned forward, and for the first time, fixed a steady gaze on Trysten. "And why would the Confederacy bring four Drednots to the rendezvous?" he asked. "Why bring any Drednot at all? Unless —"

"The Confederacy was prepared for war," Trysten said, rising from his chair abruptly. He walked back to the glass wall and stared intently out at the incessant waves crashing on the shore. "Why? Did Milos refuse to give them the Stryker?"

There were too many questions. Even the normally unobtrusive and daft Wultoph was brimming with them.

"And why meet at Totori when Alameda is right next door?" Wultoph said.

He had a point. Totori was a nearby system . . . .

Even though there were far too few answers, Trysten had one for this particular problem. He turned toward Wultoph, smiling.

"It's Milos," he declared. "He had to have picked Totori because of the asteroid belt. That's one damn good spot to hide."

"But, Lord Paramount," Wultoph protested in a rare show of boldness, "why would Milos hide? He's the one who wanted to hand the Stryker over to the Confederacy."

"Something must've changed. He refused. The admiral attacked. What I don't understand is how an obsolete ship like the *Endeavor* could destroy a Drednot. Are you sure the information is correct?"

"Yes, I'm sure. A Drednot was destroyed. My source tells me that the Confederacy is about to declare the *Endeavor* a rogue ship and announce a bounty on it."

"What?"

Wultoph slinked backward into his chair, clearly rattled but his tone. Any other time, Trysten would've reveled at the effectiveness of his power over Wultoph, but not this day. Wultoph was a valuable tool — his House a trusty ally for three generations — and Trysten needed to keep him loyal at this critical juncture.

"Are you sure?" Trysten asked, his voice practiced and calm this time.

Wultoph nodded. "That's what my source said."

"We have to find them before the Confederacy does." Trysten rapped his desk, his mind racing once more to assess the possible damages if they failed.

"Don't worry, Lord Paramount. We'll find them," Wultoph said, nodding eagerly. His watery brown eyes brimmed with hope. "The Confederacy forces are stretched thin. Outside of the prime planetary regions, their presence is laughable at best. And that Milos is too crafty for the likes of Admiral Kanaa."

Trysten didn't want to scare Wultoph again, but he knew his cold gaze had turned glacial when he looked up at the man. "Milos is crafty for anyone, Wultoph. He's as smart as they come. Before he destroyed a Drednot, he slipped past us. He won't be an easy catch for anyone, including us. Keep that in mind."

"I-I . . . my apologies," Wultoph stuttered. "I understand."

"I hope you do," Trysten didn't bother to stop himself from snapping. Wultoph needed to wake up for his own good. "Do you realize what's at stake here? Everything — our status, our reputation — could be destroyed if the Confederacy gets its hands on the Stryker."

Trysten didn't say it out loud, but the fact was, they could even be tried at the Galactic Senate for toying with dangerous alien technology. And if proven guilty —

"What's the plan, Lord Paramount?" Wultoph interrupted at the perfect moment, scattering the fearful thoughts.

"Like I said, we find the Stryker before anyone else does. They couldn't have gone far after a brawl with four Drednots. Get people to look at every system around Totori."

"Already have. I have a team analyzing the region to determine a possible refuge."

"Good. Let's also get the core committee together. We need every ally working for us."

Wultoph shifted uneasily. "But . . . but they don't know about Sector 22. How —"

"We'll tell them it was confidential research. We'll tell them the Confederacy is trying to steal it from us. That has happened before, so it won't be hard to believe."

"What if they refuse to help when they hear about the Locustan bit?"

Trysten scoffed, and then let out a long chuckle. "When they understand how much money is to be made, they'll all fall in line. Besides, we don't need to share every detail with them. We can keep a few things out of the discussion."

"Understood," Wultoph said, hurrying to get out of his seat. "I shall get that arranged."

"Thank you."

Wultoph had almost reached the door when Trysten called. "Wait, there's one more thing I need you to do."

"Yes?"

"Find out more about Totori. I want to know the extent of damages on the downed Drednot. Find out. I don't care how much it costs."

"Yes, of course," Wultoph replied.

"Thank you."

The doors closed behind Wultoph, a hush engulfing Trysten once again. It was a welcome quiet, a needed pause to let him think.

Trysten Kiroff didn't become Lord Paramount in a day. He had worked his way up to the title, slowly acquiring riches, building influence, and then asserting it across the galaxy. He liked to think he had a sharp mind; his thoughts were ahead of most of his peers. Not being in control flustered him like nothing else. Now it was even worse. He could hardly make sense of what was going on.

What the hell was Milos up to? Was he planning to use the Stryker as leverage? Perhaps the man needed money. The Confederacy would pay handsomely to get their hands on the craft, and Trysten himself would happily part with a billion lieres.

No, Trysten struck that idea off. He had known Milos—his father's favored underling—most of his life. Milos was smart, brave, and scrupulous. Pawning things that didn't belong to him was not in Milos's nature. There had to be something else. But what?

Then there was the matter of the destroyed Drednot. That gnawed at him endlessly. The *Endeavor* was a Class II battleship from before the Locusta-Vanga war Even if Milos had it retrofitted with modern weapons, it couldn't stack up to a standard-built Drednot, a Class V model. It was impossible. Yet, it had happened. The *Endeavor* had fought and won a battle against not just one, but four mighty

Drednots. And destroyed one. That brought him to the even more unbelievable thought: What if it was not the *Endeavor's* doing? Could the Stryker have caused the damage?

Trysten quickly quashed the thought. It was impossible. The pilots chosen for the Stryker program had all been vetted thoroughly. It had taken years to find people who were just as loyal as they were skilled. These pilots would only answer to a Kiroff, and fly only for one. There was no way in hell a pilot would use the Stryker to attack a Confederacy ship. They'd know such action would compromise the program and they'd die a million deaths than do such a thing.

What if . . . what if the pilot was dead?

Could someone else — one of Milos's ratty crew — have flown the Stryker? But how? The Strykers were not just any spacecraft. They had been fused with Locustan Virikhshis, evolved AIs that wouldn't allow anyone to take control of the craft unless specifically programed to do so. In the development phase the Strykers were currently in, they were paired with just one person — the pilot — who could command the craft. Only one thing in the universe would supersede that: a Kiroff directive.

Trysten rapped the edge of his desk, trying to wither the frustration before it turned into an inferno in his head. This was an impossible situation. Perhaps this last Stryker had gone berserk just like they had earlier in Sector 22.

"Damn!" Trysten slapped the back of his chair while he ran his other hand through his hair. Were the Strykers a mistake? They had caused enough trouble already — wiped out an entire GSO fleet and killed thousands before going missing. And now, the one Stryker that still remained had mounted a direct assault on a Confederacy ship?

Trysten's mind almost ground to a halt as worries streamed in like a draft of frigid winter air and chilled his insides. Was this going to be the end of his illustrious career?

Trysten fell back into his chair and rubbed his temples. Even after the destruction of the GSO fleet at Sector 22, he had avoided the expected uproar, mostly because of his younger brother, Lynden. Fifteen years ago, Trysten had moved the stars to get Lynden into the High Council of the Confederacy. It had been a good move. The boy had done well to prevent fallout over the recent incident in Sector 22. So far, none of the nosey folk in the Senate had demanded an inquisition. Hell, people barely knew.

Trysten had hoped to find the missing Strykers while Lynden resisted the political consequences. But he hadn't expected the search to take so damn long. A full week had passed. What if Lynden couldn't hold out any longer?

Perhaps trying to get a rogue Stryker back was a waste of time. Maybe he had to start thinking of containing the fallout instead before it was too late. Perhaps it was time to cut ties? Maybe he could hush up the evidence that tied him to the Stryker?

No, not yet. He couldn't give up.

Trysten's fists curled into balls and his jaw tightened. He had done nothing wrong. The Confederacy had known what he was doing in Sector 22. Not every detail, but they had known he was investigating Locustan tech, yet they had not stopped him. They couldn't make a scapegoat out of him now that the experiment had hit a snag. He wasn't going to let them. He was going to find that Stryker and find out what happened in Sector 22.

But first he had to locate the *Endeavor.* Wultoph was already on the case, but he needed to do more . . . much more. Trysten angrily paced the room, brows furrowing deeper as he walked back and forth between the desk and the glass wall. On his sixth turn, he stopped abruptly and ran his fingers over a control panel on his desk. The air above the desk momentarily shimmered, and a minute or two later a holographic bust of a man wearing the blue uniform of the GSO appeared.

Trysten nodded to greet the man. "Lieutenant Gael Arlington."

"Lord Paramount Kiroff," the hologram nodded back.

"You took your time."

"You'd be surprised how slow I can be sometimes."

Trysten's eyes narrowed just a tad at his reply. Cheekiness was not unexpected from Gael Arlington and Trysten had learned to let things like that slip. To be dreadfully honest, he enjoyed the young man's pluck.

"Have you heard?" Trysten was purposefully tacit but the lieutenant seemed unfazed.

"If you mean the *Endeavor's* little encounter with the Confederacy fleet, then yes, I have."

A smile curled at the corner of Trysten's mouth. The affection he felt for this young lieutenant was odd. Gael was the son of his staunchest corporate enemy, Tuck Arlington. Not even a day ago, Gael had been beaten soundly by Milos. To top it all off, Gael was looking Trysten in the eye and being quite uninhibited in his responses, which would have sent Trysten into a fury, but for some reason he couldn't find a shred of anger inside him to hurl at the lieutenant.

"And what are you going to do about it?" Trysten said simply.

"Have you heard of Nebeca 21?" Gael asked.

Trysten relished the slight rush of adrenaline at Gael's words. Now they were getting somewhere. Just like he had hoped, Gael Arlington had thought of something out of the ordinary.

The man reminded Trysten so much of himself at that age. Bold and ambitious, Gael had been begging to be put in the spotlight when Trysten had first noticed him. It had taken a few inducements, including some long and unpleasant negotiations with Gael's stubborn and loud-mouthed father, Tuck, to secure House Arlington's loyalty, but Trysten had no doubt about the soundness of his decision. Every conversation was Gael was refreshing.

"Nebeca 21, eh?" Trysten said. "It's a space station off the Darren-Wu system, the last fueling stop between the inner colonies and the Fringe. What about it?"

"You said it. It's the last fueling station before the Fringe. And the one notorious for its lax security," Gael replied. "If the Confederacy flags the *Endeavor* a rogue, where do you think they'll go?"

Trysten chuckled. No doubt the lieutenant was planning a trap for the *Endeavor* at Nebeca 21. That was good, but it would have been even better to find the *Endeavor* before Nebeca 21.

"Searching every star system around Totori is pointless," Gael said, perhaps seeing the lack of zeal on Trysten's face. "A waste of time."

"Maybe," Trysten said. "Where are you now?"

"Near Totori. I tried to get to the scene of the encounter, but Admiral Kanaa isn't allowing anyone other than DSI units near. Even the GSO isn't good enough anymore."

Trysten gritted his teeth. The DSI, or the Deep Space Intelligence, was a core investigative unit of the Confederacy. Unfortunately, he didn't have any surrogates in the DSI; the organization was airtight.

"Anything you picked up from the distance?"

"The weapon used to destroy the Drednot was similar to what was used on the GSO fleet in Sector 22. I picked up a piece of debris. It has similar signatures to the ones we have from Sector 22."

Trysten held his breath. His suspicion was correct. The Stryker was indeed at the bottom of all this. But how? Did the pilot go rogue? Or had the Stryker?

"Lord Paramount," Gael said, halting Trysten's mind from bounding into woeful conclusions. "We'll find them. And this time I'll be prepared for Captain Milos."

"Yes, please do. But don't underestimate that man, Gael," Trysten said distractedly. "He's good. He's a legend for a reason."

"I know."

"And you be careful." Trysten winced inwardly as soon as those words left his mouth. It was not like him to care, yet he always saw something in Gael that was more than just a tool to further his designs for House Kiroff. Gael was as capable as Trysten had always been, someone he could trust, a compatriot, and a worthy successor to his legacy. If only the fates had been kinder . . . Sonya could have borne him a son like Gael.

"Lord Paramount, if I may ask something?" Gael chimed in. "I know it's not my place, but since I was present at CAWStrat when . . ."

Gael's voice trailed off, but he had said enough to steel Trysten's insides. Trysten was busy cleaning up the Stryker mess, but this problem had to be dealt with sooner or later.

"She's . . . missing," Trysten said as offhandedly as he could without saying his daughter's name. He avoided looking at Gael.

Gael simply stared at him, then a frown came over his face. "And?"

And nothing. He couldn't announce to the universe that his daughter, the Kiroff heir, had left CAWStrat without permission to who knew where. That she of House Kiroff had slinked out of the institute like a worthless delinquent. What would that news do to his reputation?

It was bad enough that Leona, that bitchy administrator at CAWStrat, knew. Trysten could tell she was tittering inside as she broke the news to him. He wanted to drag her to a hearing and hold her accountable, but then everyone would find out. His stupid daughter had even left a note, announcing her displeasure at how her father controlled her life. So instead of throwing a mismanagement charge at Leona, Trysten had to threaten her to keep it quiet. Then he had to tempt her with a deal just to make sure she kept it quiet.

"Lord Paramount?" Gael called again. Trysten drew a long, jagged breath. Gael had an annoying habit of poking people like that, making them face truths they didn't want to admit existed.

"I'm looking for her," Trysten said. He had sent a team of investigators to CAWStrat, but beyond that he didn't have a plan.

"Can I help?"

"No," Trysten snapped. Ramya was his responsibility, his failure, his shame to bear alone. Besides, Gael had more important matters to attend. "You go find me my Stryker."

"Yes, Lord Paramount."

After Gael's image flickered and disappeared, Trysten lumbered over to the glass wall and the breathtaking scenery it framed. A faraway look had descended on his usually sharp blue-gray eyes, and from the way the corners of his lips drooped it was easy to tell he was not enjoying the view.

Trysten rubbed his chin, his thoughts swirling. He had done his best to get Ramya trained to be a worthy heir. He'd tried to toughen her, temper her, exposed her to the best upbringing in the galaxy money could buy. Still, somehow, he fell short. The hope he had nurtured of seeing in Ramya the passion to lead House Kiroff had never materialized.

The cards were stacked against her from her first breath: his firstborn was a girl. As was tradition, the firstborn was heir apparent, and Trysten had made his disappointment known to her. He acknowledged the near-unsurmountable social hurdles she'd face as leader of a major House, acknowledging the inevitable setback House Kiroff would have to deal with during her times.

But the more he wanted to forge Ramya into a weapon worth reckoning, the more she turned into emotional mush. Trysten often wondered: was this weakling who cried up a storm if he as much raised his voice even his progeny?

As if all that was not enough, Ramya had run away. She'd somehow left the CAWStrat undetected and who knew where she was. Perhaps it was time to let her run. But if she wasn't found in ten years, by the Confederacy's laws of inheritance, she'd lose the right to lead House Kiroff.

No! Trysten shook his head and shoved the dark thought down into the depths it had come from. Incapable or not, Ramya was his daughter. She had his blood in her veins, she bore his name. He couldn't let her disappear into oblivion.

Striding back to his desk, Trysten grabbed the red folder on his desk. On the cover it read "Confidential," and inside was a dossier of five bounty hunters, supposedly the best in the galaxy. He was going to send one, or five, to get Ramya back to Somenvaar. And this time, once they got the idiot girl back, he would send her straight to her nuptials.

But before that, he had a few more things to do about the Stryker mess. First, he needed to call on his brother, Lynden, again. The incident at Sector 22 had been contained, but the one at Totori was much more public. And with the DSI being called, Trysten was sure the shit would go flying soon. He had to get Lynden ready for that. War was coming.

Don't forget your enemies, for they won't forget you.

-Mwandan proverb

1

It's one hell of a view at least, Ramya Kiroff mused as she tried to find a more comfortable position in the pilot seat of the Stryker. The sixth planet of the Kashiyap system—an ice giant with thick blue striations—hung next to them. Beyond it was the bright red orb of the fifth planet and the inner planetary region of the Kashiyap, where they were headed.

Ramya glanced one more time at the mesmerizing blue striations of the ice giant before hastily tearing her eyes away from its looming form. You only needed to look at a planet as massive as that once to understand how insignificant one human was in the galactic scale of things. Ramya shuddered. Being insignificant . . . that was the story of her life.

Fists curled into balls so tight that nails dug painfully into her palms, Ramya breathed in long and deep. Now was not the time for a pity party. She wasn't about to let those dreadful flutters at the pit of her stomach grow any bigger, or let those nervous tingles spread beyond her fingertips. Not when she had a ship to find and friends to rescue.

Ramya forced her thoughts on the most pressing issue: finding *Endeavor* and its crew. Only a few hours ago, with help from Ross and the Stryker's AI, Dakrhaeth, she had fought off four Drednots of the Confederate fleet, barely escaping their vicious attack. Ramya checked the rear scopes for signs of any Confederacy ship following them but found none. Unfortunately, she couldn't find any signs of the *Endeavor* either.

They were lost without the *Endeavor.* The Stryker was an excellent craft, but it was built for battle and not for traveling long distances. Besides, there was no chance of giving anyone the slip in the Stryker. The craft's unusual looks would attract the Confederacy's attention in no time.

"We better find them on Morris II," Ramya muttered to herself. With no means to contact the *Endeavor*, their only hope rested on correctly guessing where Captain Milos would likely land the ship. Ross had suggested Morris II, and that was where they'd headed.

Ramya blinked to clear her vision so she could pinpoint their destination and assess travel time. The Stryker had just exited the Super Luminal Highway, the SLH, and was heading steadily toward a distant red dot in the darkness that was the system's lone star, the Kashiyap. Next to them was the Kashiyap's sixth planet, and the planet beyond was a much smaller red one, which Ramya guessed was a tad bigger than Nikoor, her home world. Barely visible beyond the red planet's orbit was their destination, the dark orb of Morris II.

Just like she had done a zillion times since escaping the Drednots, Ramya scanned the instrument panel spread out in front of her and took stock of the readings. All seemed well. Ross sat in the co-pilot's seat next to her. He stared out the window and was unusually quiet since their encounter with the Confederacy and its four Drednots.

After the Stryker had fled into the SLH, Dakrhaeth, the craft's AI and the self-proclaimed soul of the Stryker, kept watch. Dakrhaeth had even suggested that Ross and Ramya take a nap, but as enticing as that sounded, neither had chosen to rest. Instead, they sat, staring outside and scanning the Stryker's instruments over and over as they streaked though the SLH.

They had come a long way. The Super Luminal Highways made travel faster, and the Stryker had made it from Totori to Morris II, located in adjacent star systems, in a little less than an hour thanks to faster-than-light mode of travel. If they had to use sub-luminal speeds, the same journey would have taken days. But now that they were out of the SLH, the distance between the AP or the Access Point of the SLH to the final destination would have to be completed in regular sub-luminal mode. And even though the Stryker was fast, it was going to take some time to reach Morris II, two planets away from the

AP.

"Feeling well, Mihaal?" The sudden question almost made Ramya jump. She had expected Dakrhaeth to be alert and awake, yet his voice—always smug and now somewhat chirpy—rattled her a bit.

Receiving no reply from Ramya, Dakrhaeth went on. "We're on course. By my calculations, we'll arrive on Morris II in fifteen minutes."

And then what? From what she knew, Morris II was quite large. How would they know where the *Endeavor* had landed? Who knew if it had come to Morris II at all?

Stop worrying, Rami! Focus. Think.

"Tell me about Morris II again, Dakrhaeth," she said. She had studied the basic information on Morris II a few times already, but she kept stumbling at the enormity of the task ahead of them.

"Certainly, Mihaal. Morris II is a terrestrial planet, orbiting the Kashiyap, a red dwarf. It has thirteen thickly forested continents, which make up sixty-five percent of the planet's surface. It has no moon."

"Thirteen continents," Ramya muttered to herself. How in the stars were they going to find a spacecraft on a planet that was sixty-five percent land?

"Morris II is approximately 1.2 Terras in size."

That was fairly large, about three times the size of Nikoor, where she had been born and raised.

"That will take a long time to scan?" Ramya asked.

"Yes."

"Well, at least no one is chasing us."

"Per our current knowledge, yes."

Dakrhaeth was as optimistic a personality as anyone else she'd met on the *Endeavor*. Ramya stifled a chuckle before scanning the rear scopes once again to make sure no one was behind them. They had disabled all of the Drednots at Totori before escaping into the SLH and Ramya was sure none of those had followed. But who knew what the Confederacy had done since? For all they knew, a whole fleet could be tracking them now.

"We have to find an efficient way to locate the *Endeavor*, Dakrhaeth," Ramya said. "We can't just keep flying around the planet."

"Yes, I agree."

A thought niggling at the back of her mind suddenly rammed to the forefront and made her recheck the power gauges. There were no alarms yet, but Ramya still worried. The Stryker was a space fighter, not designed to fly long distances, and hence couldn't be equipped with a massive reactor-based engine like the *Endeavor*. Whatever fuel supplies it had was sure to be depleted fairly quickly. And they had already been flying for a long time.

"Dakrhaeth, how does the Stryker's fuel supplies look?"

Silence. Dakrhaeth's silence always raised Ramya's hackles.

"Dakrhaeth?"

"Not too bad, Mihaal. But not optimal either."

Perfect, Ramya thought caustically. That was the one worry missing.

"I'd be able to regenerate the supplies fairly quickly." But there had to be a catch somewhere. "If we could land."

Ramya released the breath she'd been holding. Land? In a Mwandan sanctuary? To be honest, there was no avoiding landing. Ramya had hoped they could keep it to the minimum, and only after they'd spotted the *Endeavor*. But now it seemed like they'd have to do it far sooner.

"You need to consider your own needs also, Mihaal."

"What do you mean?" she asked, tapping the handle of her seat distractedly.

"I mean food, of course," Dakrhaeth replied. "I do not see any supplies on board. Although the Stryker has a storage unit that can hold enough food for two persons to last seven days, it's empty at the moment, unfortunately. I've noticed your species prefers food with high fat content, as well as exotic beverages. Before our next flight, I suggest you—"

"Has anyone ever told you that you talk too much?" Ross interrupted sullenly. He looked around with bleary eyes.

Ramya couldn't help a smile. Dakrhaeth was a test of patience. He was, to quote the very best of her father, Trysten Kiroff, "a vat of jabber." But she also had to acknowledge that Dakrhaeth was invaluable. Without his help, they would've been fried alive by the Confederacy. His jabber was an obligatory and indispensable torture.

"I'm sorry if you're offended by my intention to impart knowledge," Dakrhaeth said. He was not one to take one on the cheek lying down either. "I was taught your species says information is a source of power."

Ross sighed noisily. "Yes, you've heard right. But there's also a saying about too much information being bad. I'm guessing you didn't hear that one?"

"I cannot imagine why any amount of information would be bad for a sentient organism."

Ramya had no interest hearing any more of the back and forth, so she desperately hurled herself into the conversation. "All right, Dakrhaeth, that's enough. Can we please think about the problem on our hands? You realize that finding the *Endeavor* on a planet the size of Morris II is like looking for a needle in a haystack. A microscopic needle in a . . . massive haystack. Besides, Morris II is a Mwandan sanctuary. We'll not be welcomed there, forget finding any help. So how are we gonna do this?"

No one replied. Then Ross threw a mocking glance backward at the entryway behind them where the sphere—the only physical manifestation of the Stryker's AI—rested inside a glass column.

"The know-it-all should have a plan," he said.

"Well, he clearly doesn't," Ramya snapped. Ross was being petty, sparring with Dakrhaeth like an impetuous kid when they should be focusing on important matters. The bickering was getting tiresome and she had to find a way to distract them.

"Dakrhaeth," she called, "how long to the planet surface?"

"Eleven minutes."

Ramya's mind raced. If they could be sure the *Endeavor* had come this way then at least they'd know this was the right track. "Do you see any evidence of the *Endeavor* having passed this way?"

"I did notice some debris, but it could be from any spacecraft," Dakrhaeth replied.

So much for clues.

"Well, they couldn't have passed through here too long ago, right?" Ross chimed in, and Ramya was happy that instead of the usual arguing he had something useful to say.

"That's correct," Dakrhaeth replied. "According to my calculations, they should have been right here about twenty minutes ago."

"And that means they haven't yet reached Morris II, right?"

"They could if they were faster than us, but we can safely assume they're not. So, yes, you're correct again."

"All right," Ross said, suddenly invigorated. "How well can you see Morris II from here?"

"Not well enough to help," Dakrhaeth replied. *Chatty he may be, but no one can call Dakrhaeth insincere*, Ramya mused.

Ross sighed noisily. "Can you at least tell which continents are facing our way now? That could narrow things down a bit."

Ramya mulled over Ross's words. It made sense—the battered *Endeavor* would likely land on the first landmass it came across. If Dakrhaeth could make out the continents directly facing their path to the planet, it could give a rough idea of the area they needed to scan.

In the case of most other habitable planets, it'd have been easier to discern the landmasses, but Morris II was very dark, and the dim star it orbited didn't make spotting things any easier. Ramya squinted hard but saw nothing but a dark ball in space. Not surprising, since even Dakrhaeth was taking so long to answer.

"The largest landmass facing us right now is in a continent they call the Masumm. It is supposedly of a mountainous terrain. It has significant settlements of Mwandans as well."

"Damn!" Ross voiced Ramya's own frustration. A mountainous terrain meant it'd be difficult to land the Stryker, and it would also be difficult if they needed to go looking for the *Endeavor* on foot. And that wasn't taking into account the threat of an inhospitable Mwandan populace.

"Can't we go any faster?" she asked, twiddling the controls.

"We're at optimum speed," Dakrhaeth replied instantly. "I'd suggest you keep it at that. Starlight is sub-optimal in this system, so the fuel packs are replicating at a lower rate. We do not want them to fail."

Ross nodded. He said, "We'll just keep heading straight to Morris II, scan the continent we're aligned with, and . . . there are too many unknowns."

He was right—getting stranded on a Mwandan planet was not an option. Ramya thought of asking Dakrhaeth for detailed maps of Morris II but quickly discarded the idea. There was no point studying the topography when they didn't know where they'd land on Morris II.

Ross cleared his throat and threw a guarded look in her direction. "You haven't told me how you'd found a way into the Stryker," he said in a voice that was as cold as the look he gave her.

Ramya's heart skipped a beat. And then another. The question would come up sooner or later, but now was not a good time, as they were encapsulated in the Stryker and hurtling into the unknown. From what she knew of Ross, he couldn't take the news of her hidden identity quietly.

"Lost your tongue?" he quipped.

"Why is it relevant?" Ramya tried to stall. Nothing good could come of this, and if there was a chance to diffuse the situation, she had to try to use it. "We should be studying Morris II."

"You know there's no point in doing that until we get closer and find out where we're landing," Ross replied snippily, his eyes narrowing. "What are you trying to hide?"

It was only getting worse. If she wasn't going to succeed in stalling anything, it was better to let him have it straight.

"I belong to House Kiroff," she said, watching the muscles on his face tighten. Then his nostrils flared.

"House Kiroff?" he said slowly, lingering over each word, each syllable almost. Before Ramya could say a word, he turned away to look at the red planet they had left behind. When he looked back at her, every feature on his face was frozen, his lips barely parting as they hissed out the next question. "The captain called you Ramya. Are you *the* Ramya, Trysten Kiroff's daughter and heir?"

That was one precise question. It left no wiggle room. And just the question worried the heck out of Ramya. She didn't care as much about Ross, but Dakrhaeth? The AI had allowed her access to the ship because he sensed her Kiroff genetics and likely mistook her for her father. What if the AI was only helping them because it assumed she was the head of House Kiroff? What if it chucked them out into space on knowing she was not?

"Why can't you answer a simple question?" Ross said, his voice rising.

"I am," Ramya snapped, anger spreading its fiery tentacles into her head. She forced the loathsome words out of her mouth. "I am Trysten Kiroff's daughter and heir to House Kiroff."

There . . . you heard it. Happy now?

Ross was far from happy. But he didn't look smug like Ramya expected him to be. Didn't burst into a screaming ball of anger either.

"What are you doing on the *Endeavor*? Why did you lie to us? To the captain?" Ross whispered. Pale, gnawing on his lips, Ross looked just as upset by the revelation as she had expected.

Ramya bit the inside of her cheek as she struggled to frame a safe answer. "I didn't lie. I didn't disclose my identity because I'm trying to . . . avoid unnecessary attention."

"He found out?" Ross asked.

Ramya assumed he was talking about Captain Milos. "He knew from the moment he met me. So he said."

"Who else knows?"

"Fenny."

The veins on his temples jutted out. His nostrils flared again. "How long has *she* known?" he asked.

It hadn't been too long, but Fenny had promised her, as had the captain, that they'd keep her identity a secret.

"For a bit," Ramya replied guardedly. "I asked them both to keep it a secret."

Her defense for them didn't have an iota of effect on Ross. Unless she considered the mocking twist of his lips and the grunt, neither of which Ramya was aiming for. He turned away toward the darkness outside, robbing Ramya of the chance to gauge his emotions.

Quiet seconds turned into oppressive minutes. As expected, he was angry with her for not disclosing her true identity. Maybe he was let down more because the captain and Fenny didn't tell him about her.

Either way, Ross refused to look at her. He didn't even press on why she was on the *Endeavor*, traveling incognito. In hindsight, it was good he didn't probe further because Ramya wasn't eager to share that she was running away from her father, Trysten Kiroff. Ross was no Fenny and he certainly was no Captain Milos. He had never felt like a friend, and he was far from someone she could share secrets with. Besides, that secret was better not told in Dakrhaeth's presence anyway.

It was always tight inside the Stryker and now the stifling silence, like a heavy carpet wound around her head, was starting to make it feel like a coffin. How long until they touched down on Morris II?

Just then, Darkhaeth shouted, "Mihaal, I see a craft! It's just entered the atmosphere of Morris II."

Ramya sat up. Ross did the same but didn't say a word. Ramya tried to push him off her mind. He could lick his wounds for as long as he wanted because she had more important things to do than pamper his hurt psyche.

"Can you tell if it's the *Endeavor*?" Ramya asked.

"No, I can't. But I doubt the Mwandans would have too many spacecrafts flying in and out of the planet."

Dakrhaeth was right. Mwandans were reclusive to a fault. They always had decent tech and access to all of the Confederacy's technological know-how, but the Mwandans refused to use it to spread across the galaxy. The chances of this being a Mwandan spacecraft were less than minimal.

"Follow it then," she instructed.

"I am, Mihaal. Following it closely."

Ramya slumped back against her seat and let out a long, torturous breath. Her head throbbed, and her aching muscles longed for a good night's sleep in a warm, soft bed. Her mind drifted.

"Mihaal," Dakrhaeth's sharp call jolted her. Did he sound worried or was it just in her mind?

"Yes?"

"I detected an explosion on the planet's surface. It roughly matches the trajectory of the craft I saw earlier."

Ross spun around to look at her, his face drawn. Ramya could guess she looked just as shocked.

This couldn't be happening. Dakrhaeth couldn't be right. What he saw couldn't be the *Endeavor*. They couldn't lose the *Endeavor*.

"Should we hold our course, Mihaal?"

There was no doubt about that. Even if the *Endeavor* had crashed and gone up in flames, they had to go down and make sure.

"Yes, of course."

"May I note, Mihaal, this could have been caused by a Mwandan defensive. If we follow the same path, we will be heading straight into a similar fate."

Perhaps. But no matter what, she had to find out what happened.

Ramya breathed in long and slow. "Get us there as quickly as you can, Dakrhaeth," she ordered.

There was no way in hell she was bailing on her captain and crewmates.

2

Ground cover had a different meaning on Morris II. As the Stryker approached the surface of the planet, Ramya held her breath. The dark vegetation had wide swaths of plants in all sorts of shapes and sizes and there was barely a spot or two of the ground not covered by it. The dim light of the star made the entire scenery murky and depressing.

Dakrhaeth steered the Stryker steadily in the direction of the explosion they had seen earlier and Ramya could barely think straight. She didn't hope for much. Better to prepare for the worst — the *Endeavor* had crashed and no one had survived. But even considering that didn't clear her head. She still couldn't think beyond finding the crash site and it didn't help that Ross sat rigid and stony-faced next to her, refusing to speak.

She wasn't going to give in to him. He could fret and fume as much as he wanted. Her eyes were glued on the landscape below, the thudding of her heart growing steadily like a war-drum beating faster and louder as the time of first encounter drew near. As time crawled on they crossed more ground, but there was no sign of a crashed spacecraft.

"I'm locked on the explosion site, Mihaal."

Ramya sucked in some air and braced for the inevitable. The *Endeavor* would be in pieces and everyone in it — dead.

She reached for the flight stick. No one could alter the grim truth, but at least being in charge when facing it would give some sense of control even when there was none.

"I'll take over Dakrhaeth," she announced. Grabbing the flight stick, she leaned forward to look outside. A thick plume of smoke rose a short distance away, right from the middle of the dark expanse of the forest. Dakrhaeth had scopes and sensors at his disposal to see more, Ramya figured.

"What do you see, Dakrhaeth?" she asked, ignoring the throbbing lump that seemed to expand in her throat.

"It is interesting. I do not see any spacecrafts. A building seems to be on fire."

The breath Ramya had been holding made out of her in a slow relaxed wave. There was still hope! Maybe the *Endeavor* had landed somewhere safely. Maybe its crew was still alive. Regardless, they needed to check out the explosion site and make sure it had nothing to do with the *Endeavor*.

Ramya pointed the Stryker's nose directly to the swirling gray column. As the Stryker drew closer to the plume, she saw the source of the smoke clearly. Dakrhaeth was correct—there was no spacecraft in sight. At the center of the site was a building complex of some sort, built of a dark-brown material. The centermost structure was shaped like an ovoid. An explosion had ripped it in half and smoke billowed out of it. Ramya could see the raging fire and people—Mwandans were humanoids, so they looked just like regular people from afar—running in and out of the area.

Dakrhaeth sounded a cautionary note. "Mihaal, they're looking. I suggest we get out of here."

"I agree," Ramya muttered under her breath as she tugged the flight stick to turn the Stryker around. There was no *Endeavor* here, so whatever else was going on down there was none of her business.

"Watch out!" Ross shouted.

Ramya pulled on the flight stick and pressed hard on the throttle, but it was already too late. Something hit the right side of the Stryker in a series of soft plops. It didn't sound harmful, but the craft tipped sideways and the alarms went blaring.

Ramya threw her weight on the flight stick and pushed the throttle down. The Stryker turned and pulled forward but not as quickly as Ramya wanted it to. For a second, her vision turned blurry and the world seemed to recede from her, but she held on. By the time they'd cleared the vicinity of the explosion site Ramya was gasping for air. It had to be the rush of adrenaline, or maybe it was her empty stomach. The alarms assaulted her senses with their unending screech. The entire control panel was blinking red, as if everything on the Stryker was falling apart.

"Dakrhaeth," Ramya shouted as soon as she had put some distance between them and the building. "What happened? How bad are we hit?"

The alarms quietened abruptly. The silence that followed told Ramya there could be nothing good to hear.

"I'm afraid it's bad news, Mihaal," Dakrhaeth said. "We were struck quite efficiently. Whatever the weapon was, it took out a good chunk of our right wing. And unfortunately, navigating in these atmospheric conditions requires working wings."

First the failing fuel packs. Now this? Could they ever escape Morris II?

"You idiot," Ross snarled so viciously that Ramya jumped and shrunk back. "Did you forget to have the damn shields up?"

Ramya fumed. That was no way to speak to a compatriot, human, AI, or otherwise. "Neither of us asked him to check on the shields," she reminded as gently as she could. Even though she didn't want to engage in a heated argument with Ross again, she wasn't about to let it slide altogether.

"He's supposed to take care of the Stryker." Ross spat the words out. "It's not my job."

"I'm sorry," Ramya replied caustically. "I forgot. Your job is yelling at people. With or without reason."

His glare burned into the side of her face. "You're going to take that stupid AI's side now? But of course, you two are in on it together. How could I forget he's your lackey? That you infiltrated the *Endeavor* together."

Infiltrated? That's what he thought she had done? Was he delusional? Whatever it was, she had to put an end to it now.

"You know, Ross, you're behaving like a twelve-year-old," she blurted. Her voice was icy and her words scathing, and his stunned stare was expected. Ross was not only older but superior in the hierarchy of things on the *Endeavor* as well. But Ramya had had enough. With the *Endeavor* lost and the Stryker's wing shot, their chance of getting out of this alive was getting dimmer every minute. The one thing they needed was to put their heads together and find an escape route.

"Quiet," Ross growled. He had been shouting at her for quite some time but never had he sounded so angry. And even though she didn't want to admit it, his voice scared her.

Ross had a lot more to say. "Right now, we have to find the *Endeavor*, the captain, and the crew. That's the only reason I'm putting up with you." He spoke through gritted teeth, nostrils flaring, and his face turning an indignant red. "But the fact remains that you're an imposter. A Kiroff spy. I'm going to get to the bottom of your treachery, I promise you that."

His words stung even though Ramya had tried her best to steel herself. Treachery? She had simply tried to escape an infernal life. She hadn't wanted to betray anyone. Why didn't he understand? Frustration and anger raised their head again. Before Ramya could retort, Ross held up a hand.

"I'm not done speaking," he said. "You may be the boss of the Stryker and its AI, but I'm your commander. I'm the one in charge of this mission and you better keep that in mind."

Or what? Ramya was about to snap at him, but she decided against it. He was right. Whether she liked it or not, Ross was in charge of the mission. Captain Milos had put him in charge, and she had to defer to the captain's judgment.

"You're right. I'm sorry," she said hastily, almost afraid that she'd change her mind before the words made it out of her. She hoped for peace, however temporary.

"Sorry to interrupt your conversation, Mihaal," Dakrhaeth spoke before Ross said anything. "We *have* to land."

People didn't land on a Mwandan planet without permission, not unless it was the last resort. She'd hoped they'd land only after they had located the *Endeavor*. That'd be one thing. But the wing situation had to be bad for Dakrhaeth to suggest immediate landing.

"I know the perils of landing in a Mwandan sanctuary, Mihaal," Dakrhaeth said. "I've been taught the protocols of your world for years. But we do not have a choice. As I informed earlier, the wing has taken a direct hit. I can regenerate it, but that needs a lot of power. If we keep flying, the regeneration rate will be miniscule. The only way to do it quickly is by diverting power from the engines to the repairs. The fuel cells are sub-optimal also."

Ramya didn't quite understand what Dakrhaeth meant by regeneration, but that detail was not as important. Not right now anyway. They had bigger issues to deal with at the moment.

"So, we *have* to land?" she asked.

"Yes. It's not advisable to be airborne in our condition. With those holes in the wing, we're quite unstable. I'd go easy on the throttle, Mihaal."

Ramya released the pressure on the throttle and let out a sigh. They had run out of options. The Stryker needed to be in perfect condition if they hoped to get away from here. And a broken wing was far from perfect. The time to break protocol and set foot in a Mwandan sanctuary had arrived.

"By the way, Commander Ross," Dakrhaeth's snippy voice scattered Ramya's thoughts, "I did have the shields up, but the weapon tore through it. I have not finished analyzing it yet, but I will inform you about the composition of the weapon as soon as I do."

Dakrhaeth went silent but his words kept badgering Ramya. What sort of weapon could tear the Stryker's shield so easily? This was the same Stryker that had quite efficiently held up against the Drednots.

"Some weapon," Ross said aloud.

Ramya nodded. *Some weapon indeed.*

"Let's find a good place to land. Away from settlements," she said. They needed a place where no one would notice an alien craft. But where could be safe on a Mwandan sanctuary?

"Maybe somewhere where there isn't much ground cover?" Ross suggested. "That way, we'll at least know if someone tries to ambush us."

That was a good idea. Little was known about the reclusive Mwandans except they were experts at camouflaging among the native vegetation. If they could find some rocky ground, they'd at least spot any approaching Mwandans easily.

"I see a small mountain to the north, Mihaal. It has a ledge where we could land," Dakrhaeth said.

Even though Ramya couldn't discern the ledge, she picked out the dim outline of the mountain. It rose above the surrounding forest, its rounded top uncharacteristically bare of the typical dark vegetation. It was also a good distance away from the explosion site, so whoever spotted the Stryker there would need some time reaching the ledge.

Ramya yanked the flight stick, then she pointed the Stryker in the direction for the mountain and pressed on the throttle a bit. They had to reach the ledge quickly and fix that wing before any more intrusions.

3

Other than a few unexpected rolls to the side, the Stryker made it safely to the ledge. Their landing spot was a rock jutting out of a small mountain. The top of the mountain was unexpectedly bare; vegetation stopped abruptly a distance below the ledge. The ground was a dark red, or perhaps it looked redder in the red light of the Kashiyap. It was crumbly, and the Stryker's landing gear sunk deep into the ground before the ship came to complete rest. Ramya turned the engines off and the soft purr she had gotten so used to having around her ebbed away slowly.

"Dakrhaeth, an estimate of the repairs, please?" Ross asked. Ramya had to look askance at him. His question and the courteous way he asked it was not something Ramya had expected. He sure sounded different. However, a deep frown still graced his forehead.

"Three hours or four, Commander."

Ross nodded at Ramya. "We should check outside. Make sure the area's safe."

"I detect no signs of life in the near vicinity," Dakrhaeth informed.

The gears in Ramya's head spun steadily. To survive this they had to stick together and more confrontations were the last thing they needed. The safest way to keep things quiet was to keep Ross away from Dakrhaeth and busy. And getting out of the Stryker was the best business she could think of.

"Let's go check it out," she said eagerly to Ross, ignoring Dakrhaeth's comment.

"The air is breathable, right?" Ross said, unstrapping himself from the seat.

Morris II had a breathable atmosphere. Apparently, the oxygen content in its air was better than the eighteen-percent level on Nikoor where she grew up. But getting out on a planet she'd never been on before needed more than relying on her memory.

"Dakrhaeth," she called. "Can you check on the air outside? Do we need suits?"

"No, Mihaal. No suits necessary. I have run a test of the air outside. It is 74.65% nitrogen, 24.38% oxygen, 0.91% inert gasses, 0.06% carbon dioxide, and some water vapor. You shouldn't have any trouble breathing."

It sure sounded good. Ramya unstrapped herself and followed Ross to the exit of the Stryker. The door parted with a low hiss as soon as they were close.

Ramya's eyes ran over the scene outside. The first word that came to her mind was "dull." Thanks to the dim red light of Kashiyap, everything was exceedingly morose. Ross peeked out and a second or two later he jumped down to the ground below. Ramya noted that the surface was crumbly, clear from the way Ross wobbled a little when he touched the ground and how he left deep impressions on the soil when he walked. The ledge had to be covered with a layer of rock dust a few inches thick.

Ramya watched Ross walk around for a bit before approaching the door. Stopping at the threshold, she breathed in deep. A funny smell — somewhat pungent and a bit sickly — hung in the air. Perhaps it was her empty stomach, Ramya couldn't be sure, but her insides churned a little.

She ran a hand over the weapons strapped to her right thigh — two blasters. Ross had a blaster and a slightly bigger gun on him, neither of them impressive. When they had picked up those weapons before boarding the Stryker, the plan had been a simple — let the Stryker down on an asteroid and leave — handoff with the Confederacy. Had Ramya known how things would change, she surely would've picked bigger guns. Now her weapons seemed utterly inadequate. How far would their puny blasters go against something that could break through the Stryker's shields? They had no choice but to make do with what little they had.

She was about to jump outside when Dakrhaeth spoke. "Mihaal, here is something you need to remember. When I'm in the middle of the repairs, I won't be able to reroute power back to the engines without risking a total breakdown of the repair process. That will be a waste of resources and should be avoided."

"That means we will be stuck in this area for the next four hours, right?" Ramya asked.

"Yes. So I suggest you complete a basic recon of the area before I start. I do not expect you to find anything different from my observations, but since the commander wants so, perhaps it's best to give him what he wants."

Dakrhaeth and his snarky commentaries, Ramya had to suppress a chuckle. The AI was correct though. While Ross seemed to let go of his anger for now, Ramya knew the quiet wouldn't last long. The best way to appease him now was to let him go about commandeering the mission.

"Got it," Ramya shouted before joining Ross outside. The surface, just like she had expected, was soft and a tad slippery, but it felt good to have ground under her feet nonetheless. All around them, an unending sea of dark foliage stretched in all directions. Ramya looked around and up at the sky. The Kashiyap was still quite high, so there would be daylight for a while. If they were lucky, the Stryker would be fixed before nightfall.

Ross had already walked to the other side of the Stryker so Ramya followed. She found him staring at the Stryker's damaged right wing. A series of perfectly round holes with smooth charred edges dotted the wing. Individually they were small, but they were many and altogether had turned a part of the Stryker's wing into a net.

"It's as if a bunch of bees flew through the wing. Weird, right?"

What better could they expect? They were on a weird planet inhabited by a weird race they hardly knew anything about. If it started raining fire, Ramya wouldn't be half surprised.

She scanned the horizon, her gaze lingering on the plume far to the south, which had grown thinner now. She kept looking for any signs that could indicate a Mwandan presence. There was nothing other than an endless expanse of shiny dark foliage for as far as she could see. There wasn't even a breeze.

"Dakrhaeth will be locked on the repairs once he starts," she told Ross. "He wants us to tell him if he can begin."

"I don't see anything out of the ordinary," Ross said. "The AI didn't pick up anything either. Only thing is . . ." His words trailed off. He was staring worriedly at the large form of the Stryker. Ramya immediately guessed why he was frowning; the dark, shiny Stryker was like a beacon on the ledge. Even though its wings were partially tucked, sharp eyes could easily spot the Stryker's hulking presence.

"Damn! We have to cover it with something," Ramya said. "Whoever shot at us knows there's an alien craft around. They might come looking."

They crossed the distance to the Stryker's entrance with frantic steps.

"That was quick, Mihaal," Dakrhaeth greeted. "I doubt you have found anything more than what I already observed. So do I have the commander's blessing to start the repairs now?"

Ramya had to use every bit of her willpower to stop from snapping at Dakrhaeth. Did he think his cheekiness was going to help their situation?

"Well, there's an issue," Ramya said with as much calmness as she could muster. "The Stryker's sticking out like a flare on the ledge. They'll spot us in no time."

"Oh, that!" Dakrhaeth said as if he had heard the silliest thing. "I can turn my cloaking on. That will stretch the repairs another hour longer possibly, but you are correct, we cannot have Mwandans poking around."

"You have a cloaking device too?" Ross asked. He sounded almost as incredulous as Ramya felt herself. Why didn't Dakrhaeth tell them about it when they were fighting the Confederacy? Cloaking would've been a useful tool.

"Yes, I do." Dakrhaeth almost sounded bashful. "Although a rather primitive one, I'll admit. It can only be used when the Stryker is stationary since it likes to guzzle energy." Ramya and Ross looked at each other and shrugged. "I'm turning the cloaking feature on now," Dakrhaeth announced.

In the blink of an eye, the Stryker started fading. A few seconds later, the Stryker went completely invisible. Ramya chuckled. No one could have guessed the presence of a spacecraft if they were to look at the ledge now.

"Mihaal, I'm commencing the repairs now. Please understand, I shall go into Sleep Mode," Dakrhaeth's voice floated through the air. "I will need five hours to get back. I advise you not venture too far from here while I'm away. We don't know enough about Morris II and I worry about your safety."

"Yes, understood," Ramya said bit grudgingly. Her insides felt leaden, and even in the superior atmosphere of Morris II, she had trouble breathing. She didn't want to let Dakrhaeth go, although she knew he wouldn't really be gone.

"And, Mihaal, be wary of the trees."

Ramya nodded distractedly. Too many what-ifs crowded her head. With Dakrhaeth in Sleep Mode, they were even more defenseless on the alien planet. And Ramya found little to cheer about. Still, the wing needed to be repaired, and Dakrhaeth needed the time.

"I'm going to check on the other side of the mountain, all right?" Ross said. "You could come if you want."

Ross didn't smile. Though his face was rigid, he wasn't frowning either. At least he'd invited her to come along. That was a good sign. Maybe they could spend the next few hours amicably. Ramya wasn't looking forward to more arguments.

"Let's go," she said.

The path to the other side was a thin trail that hugged the side of

3

the mountain. It was relatively flat with a few places that needed careful stepping. The gravelly surface provided little foothold and it took close to twenty minutes to make it around with a whole lot of slipping and sliding. The other side was a sharp incline that descended steeply into a ravine. They couldn't have seen it from the ledge, but the ravine stretched a long way to the north in a straight line. Just like most other places in Morris II, the ravine was brimming with foliage.

They had been staring at the landscape for a few seconds when Ross suddenly said, "Do you see that?" He pointed at a depression in the foliage. "It almost looks like the plants got squished by something."

Ramya frowned. The surface did look a tad uneven in the region Ross was pointing, but nothing stood out to her.

"There's something over there," Ross said, and scrambled to a rock that extended a bit over the ravine. His feet slipped once, but he quickly regained his hold.

"Be careful, Ross," Ramya yelled. They were in enough trouble already, and she didn't need Ross to fall and break his neck or limbs.

"I'm fine," Ross shouted back. Perching near the tip of the rock, Ross shaded his eyes and squinted again. "It's weird," he declared. "You could say the shape of the foliage in that depression sort of matches a Class II battleship. See that rounded top? And the pointy rear end? It's almost like . . ."

Even though Ross didn't finish the sentence and she could hardly make out the depression he was talking about, Ramya's heart leaped at the possibility. *Could the* Endeavor *be down there?* She squashed the hope with a strong hand. How was that possible? If a spacecraft fell into the ravine, the plants couldn't keep standing; they'd be buried under the craft's bulk. Here though, it seemed like the foliage had made way for the ship to sink through them, and then encased it like a cocoon.

"Rami!" Ross's shout made her jump. For a second she thought he was ill. Eyes bulging and mouth open, he was heaving as if he had just run a mile. She was about to ask what was wrong when she noticed he was pointing at the comm unit on his wrist. The unit—a silvery strap with four buttons on its face—was blinking green.

Ramya forgot to breathe. Her thoughts blurred until they slowly settled on the one obvious conclusion: They were within range of the *Endeavor's* main radio.

As Ramya stared almost disbelievingly at his wrist, the thudding of her heart deafening, a chuckle bubbled up. All was not lost after all. The *Endeavor* was close, somewhere very close.

4

The path down from the ledge was as narrow as it was slippery. Ramya held her breath as she followed Ross down the treacherous incline. *This is madness,* she thought, but the only option was to embrace the madness. Overjoyed on finding the *Endeavor* somewhere near, they had tried using the comm to contact the ship, but that hadn't worked.

"Maybe the radio's damaged," Ross had declared on hearing the dull as-good-as-dead buzz from the comm. "Or something else. We have to go find them."

Ross had jumped headlong into this rescue mission and she had agreed wholeheartedly. But even as Ramya strode deeper into the murky forests of Morris II, there was little confidence in her steps. They were venturing into unknown and unfriendly territory. Besides, the Stryker was out of commission, which meant no back up in case they needed to evacuate in a hurry. Even knowing all that, they had decided that trying to find the *Endeavor* was the right thing to do.

Ramya and Ross descended below the canopy of dark foliage and the dimness underneath was downright creepy. It was not just the lack of light but something else that Ramya couldn't put her finger on just yet. Something unnerved her, sending jitters up her spine every few steps into the forest.

Ross stopped when they had reached the bottom of the hill and pressed his wrist-mounted comm for the zillionth time. Like before, nothing but a buzz came out of it. He looked at Ramya next, brows furrowed.

"Are you all right?" he asked.

She wasn't anywhere near all right. All she had wanted was a ride off Nikoor. She'd hoped the *Endeavor* would carry her out to the Fringe, or as close to the Fringe as possible. Then she could go looking for the Moanus and Uncle Brynden. Now those goals seemed so far removed, her existence swamped by the trouble with the Strykers. When and if she could get back to her hunt of the Moanus was the question on the top of her mind. And she had no answers.

"I'm fine," she replied. She didn't want to snap at him, but she couldn't damp down the sharpness of her voice.

Ross's face tightened. Ramya expected a stinging retort but oddly he shrugged and flashed a contrite half-smile. "You're worried. And you should be. You're right to be concerned about this mission," he said, surprising Ramya with his choice of words. "I know it's risky. But we can't wait until the Stryker's back in play. What if the *Endeavor* can't last that long?"

He'd already argued his case once and it didn't matter if he said it all over again a thousand times. Ramya acknowledged that time was of the essence, and trying to find the *Endeavor* was the right thing to do. But the risks were enormous in a Mwandan sanctuary. They were defenseless, armed only with puny blasters, and not even knowing where they were headed.

"The question is, how long will we last?" she replied.

"Let's at least try?"

"We are trying, but . . ."

Ross let out a long sigh and stepped closer. He pulled out the piece of paper on which they had sketched a rough map of the area. He tapped the depression in the forest where they were headed.

"Gauging the distance, we should reach there in less than an hour or so," Ross said. "From what I remember of the information the AI was spewing out, this area is relatively low on threats. There are no significant settlements and no known predatory animals in this zone, so we should have a relatively quick stroll across the forest and back."

It sounded so easy, too darn easy for comfort, and that was what worried Ramya the most. But she couldn't show her fear to Ross. Not because he'd laugh at her, but because he didn't need doubts to cloud his mind right now.

"Let's go," she said, forcing conviction into her voice. "Let's get this done."

They lumbered on, due north, blasters drawn. The forest floor was eerily quiet. Every forest she had been in had an ambient noise, sounds of insects humming, birds chirping, and wildlife stomping around the foliage. This — absolute silence — was abnormal.

"It's so quiet," she whispered, noticing how Ross's jaw tightened at her comment.

"It is," he said, nodding gravely. "This is creepy."

Did he sound a smidge nervous? Perhaps. A shudder sped up Ramya's spine.

"The trees are sentient, aren't they?" she whispered as they walked onto a narrow trail that cut through the undergrowth.

"Yes, so I've heard. Supposedly, they sense emotions," Ross said.

The forest was likely sensing their fear or channeling something else. Clearly something was up and it couldn't be good.

They continued on, Ramya following Ross. She stepped as noiselessly as she could through the dense undergrowth, scanning her surroundings as she went. Above them, trees grew dark and thick. After some time, Ramya heard a whisper. She paused. It wasn't a human's whisper but more like the sound a breeze would make passing through leaves. Only this was far to organized to be a simple rustle.

Ramya looked up and around her. The leaves were indeed moving. To be wholly accurate, the whole forest was moving, swaying in unison, in a rhythm that was fierce and grew fiercer by the second. Ramya held her breath and felt for a breeze. There was none. The treetops were swaying by themselves.

Gripping her blaster tighter, Ramya firmly grabbed Ross's arm and he stopped as well. His eyes were like headlamps behind his round eyeglasses, his lips taut.

"Something's going on," he muttered, stepping closer to Ramya.

"I hope *we* haven't angered them somehow," she whispered. Ross shrugged in reply.

Around them, the storm grew. Branches swayed back and forth like spell-casters around a magic circle. Torn leaves flew across their faces, and twigs crackled and snapped.

Ramya's heart picked up pace. She had no idea what these trees were capable of, but she doubted the blaster was of any use. They could thrash her to oblivion and just as easily pick her up and chuck her into space. Besides, they were outnumbered one to hundred. In a situation like this, a gun was useless. Nevertheless, she tightened her ice-cold grip on the blaster.

"Let's keep pushing forward," Ross suggested, and they plodded forward immediately.

It wasn't their presence causing the storm, that fact was clear right away. The reeling of the trees didn't change much at all as Ramya and Ross walked past. Their wild throes didn't ebb; it seemed completely unrelated to the humans' presence.

"Perhaps this is just some sort of a natural phenomenon on Morris II," Ross muttered a few paces later, his shoulders relaxed just a bit. The corner of his lips curled and he gave Ramya an amused look. "Maybe it's called a 'treestorm.'" He paused a second. "You know, like a thunderstorm or a snowstorm."

Lousy joke, but by the stars, Ross was joking, and with her, the "treacherous Kiroff infiltrator." Ramya let out a low chuckle and nodded. Internally, she scoffed. As if she was about to fall for a cute joke after all his jibes and accusations.

"There's a clearing coming up," she said, spotting a lightening of the background some distance away.

"You're right," Ross replied. Looking around quickly, he held his blaster up and sprung forward. Ramya followed, throwing cautious glances around as she hopped from behind one tree to the next. Ross had already reached the edge of the clearing and he held his fist up, signaling her to stop. Ramya halted and watched as Ross's face turned pale as he looked at something beyond the border of trees. He had to have spotted something. Blaster clutched tightly with both hands, Ramya bounded to his side and peeked.

The clearing was actually an unpaved road. It seemed to stretch from south to north, long and straight across the forest. The scene Ross was staring at, ashen faced, was unfolding to the south of where they stood. Two oblong saucer-like crafts stood to one side; one of them was upside down, and the upright one was much larger and marked with red stripes that reminded Ramya of the Mwandan flag. The striped vehicle possibly belonged to the Mwandan government, she deduced.

There were four people crowded about twenty paces from the two vehicles. Two of them wore red striped uniforms. Mwandan police perhaps? Of the two civilians, one was lying spread-eagle on the road, a brown patch spattered like a halo around his head. He or she was surely dead or grievously injured. The other civilian was small and wore a blue bodysuit. They were all throwing punches at each other, the civilian clearly fighting a losing battle against the much heftier officers.

"That's just a kid. We have to do something," Ramya whispered as one officer kicked the kid and sent him flying backward.

Ross threw her a look that screamed, *Are you out of your mind?*

The kid recovered quickly and butted the officer with his head. The officer fell to the ground, but his partner charged, his baton-held arm raised menacingly. He tackled the kid and pounded him. Ramya cringed at the ferocity of the blows. The other officer was back on his feet and he, too, joined the merciless beating.

The forests started to howl. Ramya and Ross stared at each other in confusion. Ramya couldn't believe her ears, but the trees made a sharp sound — a plaintive wail almost — that ripped the quiet. It was as if they were protesting the two officers beating their fugitive.

"We should do something," Ramya said again, leaning closer to Ross.

"Like what?"

"They'll kill the guy," Ramya said. "Can't sit back here and watch them beat someone to death."

Ross gave her an exasperated look. "What can we do? We don't know what's going on. They could as well be tackling a mass murderer. We can't be sure." He paused for a second and shrugged. "Besides, we're trespassing. We don't need them coming after us next."

"But, Ross, this isn't fair," she protested. "This isn't an even match. I mean, look at their size. Clearly that's a juvenile they're beating up. And even if he weren't a kid or innocent, no one, not even enforcers of law, can beat people to death like this. There's a system of justice, the courts and councils decide the punishment. That's the rule of the Galactic Confederacy."

Ramya stole a look at the continuing tussle on the road. Thankfully the kid was made of sterner stuff than his dead partner. He had fought off the two officers somehow and now he was kicking and shoving and punching like a madman trying to make some space around him. But his actions were getting slower, Ramya could tell even from a distance. They didn't have much time to debate on whether or not to help. The kid's situation would soon be beyond helping.

"Mwandans have never really accepted laws of the Confederacy," Ross said. His face was drawn and he flinched every time the two officers landed a hit. The officers landed a particularly vicious strike and the kid collapsed in a heap to the ground. The forests shrieked in protest.

Ross shook his head. "This isn't good. But we can't get involved in this. We're already in too much trouble."

Ramya breathed with difficulty. She was never one to back down from a chance to help anyone in need, and this situation was clear as heck. That Mwandan in blue needed help. But her situation with Ross needed help as well, and Ramya didn't want to jeopardize the façade of normalcy that had settled between them. She forced herself to turn away from the scene of the vicious beating.

"Let's keep going then," she said reluctantly.

"No, let's not," Ross said, surprising Ramya. "We'll do something to give the guy an opening. And after that we leave."

Ramya's heart leaped. She already had an idea. "Let's shoot at their vehicle. That'll distract the officers for a bit and it that should give the kid enough time to run away, or at least catch his breath."

"Good enough for me," Ross said as he raised his blaster. With a chuckle, Ramya lifted her own blaster and aimed at the striped saucer-like vehicle on the side of the road.

"Ready . . ." Ross said, and he paused a moment. "Fire."

They fired in unison, energy streaking from their blasters and impinging on the craft with a loud bang. Smoke curled up like a dark tendril.

"And hold," Ross said.

The shots had the intended effect. The two officers fell away from the kid and turned to look at the smoking vehicle. That moment of inattention was all the kid needed. He kicked one of his pursuers on the leg, cutting him off at the knees. He jumped to his feet, and as the other officer rushed forward, the kid fell back a step and lunged, head-butting his opponent squarely in gut. In the second that both officers were incapacitated, the kid broke into a desperate sprint toward the forest. Something, Ramya couldn't figure what, changed around them.

"Damn! He's coming our way," Ross said in a low voice. The kid was indeed heading in their direction toward the fringe of the forest on their side. "Fall back," Ross ordered. With long steps he hurried back deeper into the forest.

The trees! Ramya suddenly realized the forest had stilled. Not a leaf moved, not a branch crackled. There was no howling, no moaning, not even a whisper. It was as if the entire forest was holding its breath just like Ramya.

"Rami, get back here." Ross's voice, urgent and tight, reached her ears, but Ramya's feet wouldn't budge. She desperately wanted to see if the kid had made it. Her eyes flitted from his sprinting form to the two officers who had now hobbled to their feet. They pulled something—weapons presumably—from their hips and pointed it toward their fugitive.

The forest howled. No, it screamed. It was a gut-wrenching, ear-splitting ruckus that shook the world. Ramya clutched her ears, and her legs buckled under her. She sank to her knees, her eyes trying to hold on to the scene playing out before her. Bright yellow flares shot out of the officers' weapons and streaked across the road toward the kid who was still a few paces away from the edge of the forest. Just before Ramya blinked, he dove into the trees. The yellow flares, now pointy and streamlined like a pair of javelins, landed on the trees where the fugitive had disappeared.

Another howl ripped the skies as the assaulted trees fell apart and collapsed in a fuming heap to the ground. The pain in her ear intense and nearly unbearable, Ramya writhed on the ground. A few steps away, Ross was doubled over. The noise didn't show any signs of abating.

Ramya looked askance at the officers. They were clearly not affected by the sound, but they weren't hurrying after the fugitive either. The duo animatedly discussed something among themselves and a moment's hesitation later, marched toward the forest. Hands clasped over her ears, Ramya stumbled toward Ross. She could barely think straight with the ear-splitting ruckus that churned her guts, but they couldn't let the two officers run into them. Together they stumbled deeper into the raucous forest, barely seeing where they were headed.

Low branches tore into her arms and legs and thrashed against her face. Ramya's vision was blurry and her throat was parched. Then her foot caught something—a root or rock—and her heart lunged into her throat as she went flying. She landed face first on the forest floor, unglamorously like a pile of mud. The world faded a little, slowly at first. Then, in an instant, it turned black.

5

A pair of glittery red eyes that were set on a deathly pale brow-less face peered at Ramya. No, not just pale. It was gray, a shade of death. It was hairless with a brown-streaked neck. It reminded her of the Somfero mushrooms that were famous on Nikoor. As much as Ramya struggled to focus on the immediate, her energy-starved mind drifted impishly into thoughts of a sumptuous meal of long ago.

Somfero . . .

Ramya loved the Somfero—meaty, a little tangy, and perfect when toasted with a bit of pepper. Her father hated the Somfero as well as her love for them, Ramya recalled, grimacing.

"You have a peasant's taste in food," her father had growled at Ramya once as she gorged on a generous helping of the Somfero. She had cringed at his disapproving tone and set her spoon down. She had looked across the table hopefully. Her mother, the shadow of a presence on the other side of the table, had raised a curious brow. Like always, Lady Sonya had said nothing but simply gone on with dinner without a care.

"Hello," the small figure said in a voice that tinkled like a glass chime and cut through the haze of hurtful memories. "You be all right," he added.

He? Ramya couldn't tell for sure. The telltale brown stipes of a Mwandan male was present on his neck, but they were faded at best. If this was a male, he had to be a very young one. Ramya squinted, noting the enlarged oblong cranium typical of Mwandans, the overhung head in the back, and the lacking hair. He was wearing a blue bodysuit that fit snugly like a glove on a fist. Blue like the color of the sky in Nikoor.

Wait! A blue bodysuit? This *had* to be the Mwandan kid they were trying to help. The events leading to her fall and eventual blackout hit

Ramya like a Drednot's bulk. She sat up and looked around. Her neck felt stiff and weak as if it had gathered a decade of rust. The Mwandan stranger looked on curiously as Ramya pressed her throbbing temples and scanned her surroundings. The forest was quiet, far from the shrieking presence it had been when she'd tripped and fell.

She stiffened. *How long had she been passed out? Where the hell is Ross?*

"He gone foraging," the Mwandan tinkled as if he had read her mind. "You both quite . . ." — he paused and tapped his smooth gray chin — "*famished*. That appropriate word, believe so. I send him out foraging."

Even in the stilted, oddly formed sentences the young Mwandan strung together with obvious difficulty, the description made Ross sound like a bovine. Ramya's nose crinkled.

"Forage?" Ramya said. "For what? Food? There's food around here?"

He raised both hands up at the canopy of trees above them. "There food everywhere in forest. You only need eye to see."

Ramya scrambled to her feet, once again reeling from the dizziness and a sharp pang of hunger. She and Ross couldn't tell one tree in the forest from another on Morris II, so how was he going to forage for food? He could eat a poisoned plant and kill himself. She steadied herself. Ross was her last link to the real world, she couldn't lose him.

"What the matter?" the Mwandan asked.

"We don't know enough about Morris II, let alone its vegetation," Ramya said. "Ross wouldn't know what's good for him. I need to find him and stop him."

"You should keep faith in partner," the Mwandan said. "He be back. You have these." He stretched an arm and opened a gray palm. About ten black-and-red berries sat at its center. "Please, have."

Ramya looked from the Mwandan's gray face to the berries and back. She wanted to eat them so badly, but she knew nothing about this stranger other than the fact she and Ross had aided his escape. Ramya forced her eyes off the berries and focused them on his red glittering eyes.

"What's your name?"

The Mwandan's eyes dulled. His fingers curled over the berries. "You not have faith in me?" he asked.

Ramya shrugged, her eyes lingering on his closed fist more than was necessary. "I don't know you."

"But I know you. You save my life," the Mwandan said. "You and Ross. I obligated to you both."

Ramya flinched. She could do without the obligations. Her father was big on debts and gratitude and loyalty and obligations. She had heard those words far too many times to even tolerate them anymore.

"I only try repay my debt to you," the Mwandan went on, possibly not even noticing her frown. "This food is paying of debt."

He was likely harmless. Possibly. But could she take a chance and try one of those berries? Another sharp pang in Ramya's stomach struck at her will to hold out. She looked around one more time. Where the hell was Ross?

"You didn't tell me your name," Ramya said, suddenly remembering a forgotten thread.

"Ahool. Ahool Petta my name," he said. "You Rami, I know."

Ramya nodded. "Yes, that's me." Ross had not divulged her true identity, thank goodness for that. She could do well without the entire universe knowing who she really was.

Suddenly Ahool's eyes glittered merrily. He was looking past her, Ramya realized. One glance back and she spotted Ross marching toward them. Ramya blinked. What was going on with Commander Ross? He was grinning in a silly, happy sort of way, Ramya had never seen before. He carried his blaster in one hand and a small red packet in the other.

"You found them," Ahool Petta squealed like a kid who had found a long-lost toy.

Ross kneeled near Ramya and opened the packet he'd been carrying. It was full of leaves. They were dark just like every other foliage on Morris II. In addition, they had red veins crisscrossing them from tip to base.

"These perfect. Crisp," Ahool said as he ran his fingers over Ross's collection. He picked a couple, shook them a little, and held them out for Ross. "Chew. Chew lot. They give you strength and build immunity."

Ramya stared incredulously as Ross stuffed his mouth and started to chomp. All without a word or a question. For as long as she had known him, Ross was the suspicious kind. She couldn't understand why he would eat these strange leaves because a strange Mwandan told him to. She blinked a few times as Ross shoved another large wad of leaves into his mouth.

Ross had clearly noted her disbelieving look. It was hard to miss anyway. "It's all right, Rami," he said as soon as he had finished. "Ahool is a Berkari. He's also training to be a doctor."

Ahool reached into his suit and proudly flashed a golden medallion on his chain. Ramya didn't know what that meant, but she presumed it was some sort of official certification of his medical knowledge, and Ross apparently knew what it meant.

Ross continued vouching for the Mwandan. "He knows his stuff. You should try some of the berries. It will make you feel better. I was starving, but now . . ."

Ramya looked askance at Ahool Petta who was observing Ross with keen glittery eyes. As soon as Ross stopped speaking, he opening his palm again, revealing his offering of berries to Ramya.

The Berkari . . . Ramya tried to recall what she knew about that. It was hard to think. Pangs of hunger were clawing at her stomach and soreness was spreading through her bones. The Berkari was a radical faction among the Mwandans, she recalled. They didn't agree with the Mwandan government who kept the Mwandans isolated from the rest of the galaxy. The Berkari wanted the Mwandans to be an active part of the Confederacy, a sentiment outlawed by the current Mwandan government.

But did that automatically make Ahool their friend? Likely so. "The enemy of an enemy is a friend," so the ancient saying went. It was her father's favorite saying. Lord Paramount Trysten Kiroff didn't shy away from attributing his fortunes to following that adage, so it had to be worth something. They were trespassing in a Mwandan territory, and the government wouldn't like that one bit. In that case, the Berkari was their best ally.

Ramya grabbed a handful of berries from Ahool. They were sweet and . . . just the most wonderful taste. Ramya was sure she hadn't had anything half as wonderful in her life. They left a cool sensation inside her mouth, throat, and chest, and a few mouthfuls later, the dizziness had just about disappeared entirely.

"What now?" she asked Ross.

He promptly handed her one of the leaves from his basket. "Have this. It'll help you adjust to Morris II. Apparently, the trees here release minute spores that can be toxic to aliens . . . meaning us."

The berries had certainly helped so Ramya didn't argue. Ahool's face broke into a huge grin when Ramya took a bite of the leaf. A sharp sour sensation hit her taste buds and Ramya barely managed to stop from cursing out loud.

"Ahool has offered to take us to the Grove of Stillness," Ross explained as Ramya forced some more of the sour leaves into her mouth. "That's where the *Endeavor* seems to have crashed. Trouble is, that's sacred burial ground for Mwandans and we don't have long to get the crew and, hopefully, the whole ship out of there before the government comes looking."

Ahool nodded eagerly. "Fortunate that Grove of Stillness is remote, so forces don't know about it very quickly. But still, we should hasten to help your friends."

"How long will it take us to get there?" Ramya asked. They had to rescue the *Endeavor* if they wanted to get out of Morris II, and time was running out very fast. Not just the Mwandan government, but very soon, the Confederacy would come looking as well. Her father's shadow was always looming.

"If we walk all way, an hour at least." Ahool paused to mull over something. "If we not run into squad officers looking for me. Worst case, it take much longer," he said, the corners of his lips drooping. "But if—"

"If what?" Ramya asked.

"If we fix rambler, then—"

"Rambler?" Ramya asked, fixing a curious gaze on Ahool. "What's that?"

"It's vehicle. I traveling with Moonis in it," Ahool explained. His gaze drooped and his face lost its characteristic shine when he mentioned Moonis. It seemed the gray pallor of his had suddenly acquired a bluish tinge to it. "Squad officers wreck it when they catch up with us."

Ramya cast a look at Ross. Had he asked Ahool about why the squad officers were chasing Ahool in the first place? Was it because he was part of the Berkari? "Why were they chasing you?" she asked.

Ahool let out a long sigh. Leaves rustled all of a sudden. It seemed as if the entire forest let out a sigh. "We make trouble at the squad headquarters," he said. His eyes flicked from Ramya to Ross's before drooping to the ground again. "They had us in prison. We broke out. Make a little explosion and damage the building. Squad officers not like it one bit."

Ramya fiddled with her thumbs and looked at Ross who simply gave her an indifferent look. "May I talk to you for a second, Commander?" she said, and Ross stepped away from Ahool Petta, albeit a little reluctantly.

"What?" he said in a low voice as soon as they were a few steps away from the Mwandan. His face flushed, and he almost seemed annoyed that she had pulled him aside.

"He's a fugitive," Ramya said. "The Mwandan law enforcement is after him."

Ross shrugged. "You wanted to help him, didn't you?" That was a fact. "Besides, we're fugitives too. We're wanted more than Ahool, I have no doubt."

Ross was correct, so it was back to the same old saying. In hopes of shoring up that elusive courage, Ramya muttered, "An enemy of your enemy —"

"Is a friend," Ross completed. His voice had turned hard when he spoke again. "We *have* to get to Captain Milos. Whatever it takes."

Ramya nodded in agreement. She couldn't lose sight of what was really important. They had to get to the *Endeavor*. They headed over to Ahool Petta, who was sitting with his head down.

"So, Ahool . . . what's wrong with your rambler?"

"Not wrong. Just fallen." He sat up a bit. "They fire at us. The rambler topples. Moonis dies. They try to kill Ahool, but you help."

"But what's wrong with the rambler?"

Ahool shrugged. "Maybe nothing. I not know. I no engineer. I doctor."

"Oh, I see," Ramya said.

Perhaps they could fix the vehicle. Ross had been on the *Endeavor* for a while. He had to know something about fixing vehicles. She knew a thing or two about spacecraft design also, although she'd never tried her hand at fixing an automobile, let alone a strange Mwandan version of a vehicle.

"The best option now is to check the rambler out," Ross said, and Ahool nodded vigorously in support.

"Assuming the squad officers left it there," Ramya said as they started walking to the edge of the forest in a line, Ross leading, Ahool in the middle, and Ramya flanking the end.

"Yes, they did," Ross said. "They took off in their own rambler with the dead man."

That was good news. Perhaps they'd be able to fix the vehicle and get to the *Endeavor* quickly.

"Why didn't they follow you into the forest, Ahool?" Ramya asked the Mwandan. Ramya recalled the howling forest when the officers had shot at a fleeing Ahool.

"They fear forest spirits protecting Ahool," Ahool replied. "The squads no friends of the forests. They not respect the true Mwandan ways. That's why Berkari fight."

"But I thought . . ." Ramya stopped as her thoughts drifted. Little was known about the reclusive Mwandans except for the fact that the race was closely linked to plants.

"We, Mwandans, evolve from plants," Ahool went on in a plaintive voice. "Mwandans are children of forests. We are one with them." Ahool raised his arms toward the trees that towered above them and Ramya was pretty sure they swayed just a bit, as if nodding in agreement with Ahool. "But government now want to use forest for fuel." Ahool paused and shuddered. "No true Mwandan accept that. No true Mwandan destroy ancestors."

Ancestor or not, using the trees for fuel wasn't such a great idea. Humans had long learned that. Since the near-destruction of Old Terra, cutting down of trees or making any drastic changes to the habitats on any colonized planet was enforced strictly. Either the Mwandans obviously didn't know the terrible history of the humans or they chose to ignore it knowingly.

"Not a great idea," she said. "Destroying forests is no good."

Red eyes flashing, Ahool turned toward her and nodded. "That's why I protest. And they lock me up."

Ramya chuckled. "So you blew up a building?" she asked.

"Ahool not proud of it. But he had to get out," Ahool replied. "I not know explosives so powerful. Moonis arrange that. But dome breaks in half and people get hurt. I not enjoy that."

Ramya's feet slowed as Ahool's words sunk in. "Hey, wait! Ross, could this be the same building we saw down south?"

"Could be," Ross replied distractedly. He raised a cautioning arm in the next second. They had reached the edge of the forest and only a single row of trees stood between them and the clearing beyond.

The clearing was empty. Except for the overturned rambler that lay to one side and a large brownish patch on the ground where Ahool's accomplice, Moonis, had once lain, there was no evidence of the scene of a few minutes ago.

"All's clear," Ross whispered. He pointed in the direction of the rambler. "Let's get to the vehicle. Be prepared to fall back."

They reached the rambler without any incident and after some tugging and pushing, the trio was able to straighten the vehicle.

"I try to start it," Ahool volunteered. He scuttled into the glass-covered passenger area and sat in the single seat in the front row. His gray fingers danced on a large curved panel. Ramya peeped in to observe. All control of the vehicle was achieved through that touch-sensitive panel, and Ahool seemed quite at ease with the control system.

"What's going on?" Ross asked from behind. He had been scanning back and forth in case the officers returned.

"Nothing," Ramya said. Other than some noncommittal beeps and barely reassuring *bloops*, there didn't seem to be a sign of progress as far as she could tell.

"We can't wait out here for too long," Ross said in a low voice. "The squad can be back anytime. Possibly with reinforcements." He raised the blaster in his arms. "Our weapons are no match for what those two had."

He was right. It was unwise to wait for too long at the scene of the getaway. Sooner or later, the squad officers were bound to come back to check the periphery. If Ahool Petta was indeed responsible for the explosion they had seen from the Stryker, no law enforcement worth their salt would simply shrug off the miscreant behind such pandemonium. They had to get away from here as quickly as possible.

"It getting alive." Ahool's excited shout made Ramya snap back toward him. The panel was now brighter than before, clusters of shapes and letters dancing over it. Ahool's fingers danced even faster, almost in frenzy.

"Can you drive it?" Ramya asked.

"I not know," Ahool replied. "But I try. I wake it up, didn't I?"

Somehow, even though Ahool sounded nothing short of confident, Ramya couldn't feel enthusiastic about the ride. Ross's face was equally dim.

"Is it all right?" Ramya asked again. "Safe?"

"There trouble with fuel line. Blockage, report say."

"Can you fix it?" Ross asked.

"Nothing to fix. We take chance. Go as far as we can."

What if they went up in a ball of flames? Ramya looked at the panel. A zillion words in some unrecognizable Mwandan script flashed all over it. She couldn't read it and asking Ahool to translate it all would take a long time. Time they didn't have.

They had to follow Ahool. There was no other option.

"Come up," Ahool invited. His eyes were like rubies, and a nervous smile stretched unsteadily on his lips.

The stars help us, Ramya thought before jumping into the rear seat of the vehicle. The window next to her was shattered, a reminder of the attack that killed Ahool's companion, Moonis. Ramya suppressed a shudder and forced her eyes ahead.

As soon as Ross climbed in next to her, Ahool let out a joyful, chirpy sound. "We go now," he announced. "We follow road for ten minutes, then find fork to Grove."

The rambler lifted off the ground slightly and teetered. For a second, nausea returned to fill Ramya's guts. Then, with a bone-chilling hiss, the rambler shot forward.

Ramya had barely let out the breath she had been holding when the shadow fell across the clearing. The shadow's immense size and the suddenness with which it appeared made everyone look up through the glass roof of the rambler. Ramya's heart skipped a beat.

There was no mistaking the hulking craft north of them. It was blood red, a color typical of a Norgoran spaceship. It reminded Ramya of a torpedo. Its flaring rear end shaped like the tail of a fish was spinning, which was characteristic of the Norgoran Glasspointe, the fastest scout ships in the galaxy.

"Ahool, take cover," Ross yelled immediately. "Right now!"

Unsteadily, the rambler scrambled to the edge of the clearing.

"Should stop?" Ahool asked in a rushed voice, his face tinged with fear.

"No, keep going straight up," Ross instructed. "Don't turn toward the *Endeavor*. We don't want to point them that way. Just keep going. Stay in the shadows."

The Glasspointe hovered over the clearing, and for a while Ramya was sure it was watching them.

"Is it here for us?" she whispered to Ross.

"Why else would a Norgoran ship come to a Mwandan sanctuary?" he said before tapping Ahool on the shoulder. "Hey, Ahool, have you seen Norgoran ships out here lately?"

Ahool shook his head vigorously. "Never seen ship like that in my life."

Ross threw a meaningful glance at Ramya. "Only one thing has changed. Us. Our presence on Morris II."

"The Norgorans are the best seekers in the galaxy. They must be looking for the *Endeavor*."

Every race in the Confederacy was allowed to maintain their own space fleet according to the Treaty of the Races that culminated in the formation of the Confederacy hundreds of years ago. The Norgorans didn't build battleships like the humans or starbases like the Octus. Their specialty was the smaller, sleeker, and fuel-efficient scouting ships. When it came to looking for new resources in uncharted territory or scanning a disaster zone for survivors, the Confederacy often turned to the Norgorans for help.

"Besides, they're probably the only people the Mwandans would allow in here," Ross added.

Norgorans were peaceful people. They were a far cry from the other two races that actively participated in the Confederacy: the ferocious and bloodthirsty Octus, and the slightly less fierce but not entirely peaceful humans. If the reclusive Mwandans let anyone into their sanctuary, it had to be the gentle Norgorans.

The shadow above them shifted and Ramya looked up at the dark underside of the ship. It tilted then turned away southward.

"They're leaving," she whispered.

"They didn't see us," Ross said. "We just had a most lucky escape, Ahool. Let's get away while we can."

"I take you quick," Ahool said. He swerved, the rambler teetering toward the forest at a breakneck speed. Ramya's shoulder crashed into the window frame and all the soreness in her body came alive in an instant. She winced and held her breath, bracing herself for impact as the Mwandan automobile rushed headlong into a wall of trees.

6

The rambler weaved through the trees, veering madly from one side to another, back and forth, over and over again, to avoid the tree trunks. Branches and twigs smashed against the rambler's front and side like whips, and wind blew through the broken windows and lashed across Ramya's face as she grabbed the back of Ahool's seat as tightly as she could.

The worst part was the lack of control. Ramya had been through plenty of iffy situations in the last few days, but she had never been so much at the mercy of unknowns. Right now, on a planet she knew little about, guided by a person she had barely known for a few minutes, and careening recklessly into who knew where, every fear that Ramya had kept at bay for a long time now pounced back on her.

There would be no going to the Fringe. No finding the Moanus. Or Uncle Brynden. There would be no regaining of her honor back from her father. She would remain the black sheep of House Kiroff, the one who ran away from CAWStrat like a common thief.

In that dark second, Ramya's mind flew back to her final days at CAWStrat. Armand Danukis's sneering face flashed across her mind's eye. Leona's snicker floated into her ears. Her father's blue-gray eyes stared at her, murderous rage coiling in their icy depths.

Someone nudged her elbow. "Rami!"

Ramya clung on to the voice like it was the one plank that could get her out of the seas of despair. Her eyes fluttered open to find Ross looking worriedly at her.

"You all right?" he asked.

"No."

The rambler tilted to almost sideways before straightening. Ramya felt Ross grab her arm, steadying her just before her head hit what was left of the window. Any other time, she'd have hated looking so weak, but now she felt oddly comforted by his support.

"We'll never make it," she whispered, and felt his grip tighten.

"We *will* make it," he said in a steely voice. "We have to. Can't let the captain down."

He stared, hard-jawed at the blur ahead. Forests rushed at a break-neck speed on his round eyeglasses. Ramya noticed how the plated metal on the rim of his glasses had peeled in places. *Is he too poor to get it fixed,* she wondered. It was as unexpected a thought as the appearance of the Norgoran ship. She realized she knew nothing of Ross's life before he got to the *Endeavor.* Guilt twisted in her heart. It was wrong to have kept her identity a secret from him, from any of the crew. They were family now. They had to know. The first chance she got she'd tell them.

The rambler stopped, and Ramya pushed on the back of Ahool's seat to keep from falling forward. She peered outside, her head spinning. They had reached some sort of a blockade. It was a wall, not made of stone or steel but an impenetrable line of super trees. It was difficult to believe that trees could grow so close together that they almost formed a mesh.

"We reach the Grove of Stillness," Ahool announced in a breathless voice. He lifted a shaky finger at the barrier ahead. "That Sentinel wall."

"We reached already?" Ramya asked, throwing an incredulous glance at Ross.

"We make shortcut," Ahool explained. "And I drive very fast."

Indeed. They had almost flown.

Ramya quickly scanned the sky and caught Ross doing the same. "Have we lost the ship?" she asked.

"I'll go outside and check," Ross suggested. "Ahool, can we get off?"

Ahool sat the rambler down on the ground. Ramya thought the young Mwandan looked even paler than before. He had to be shaken. Anyone would be tense after such a wild dash through the forest

Ramya patted the Mwandan's shoulder before slipping out of the rambler. "You're an amazing driver, Ahool. Did you know that?"

A pink flush spread up Ahool's face. He smiled shyly and shot a quick glittery look at Ramya before nodding. "I pray to forest spirit. They help. They want keep all alive."

They most definitely wanted to keep Ahool alive. Ramya recalled how the trees had howled when the squad officers had shot at the fleeing Mwandan. He had a connection to the forest spirits, whatever that was.

Ross had been scanning the skies intently. "I don't see the Norgoran ship," he declared, "but if they picked up signs of our presence then they'll surely come back."

No doubt about that. Norgorans were a notoriously stubborn people, and once they picked up a scent, they didn't let go. It was no accident that they grew a reputation of being the galaxy's premier scouts. But they weren't hovering overhead, at least for the moment.

"Ross. Rami." Ahool stood behind them, a worried expression on his pallid face. He nodded at the mighty barrier of trees ahead. "I need ask for permission to enter."

"What do you mean?" Ross asked. "Can't we just walk in?"

Ahool shuddered and clamped his palms over his ears as if he had just heard a blasphemy. Then he shook his head violently. "Oh no, no, no! Cannot just walk in to Grove of Stillness." He stopped and pointed at the largest trees that stood at the middle of the wall. "They sentinels. We beg for path. If we go with no blessing, sentinels punish us. They kill us."

"How do we get their blessing?" Ross asked again.

Ahool gave a droopy-faced look. "I try speak to them. Never have talked to sentinels." He walked back to the edge of the clearing and sat down on the ground facing the towering wall ahead. He crossed his legs, then his arms, and closed his eyes. Then, his lips started moving as if he were chanting a spell.

Ramya let out a sigh. Thank goodness for their Mwandan friend.

It was a fabulous stroke of luck that they had found Ahool or they'd have been killed in that grove the moment they stepped in.

"This is ridiculous," Ross whispered, shaking his head at Ahool. "Who knows how long this will take."

Ramya could understand Ross's fears. The worst case scenario chilled her heart. "I hope the Grove isn't punishing the *Endeavor* for crashing into it. I have no idea what these forests are capable of, but the Mwandans do not take them lightly, that's for sure."

Ross gave a hopeless shake of his head. "We don't have a choice but to wait until Ahool wakes up. Funny how everyone starts napping around us. First that damned AI and now this guy."

Ramya was about to remind him that Dakrhaeth wasn't napping because he felt like it but to repair the Stryker, but Ross's dark and gloomy face convinced her to remain quiet. He was stressed and that wasn't unexpected, given the situation. Now was the time to mend fences, not light a fire under it.

Ramya decided to put some effort into small talk instead. "You must've known Captain Milos for a long time," she said.

Ross turned sharply, his brows furrowed. He was about to snap at her, Ramya was sure, but he didn't. "Not too long," he replied calmly. "I was the newest addition to the crew until you came along."

"Were you on another ship before that?"

"No. This is my first job on a ship," Ross replied in a thick voice.

"Where are you from? Which sector?"

His eyes flashed and Ramya shriveled a little. She had gone too far with that question. What right did she have asking about his past when she had lied about her own? But Ross didn't retort like she expected. He simply pursed his lips and turned away.

So much for small talk. Ramya was about to walk about and scan the periphery when Ross turned back.

"Halperion," he said. "You must've heard the name."

Ramya wished she had never asked. The name Halperion, the way he said it, and the seething hatred in his eyes chilled her bones.

"I have," she replied simply, holding his burning gaze as fearlessly as she could.

Ross scoffed. "The planet with the biggest Solandium deposits in the galaxy. Halperion sure is famous, isn't it?"

He was taunting her. Halperion didn't just have the biggest Solandium deposits in the galaxy, which made it one of the most sought after planetary fiefdoms; it was made more famous by the bloody games the houses played to secure rights over the Solandium mines.

Ross absent-mindedly tapped his blaster. "It used to be a beautiful place. No one cared about a bunch of hillbillies on a remote planet. We didn't mind the lack of attention either. Then someone stumbled on a vein of Solandium and all hell broke loose."

She had been just a child then, but Ramya vividly remembered the rush of activity at Somenvaar when the news of the discovery broke. House Danukis was the first to bid for mining rights on Halperion, but they were no match for Trysten Kiroff's maneuvers. Within a few months he had somehow managed to get most of the homesteaders on Halperion to sign over the rights of their lands to House Kiroff.

Ramya still remembered overhearing a heated exchange between her grandfather and her father.

"You sent in mercenaries?" Grappa Abelei had hissed at Trysten. "I can understand bidding wars, I can even understand bribes, but threatening those poor people by sending thugs into their homes? Forcing them to sell off their rights for a fraction of what it's worth? That isn't right."

Her father had looked away but his face stayed hard as a rock. A few seconds later he had replied in an icy tone, "House Kiroff is now mine to lead, Father. What is best for it is up to me to decide. I don't want to lecture you on how to spend your retirement, but if I did, I'd advise you to stay out of our business matters. You've done enough and I'm grateful. Please let things stay that way."

Ramya hadn't understood what it all meant, only that Grappa didn't speak to anyone except her in the week that followed. Then the Locusta-Vanga war started. Grappa left for the front and never returned. Thanks to the new Solandium mines on Halperion, House Kiroff manufactured fighter crafts for the Confederacy faster than anyone else in the business. When the war ended, Trysten Kiroff had become the richest man in the galaxy.

Ramya let go of the breath she had been holding while she reminisced. Ross was still distractedly tapping his blaster, his face grim.

"Do you still have family there?" Ramya asked, regretting the question immediately.

Ross looked up and studied her for a bit. "Yes, they work in the mines you own, mines that should have been theirs."

No wonder he hated her. Ramya breathed in deep but still felt pitifully empty inside.

"I'm sorry. I—"

Ross's eyes flashed. "What's your apology gonna get me?"

"Nothing." Nothing she said or did was going to change the past, but she was sorry for how unjustly the people Halperion had been treated. "If I ever get a chance—"

"Save it, Rami," Ross cut her off. "Whatever you do now isn't going to fix the lives ruined. It won't bring back my uncles who died fighting those thugs House Kiroff unleashed on us. So just let it go, all right?"

"I'm sorry." The words trickled out of her mouth.

"Please," he said through gritted teeth. "Please stop saying that." Ramya shriveled at his vicious tone. Ross stepped closer, his eyes flashing dangerously. "I dreamed of going to the university and for a bit it had seemed I could. My poor father was up in the clouds, happy that he could finally give me something worthwhile. But he was just a silly old man with stupid hopes who forgot to factor in Trysten Kiroff's greed."

Ramya held her breath. Ross's words stung and kept on stinging. Strange that she felt no anger, only guilt. No wonder Ross was always so bitter. How many more of such lives had her father ruined? How many enemies did House Kiroff have out there? Fear touched the base of her spine with ice-cold fingers and made her shudder.

Ross went on with his pitiless tirade. "I've taught myself to be smarter than my father. I don't think that just because I've been good to people, they'll be good to me. And I certainly don't trust anyone with Kiroff blood in them," he said it all in one breath. He paused for a second before spitting out the next words. "I told you . . . I need you now to get to the *Endeavor*. Besides, I have to follow the captain's orders. I just can't desert you. But don't, not even for a second, think of me as a friend. I'm not. And I don't want to be."

For a gut-wrenching moment or two they stood facing each other, eyes locked in a battle of will. Then Ross turned on his heels and marched away. Ramya turned also, a pall of gloom tightening like a noose around her neck as she stared blankly at the nearest tree trunk.

He could never forgive her. The camaraderie of the moment was only the means to an end. It would be over the second they found the *Endeavor*. What would Ross do after that? Could he . . . disclose her identity to one of the countless enemies of House Kiroff?

Ramya leaned against the tree, thankful for its steady presence. Dark, worrisome thoughts swirled endlessly in her mind, and she struggled to breathe. She closed her eyes and willed the fears away. She had to focus on the present, on getting to the *Endeavor*. The rest was going to have to wait.

"Rami!"

"Ross? Wha—"

Something black and sticky slapped her face and clung tightly, gluing her mouth shut and keeping her eyes closed. Waves of stickiness wrapped around her torso at a furious pace. Long before Ramya could panic, she toppled to the ground like a mummified corpse.

6

7

Ramya heard voices. People were talking in the distance, speaking in a strange tongue — possibly a Mwandan dialect — that she couldn't understand. The voices faded soon after, and even though Ramya strained to hold on to the distant sounds, she couldn't for long.

She gave her shoulders a frustrated shake. She didn't budge even a hair. Whatever wrapped her from head to foot in a dark cocoon was tight and strong. She couldn't as much as twitch a finger. The blaster in her hand had been ripped from her fingers when the thing encircled her so she was totally, utterly defenseless. Ramya had no trouble breathing though. The cocoon was like a full body armor — a breathable but sightless armor.

It was one hell of a restraint. Ramya had tried to fight her way out of it, and she had also tried to scream. None of it worked. It was funny that even as she braced for a painful death in the hands of her captors, she thought of her father. Trysten Kiroff would've been intrigued by such a novelty of a shackle. Perhaps he'd even build a factory or two and make some kind of armor out of the technology.

"Ahool . . ."

Ramya's ears perked up on hearing Ahool's name. Who were these people? The squad officers? Or were these some friends of Ahool's?

She wished they'd at least let her see their faces. Or maybe not. She didn't want to watch them arrange her execution. Sometimes ignorance was bliss.

The questions didn't stop coming though. Did they wrap Ross and Ahool up as well? How long were they going to keep her restrained?

Someone shrieked. It sounded just like Ahool. Ramya pushed against the body restraint but barely moved. Were they hurting

Ahool? She strained her ears, but other than some sort of a dull commotion in the distance, she couldn't fathom much. She was running out of air. It was getting harder to breathe . . .

She had to calm down. There was no point struggling. Unless they let her free, there was no way to get out of this casket. Or unless she grew some kind of superpower, but that was as incredible a dream as could be. She *had* to wait and not panic. Ramya breathed slowly . . . in and out, in and out.

Ramya had steadied her thoughts to a manageable level when she noticed the change—the distant furor outside was growing louder. The voices were coming closer. Ahool, she realized gleefully, was the loudest among others.

Someone tugged at her feet while someone else grabbed her head. They hoisted her, cocoon and all, and stood her up. There was a dull pop and then the bindings around her body fell away and the stickiness on her face vanished. Someone snatched her second blaster from its holster before Ramya's eyes fluttered open. The blurred figures came into view slowly. About a dozen or so Mwandans, dressed in black hooded shirts that covered their pale heads, were carrying weapons that looked like blasters but were longer and stouter. They stood facing her in a semicircle. Ahool stood right in the middle, and on seeing Ramya open her eyes, he rushed forward.

"You be all right," he said. He pointed at the Mwandans with weapons behind him. "They my friends."

"Some welcoming friends," Ross grumbled next to her, massaging his right hand tenderly.

"They not know," Ahool tried to explain. His face had taken on a bluish tinge, a sign of anxiety.

"What do they want?" Ramya asked. "Why did they catch us?"

"Berkari Chief come looking for Ahool. Then find you."

Ross stepped closer. "The Berkari chief? He's here?"

Ahool nodded. "Yes. He wants talk to you. Come."

Ramya and Ross exchanged a quick glance before following

Ahool Petta. This had to be good news. Based on the title alone, the Berkari chief sounded and seemed quite powerful. If only they could get him to help them get the *Endeavor* free.

Ahool led the way near the edge of the clearing to the damaged rambler. There was a larger vehicle next to it. It was almost five times bigger than Ahool's rambler and black as charcoal. A caped figure stood next to the vehicle looking up at the Sentinel wall. On hearing the group approach, he turned around.

Ramya's eyes widened on seeing his face and her steps slowed. This male — she was sure it was a male — was not gray like Ahool and the rest of the Mwandans behind them. Instead, he had deep brown skin with black stripes on his neck.

"He's an Uminato," Ross whispered. Ramya had no idea what that meant, but she was sure glad Ross knew. She took note of the light tone in his voice, so it had to be good news. There was no time to ask Ross to explain because they were already face-to-face with the leader of the Berkari. Ross gave the Mwandan a quick half-bow and Ramya quickly followed.

Ahool pointed at Ramya and Ross and spoke excitedly to the chief in some Mwandan language, none of which Ramya understood. The chief did not seem displeased. He simply nodded gravely, which was a good sign. As soon as Ahool stopped speaking, the chief addressed Ramya and Ross.

"Humans are not welcome on Mwandan sanctuaries, weren't you aware of that?" he said. His voice tinkled also, just like Ahool's, only his sentences were perfectly constructed and nothing like the rapidly and randomly strung sentences Ahool typically spoke.

"Yes, Chief, we were aware," Ross replied.

His eyes widened. "Then why are you here? Ahool tells me your mothership has crashed into the Grove of Stillness. Is that true?"

"Yes, it is true. We did not have a choice but to land here, Chief."

"Why is that?"

Ross inhaled sharply. He was clearly hesitating and that was not lost on the Berkari chief.

"You are not outlaws, are you?" he asked, the tinkle in his voice suddenly thick and heavy. Ross shook his head when the chief held up a cautioning hand. "Let me tell you that lies are useless with me. I can sense untruths just as easily I can see you standing in front of me. You could ask why I'm even telling you that. I should simply find out when you speak."

He paused, looking from Ross to Ramya, and holding Ramya's gaze for an uncomfortably long time. Ramya knew she was not supposed to open her mouth — the Berkari chief had just stopped Ross from even shaking his head — and if anyone was supposed to respond to the chief, it had to be Ross. Yet, something inside her fluttered and snapped out of control as the Berkari chief stared at her.

"You're testing us, that's why," Ramya blurted. "You're giving us this chance to choose for ourselves. If we speak the truth, you'll help us."

His eyes glittered and widened. "So, speak."

Ross didn't need another invitation. He related every part of their adventures, starting from their finding the Stryker in Sector 22 to the encounter with the Confederacy and finally to their journey to Morris II to find the *Endeavor*. Once in a while, Ramya chimed in with things she had heard from Dakrhaeth and his pilot, Habardein.

"We didn't plan to come here, Chief," Ross concluded in an earnest voice. "Neither did Captain Milos. And we won't stay here for a second longer than needed for us to get the *Endeavor* out of here."

The Berkari chief looked away from them. His eyes had lost their sheen — he had to be worried about something — Ramya knew from watching Ahool.

"What do you know about the four missing Strykers?" he asked Ramya after a sizeable silence.

For a second, Ramya's stumbled to a halt. That was odd. Why did the chief ask that particular question?

"Rami," Ross's sharp call shoved her out of the jumble in her head.

"We don't know for sure, but Dakrhaeth . . . the AI on the Stryker we have . . . he said they went to the Fringe to lay the groundwork for the second Locustan invasion to begin."

The Berkari chief crossed his arms and paced around, his deep brown coloration turning purplish for a moment or two. He was agitated, maybe even afraid. The idea of a second Locustan invasion was terrifying, but Ramya couldn't understand why it rattled the stolid Berkari chief as much.

Something pierced Ramya's thoughts like an unsettling ripple through her mind, vanishing as swiftly as it had come. Her spine tingled at the strange sensation. Ross stood stiffly next to her with a bemused expression on his face. The Berkari chief stared at them, his eyes boring into them like a pair of lasers. He had just probed their minds, Ramya realized.

"Your captain," the chief said, staring worriedly from Ramya to Ross, "He's Terenze Milos?"

Ramya and Ross exchanged a quick glance before Ross nodded. "Yes, he is."

He pointed at the looming wall of trees. "And you're sure your ship's in there?"

Ross held up his comm. "Look," he said. He pressed the large button at the center that connected radio channels for communication. The comm flashed green for a brief second, then crackled. "Wait . . . that's—"

Ramya scooted closer. All they had heard so far on the comm was a dull buzz, but this was far more.

". . . ello," a voice spurted out.

"Flux?" Ross yelled. "That's our engineer," he explained quickly to the Berkari chief. "Flux!"

"Ross? . . . you . . . tuck." The channel went dead as abruptly as it had come to life. Ross flashed a bewildered look at Ramya before tapping the button a few more times. The comm stayed quiet.

"What did he mean? Tuck? Who's Tuck?" Ross said.

Ramya didn't know, but her head was spinning, one thought circling her mind at a furious pace. The crew was alive after all.

"I think he meant stuck," the Berkari chief said suddenly. He had turned a shade of purple once again.

"We need to help them," Ross said.

The chief burst out in a Mwandan tongue, yelling orders at his men, who broke in a frenzy of activity at once. He barked something at Ahool who immediately scuttled close to Ramya and Ross.

"Come, we get inside Chief's carrier," he said, pointing to the black super-rambler.

"Where are we going?" Ramya asked.

Ahool nodded. "We go inside the Grove of Stillness, of course."

Of course? But how? The wall looked as impenetrable as ever. Ahool's prayers and chants had not made the slightest dent in the Sentinel wall.

"Does the chief's vehicle have special powers?" Ross precisely asked what Ramya was thinking. "Can it just sail through the wall?"

"Of course no," Ahool chuckled as if Ross had just made the silliest of comments. "Chief opening wall now."

Ramya spun around to look for the chief. He stood, arms crossed and eyes closed, facing the wall. She looked up at the wall of trees on the other side of the clearing. Nothing seemed to have changed. Or had it?

"Did those trees just move?" Ross said suddenly.

The trees were surely doing something.

Ramya blinked. Then again. Something was happening. How, Ramya didn't quite understand, but she was sure the opening between the two tallest trees at the middle of the wall hadn't existed a second ago. Now an even, although narrow, path that led into the darkness of the grove had appeared by some magic.

"Come, come," Ahool prodded. "We ready to find your ship."

They were indeed. By the time Ross and Ramya had boarded the chief's carrier, the path had grown wide enough to let a large vehicle to pass. A second or two later, the Berkari chief stirred. He bowed low at the wall and then rushed into the carrier. As soon as the doors closed behind him, the vehicle took off.

The Berkari chief stopped briefly near Ross and Ramya. "We will find your ship, do not worry," he said.

The chief was a regal presence and the confidence oozing out of his words was comforting. Ramya suddenly realized that they didn't even know the chief's name. In the rush of activity, no one had introduced him. They could always simply call him "Chief," but being trained in observing protocol since childhood, Ramya couldn't shake off the discomfort.

She half-bowed hastily and voiced her question before the Berkari chief could walk away. "How should we address you, Chief?"

The corner of his mouth curled a little. "I am Chief Dal Uminato. You can address me as Chief Dal."

A shadow fell inside the carrier. Ramya looked around. They had started to enter the grove. It was pitch-black inside, a darkness so deep that made Ramya shudder.

"It's closing," Ross said. Following his gaze, Ramya looked toward the back windows. The opening that the sentinels had made for them to enter the grove was slowly growing thinner. It grew smaller until the last sliver of light was wiped off and the grove shut around them.

8

Darkness was thick and heavy and the carrier seemed to plod forward through it with difficulty. The weak light of the carrier's front lamps lit a thin path ahead. Chief Dal Uminato stood with his arms on his hips, barking orders to the pilots in Mwandan tongue. A while had passed before he turned back to Ross and Ramya.

"How long has it been since your ship crashed here?" he asked, his face rigid.

Ross glanced at his watch. "Over an hour."

The chief rubbed his chin and pondered. "An hour? That's bad."

Ramya guessed that no one, not even the Mwandans, entered this grove without its permission, and the *Endeavor* was an alien craft that had crashed into it. The grove couldn't have liked that.

"Bad? Why?" Ramya asked regardless, hoping the chief had some other reason in mind.

"Reliquary groves like this one aren't meant to be disturbed, that's why," the chief said. "Trespassers into the grove pay with their lives."

"Couldn't you ask the forest spirit to forgive them or something?" Ross asked. "They didn't mean disrespect. They —"

"I asked. Doesn't mean the spirits listened. And it certainly doesn't mean they'll forgive."

"We can't lose them," Ramya said. "We have to save Captain Milos. Only he would know how to fight the Locustans. No one else would believe what Dakrhaeth told us . . . about the second invasion that's coming or about the four missing Strykers laying the groundwork for it."

"I would," the chief replied grimly. "I know."

Ross leaned forward with a deep frown etched on his forehead. "You know about the Locustans?"

The chief inhaled sharply. "I don't exactly know about the Locustans, but there's something strange afoot at the Fringe. There is a small Mwandan sanctuary on Bucifer P9, in the inner Fringe. Chief Mifek leads the Berkari faction there. We, the Berkari chiefs, speak to each other often. In his last communique, Chief Mifek said some strange things . . . frightening things. He said populations on various planets in the Fringe have disappeared mysteriously in the past week. No one knows where the people went, or why, or how. Now hearing what you just told me, I'm certain the missing Strykers have something to do with it."

"How could you have news from the Fringe?" Ramya asked. She hesitated a second before asking the question that burned in her mind. "I thought . . . I thought you shun the Confederacy and its broadcasts?" The chief frowned and Ramya hastened to explain some more. "That's what I've been told."

"You're not incorrect," the chief said. "Our government doesn't allow news broadcasts from the Confederacy. But we are the Berkari, the Mwandan outlaws. We don't agree with our government. Besides, I have other ways to get news."

He turned around to look at the path ahead. Ramya peeked also — there was nothing new to see outside, only a dimly lit path into the unending dark. But the Berkari chief had certainly sensed something because he walked over to the pilots and yelled in his native tongue. The vehicle seemed to slow down a little.

Ramya scooted closer to Ross. "Why are they slowing down?" she whispered.

Ross shrugged. He couldn't know the answer, but she desperately needed some reassurance. Slowing down was not good at all. They were already late and losing time. Every second mattered. Not knowing the Mwandan world thoroughly enough, there was nothing she could do and the helplessness infuriated her.

Thankfully, the Berkari chief came back to them quickly. "Temihula's not letting go," he said gravely.

"What? Who?" Ross asked.

The chief closed his eyes briefly before pronouncing the name again. "Temihula's one of the major spirits of the grove. He's the giver of life, the forefather of the Mwandan race. We're all descended from him."

The Mwandans, a plant-based species, understandably worshipped the flora. Their sentient forests were as powerful as they were weird and the spirits within them were gods to the Mwandans. It stood to reason that a command from the spirits was irrefutable.

"What do you mean he's not letting go?" Ramya blurted.

"He's the one who holds your ship captive," the chief explained. "And even though we have permission to travel into the grove, he's still angry at the intrusion and he refuses to release the ship."

"What does he want?" Ramya asked.

"I'm not sure yet. I'll ask when I get closer to the center of the grove. But . . ." His words faded and Ramya grimaced. A dangling "but" never was good and certainly not in this situation. One part of her didn't want to know what he thought was wrong, but she also knew she had to find out. How could she help Captain Milos and the *Endeavor* if she was scared of hearing the truth?

"You have doubts, Chief?" she forced the words out.

Chief Dal Uminato sighed deeply before nodding. "I do. Temihula isn't one to trifle with. If he makes up his mind about something, that's it. I'm not even sure he'll speak with me."

A long sigh coursed out of Ramya. Anger swirled within her, along with it fear and hurt and every other emotion that made her want to scream. Her fists curled, nails digging into her palms painfully. Ramya welcomed the grounding pain and breathed. Now was not the time to give in to fear and rage, she reminded herself. She had to think clearly. But what could she do? Temihula wasn't a person; it was a sentient spirit of the forest. How did one talk to a forest?

"Let's at least get closer and try," Ross suggested, and the chief nodded in agreement. For a second or two Ramya envied their calmness. This was something she needed more of, to build a façade of composure even when she was tearing up inside just like she knew Ross was at the moment. But it was easier said than done—emotions spewed out of her more often than not, another thing her father utterly, intensely disapproved of.

Ramya turned away, looking for a way to distract herself. She spotted Ahool. He was seated on a bench where a pillar inside the carrier formed a small nook. Ramya strode over and sat down next to the Mwandan boy.

"What are you thinking?" she asked, nudging him gently.

"I worry. The forest is angry and that's not good for Ahool," he said. "Look." He pulled at the long zip on his sleeve and pushed the blue fabric up to reveal his spindly gray arms. Reddish painful-looking welts were scattered all over his arms.

"What are these? How did they happen?"

"Mwandans sense thoughts from forest spirits. Their anger make Mwandan sick."

"But the chief looks fine," Ramya said. "Or is he getting sick also?"

"Some Mwandans get more affected," Ahool explained. "Some less. But chief is Uminato, he can channel anger better."

"You can't? That's bad."

Ahool shook his head. "Not bad. Ancient spirits bless me. I feel them more than many. But I never felt anger like this before."

The welts on Ahool's arm were getting redder and angrier by the second.

"Can you feel Temihula? What is he saying?" Ramya asked.

Ahool flinched. "Do not take his name," he whispered, shaking his head violently. For a second or two he stayed absolutely quiet. "He wants us leave," he whispered.

And let the Endeavor *die?* There was no way in hell she was going to do that. "Can you tell Temihula this is a mistake? The captain didn't intend to harm anyone or offend anyone."

"I can't talk to Temihula. Ask Chief."

She didn't have to ask. Unknown to Ramya, the chief had been standing next to them, listening to the conversation intently. Now he sighed deeply.

"Ahool is right. He wants us to leave. Look at that." The chief pointed in front of him. A storm was brewing in the murky darkness. Branches whipped back and forth, trees swung wildly. It was much like the storm they had encountered before they came across Ahool.

Ramya walked closer to the window, noticing how Ahool clutched his arms as the tempest outside grew. Ross and the chief gathered near.

"This is not safe for us," the chief whispered after he had watched for a while. "He won't let us pass. We have to turn around."

"But—"

Ramya couldn't get a second word out. The chief cut her off decisively. "There are no buts. We *have* to leave."

Ramya stared disbelievingly at the chief as he strode up to the pilot and shouted orders. Slowly, the carrier started to turn around. This couldn't be happening. They had come so close to helping the *Endeavor* and now . . .

A rush of thoughts rose in her mind in a panicky wave and Ramya cried out to the unseen forest spirit outside. "Please, Temihula! Please let us pass and release the *Endeavor*," she begged. "A whole lot more depends on it than our lives. There's more going on than you know."

Chief Dal grabbed her arm and shook her. "What are you doing? You're an alien. You can't address a forest spirit. Stop," he warned.

Ramya couldn't. If she or Ross didn't tell Temihula the whole story, who would?

She continued desperately. "Enemies . . . Locustans are coming to get us and no one else but Captain Milos understands what is happening. He knows how to fight them. He is our only hope. And if he . . . and his ship aren't released, the entire galaxy will fall. The Mwandans won't escape unharmed either. They — your children — will die too."

The chief shook his head and hissed at her. "You shouldn't do this. There isn't any way that Temihula will tolerate this. You're insulting him even more now, and this time you're doing it knowingly."

Ross grabbed her arm, his fingers icy. "This isn't working," he whispered. "Dal looks terrified. Let's not insult his forest anymore."

Ramya didn't want to affront anyone, but Temihula didn't leave her a choice. Still, she decided to try one more time to appease the forest spirit. She kneeled on the ground facing the window.

"Please, Temihula. Please let my ship go. They didn't mean to cause you or your people any harm. I don't either but — "

Something — a broken branch, likely — crashed against the window and Ramya fell back in terror. She couldn't understand Temihula like the chief did, but there was no mistaking the spirit's murderous rage. It made Ramya's core tremble, but she steeled herself.

The captain, Fenny, Sosa . . . people who'd trusted her and . . . respected her . . . were in there, trapped. Locustan threat or not, the Endeavor's crew was important to her and she was not going to give up on them.

"I care about the people you're holding, and I know they're innocent. I cannot simply walk away."

"That's enough. Stop now," Chief Dal yelled. At the same time, a loud cacophony rose from the pilot's area and a second later the carrier thudded to a stop. Ramya fell, her shoulder crashing against a pillar. Ross had held on to Ahool's chair but the Berkari chief had been thrown to the floor. He scrambled to his feet and rushed to the pilot.

"Temihula struck us," Chief Dal exclaimed. Color had drained from his face, the normal deep brown now faded and dim.

Ross glared at Ramya. "Did you have to rile him up? Now what are you going to do?"

Ramya glared back at Ross. She hadn't wanted to rile anyone. She had only seen a chance to make her case and pleaded. How was it her fault that Temihula was so stubborn and difficult?

"Well, at least I tried," she shot back.

"We have to leave!" the chief said.

"I won't," Ramya declared. "I can't."

The chief crossed his arms and frowned. "What are you going to do? Fight the grove? Fight Temihula? No one fights a spirit."

"Really? Has no one ever fought it?"

The chief looked away uncomfortably. "No one survives a fight with the grove," he said slowly. "He will kill us all."

The carrier swayed under their feet and then rocked violently as if to make a point. The pilot shouted something and Chief Dal walked away momentarily.

Ramya looked up at Ross. "You go on and leave without me," she said. "I'll go outside and see what I can do."

"Are you crazy?" Ross snapped. "A Mwandan says there's no point fighting the grove and you're not going to listen to him? You'll get killed out there."

"My life is as good as over without the *Endeavor* carrying me out of here. Without the *Endeavor*, I'll get dragged back into a life I'm trying to escape. And I'm not fine with that." Ramya paused to look at Ahool. He was staring into the darkness outside, stiff like a log. "Besides, I couldn't live with myself if I didn't try to rescue those people who are trapped in the *Endeavor*. They've appreciated me more than anyone else before, and I'd be damned if I didn't give everything I've got to get them out of that hell."

Chief Dal stomped up to them while the carrier kept rocking. "Now he's blocked the road back as well," he said, shaking his head hopelessly.

For a second or two that followed, Ramya couldn't hear a sound in the carrier other than her own ragged breathing.

"What does he want?" Ramya managed a broken whisper.

From the faded color of his face, Ramya could easily guess it couldn't be anything good.

"He's not letting us out. That's means one thing: our lives are forfeit."

"What?" Ross almost yelled. "Why? You were just trying to help us."

The chief nodded slowly. "He's offended that we are sheltering trespassers."

"It's my fault," Ramya said. "You're being punished because I yelled at Temihula."

Something fell on the roof of the carrier and moved across it like a snake. "What was that?" Ramya blurted. More falling sounds came, along with more slithering noises. The vehicle creaked as if in pain.

"Vines," Ross said, pointing at the nearest window. Thick and vicious, they crawled over the windows, wrapping the carrier in a deadly embrace. Temihula was going to crush them to death. Ahool gave out a whimper and doubled over in his chair.

A wave of guilt swept through Ramya. This was all her fault. She should've stayed quiet. Now she had gotten everyone into his mess. No, it wasn't just a mess. She had earned everyone in the carrier a death sentence.

Ramya closed her eyes and gritted her teeth. She had to fix this. Somehow. "I'm going to go out," she declared.

Both Ross and Chief Dal snapped toward her. Ross spoke first.

"And do what?"

"He will destroy you," the chief said. "You will only anger him more."

Ramya ran a nervous hand through her hair. "Maybe. But I started this. You shouldn't be held responsible for what I did."

"But you can't fix—" Chief Dal stopped abruptly and winced. The carrier rocked like a paper boat in a squall. Grabbing his throat, the chief slumped against a column and heaved pitifully, as if someone was strangling him. Ramya was too scared to touch him, barely scrunching up enough courage to ask him what was going on. Before she could speak, the chief wheezed a few words out. "He'll kill us all now."

Not if she could help it. Even though the pit of her stomach sunk like a boulder Ramya managed a nod. "Open the hatch," she yelled. "Open the hatch."

The carrier tilted sideways, shouts and screams filling the small cabin. Chief Dal, who seemed to have recovered from the agony of moment's ago, grabbed a column as the vehicle careened back and forth like a boat in a vicious storm.

"Let me out," Ramya shouted.

Chief Dal gestured at his men. One of them pressed a lever on a side panel, and with a blink and a screech, the hatch of the carrier started to open. Ramya gave a quick look around. Ross could have been carved from a stone, and the chief looked faded. Ahool had been groaning from time to time, and he now sagged to the floor like a rag doll.

"You can't go out alone," Ross said. "I'll come with you."

"No, don't," Ramya said. "Perhaps it's me he's angry with. Maybe he'll let you pass on and help the *Endeavor*."

"And that's your big plan? Sacrificing yourself?" Ross scoffed. "Are you crazy?"

"I'm going to try to survive," Ramya said.

Chief Dal grabbed Ross by the arm. "Let her go. Let her try."

Ross threw a disbelieving look at the chief. "Try? She'll get killed. She doesn't have a single weapon on her. At least give back her blaster."

The chief shook his head. "She cannot carry a weapon in the grove. The rules are clear on that."

Ross blinked a few times before scoffing. "You're going to send her out there, unarmed . . . defenseless against that . . . thing?"

"This is her choice. Maybe she's right. Maybe Temihula wants her. Maybe he'll let us go if he gets her," the chief said.

Ross shook his head in disbelief. "So we'll just throw her out to be killed just so we get to keep our hinds intact?" he snapped. "I'm sorry; I don't do that sort of stuff."

"If you survive, you get to help your captain," the chief shot back. "Does that interest you at all? Sometimes to win a war you have to lose a battle." He looked at Ramya and gestured at the half-open hatch. "If you want to go, now is the time."

The carrier rattled again as if to remind Ramya to come outside. She turned toward the door, but before she could take another step, Ross grabbed her arm and growled, "You're not going out alone. That's an order."

Ramya barely got a chance to fathom his words let alone frame a reply. A thick vine shot through the half-parted door of the carrier and wrapped around her waist.

"Rami!" Ross's scream filled the chamber.

In the next second, the vine pulled her out of the craft with a whoosh and deposited her on the forest floor. Thick darkness surrounded Ramya, and she braced herself for the unknown horrors that awaited.

9

The hatch of the Berkari carrier snapped shut behind Ramya, leaving her alone in the dark. It wasn't exactly a sightless dark; a gray and insipid light filtered through the grove. Ramya could see the gnarly trunks of trees around her side of a small clearing. The ground under her feet was soft, covered with moss.

Trees, tall and dark, stared down at her from all sides. They were huge, powerful, and quietly fierce. Vines hung from their sturdy branches like strands of jewelry. A chill drifted past, tingling Ramya's spine. It left her shaking and feeling utterly, hopelessly small.

The grove was quiet, terribly quiet . . . holding its breath. The Berkari chief's carrier stood behind her like a rock encased in vines, the only known entity in this alien world. Ramya's body shook, her fingers were icy and stiff, and an endless void filled her insides. Her feet were stuck to the ground. Her mind went blank like an empty canvas that she desperately wanted to fill in but failed no matter how hard she tried.

Then something moved. Ramya held her breath and tried to understand what it was. She couldn't tell. It could've been the rustle of a branch or a leaf falling to the ground. There was no way to tell for sure. Ramya stood, bracing herself for she did not know what. She stood for what felt like eternity . . . until she had grown utterly tired of waiting.

Every minute spent fearing was a minute wasted. And they had already wasted enough time. It was time to get it over with, once and for all. Ramya took one step, and then another, away from the carrier and across the clearing. She walked further into the darkness.

Another rustle? Maybe. She had to keep walking. Temihula was somewhere out there and she had to find him and somehow convince him to release the carrier and the *Endeavor*.

A sharp sensation in her mind, almost like a pinprick, made Ramya stop. A ripple, strong and endless, surged through her mind, and she swayed unstably. She planted her feet firmly on the ground to stop from falling.

A thought, cold and menacing, took shape in Ramya's mind and slithered through her head. It dug up pain, grief, and fear. It kept pulling, tugging at the edges of her brain, digging for her emotions. Every sad memory — lonely evenings as shadows darkened in the cavernous rooms in Somenvaar, countless instances of her father's frosty dismissals, her mother's stony indifference — flashed across Ramya's eyes, leaving her tired, cold, and vulnerable.

"Stop," Ramya shouted, pushing away the prying sensation in her head. Frustration and anger rose swiftly in her gut, making her fists curl. What a waste of time this was. "Stop prodding my brain. Let my friends go."

Leaves crackled all around, mocking her. It was not about to let anyone go. "Come on," she shouted again, desperate. "Let those people go."

Her head hurt. A wave of nausea flooded upward from the pit of her stomach.

"What sort of a god are you?" she blurted. "You are supposed to take care of your own and you're — "

The pain in her head grew brighter than a million stars. Heat flooded her insides. Ramya grabbed her temples and screamed.

The entire grove rustled again. Branches swayed giddily, as if every tree was laughing at her. A wind grew from the ground, cold and intense, swirling around her like a raging storm. Ramya wanted to run, but she forced herself to stand her ground.

Thoughts hissed in her head. Something pushed her at the knees and they buckled. Ice rushed up her legs, numbing them until Ramya barely sensed them anymore. The wind came again. It hit her like a hammer in the back of her knees and Ramya crumpled to the ground like a puppet on a string.

The presence in her head seemed to leap with joy. It had made her fall to the ground. It had won. It swirled inside her head, gleeful.

"This isn't a fair fight," Ramya hissed through gritted teeth, knowing well that she was but a toy in the hands of an entity whose strength she could not even fathom.

Suddenly, her thoughts stilled. Whatever entity was riffling through her mind stopped. Perhaps it was surprised. Or angry. Something snapped. Ramya heard the swish of something being flung. A hiss of air. She looked up right in time to catch a glimpse of the tree branch swinging toward her. Ramya fell to one side and raised her arm to stop the branch aimed at her head, barely managing to grab it. She twisted it will all her might. Her palms stung, her arms ached, but Ramya didn't let go. She wasn't allowed to bring a weapon to the fight, but she could make one. She *was* going to make one. If Temihula expected her to go down like a gentle lamb, he was in for a surprise.

A sharp crack and the branch came loose. Her palms burned. Ramya was sure they were bleeding, but she smiled regardless. Now she had something—however puny—to fight back with. Hope warmed her heart, and Ramya sat up straighter. But only for a second. A gust of wind slapped against Ramya's shoulder making her stumble forward. One her hands and knees, she pressed the stick into the ground and pushed herself to a sit upright. The wind pushed again.

Goading Temihula into a fight was a bad idea. An extremely bad idea. But as bad as it was, it was too late to walk away from the fight now. She had no choice but to take her chances. Ramya got to her feet, trembling slightly, her fingers curling over the rough surface of the tree branch like it was a lifesaver.

Weapon or not, how the hell was she going to defend herself if she didn't know how Temihula could attack? *This is as foolish as foolish gets.* Cursing herself, Ramya planted her feet as firmly as she could and tried to sense the air around her.

Everything stayed quiet for a few seconds. Then something

slithered behind her. A vine, as thick as a man's arm, struck like a snake at her leg. Ramya jumped back, swinging her stick at the clawing creeper, but she couldn't avoid it altogether. Before her stick could land on its tip, the vine hit the side of her leg. Ramya toppled over and fell backward, her back slamming into the ground. Pain from the Pterostrich attack of not so long ago, came surging back. Ramya gritted her teeth and scrambled to her feet. The vine had withdrawn momentarily, but now it rushed at her, the tip raised like a spear intent on impaling her.

Ramya fell back a few steps and swung her makeshift sword at the vine. She caught it right at the top. The vine shrunk backward and fell to the ground like a coil of rope.

A shuffling sound rose behind her. More vines, thicker than the last, rose in a line. In half the blink of an eye, one of them struck. Ramya jumped backward. The wall advanced on her, and Ramya helplessly swiped with her stick. They hit back with vicious strikes and she grunted and cried out as they lashed at her limbs, tearing her clothes and drawing blood. *I can't die here*, she thought, as she swung her stick furious, swirling it nonstop as she jumped backward, making room between her and the advancing wall.

Adrenaline coursed through her veins and she gripped the stick until her hands bled. Something pushed her from the back. The ground, dark and uneven, rushed up to her face. Ramya tried to prop herself up on her arms, but before she could it struck her side and sent her trundling across the damp ground. A branch slapped her across the face and Ramya yelped in pain. The side of her face burned and blood trickled down her cheek. Ramya ran her arm over the gash and braced herself. Then she sprung up, dashing to the side opposite to where the vines were located, where she could sense the clearing where the carrier was parked.

There was a blur of movement behind her. Vines snapped at her heels. Her mouth tasted like blood as she bit her lip in determination. She wasn't going to go down without a fight. "Come at me!" she shouted wildly, and she made a run for it, her lungs burning as she ran as fast as she could. Vines slashed at her, but she didn't stumble.

When she reached the spot free of trees and vegetation, Ramya sunk to the ground and heaved. Tears burned her eyes. She had escaped the vines. The carrier was a few paces away and still in one piece. They were all alive . . . for now. And before that could change, for better or for worse, she allowed herself a moment to give in to her exhaustion, her hunger, her pain, and she sobbed right there on the forest floor, the trees above her swaying gently in the breeze.

10

Under her feet, the ground shook, and Ramya was once again pulled from her reverie. Her tired eyes spotted a crack in the ground, and it spread like lightning across the clearing, splitting the ground open. Something—it was clearly sizable—was rising from the pit. Terror made her numb, and her thoughts stilled. Ramya held her breath and raised the puny stick to defend herself. A dark shape shot out of the ground.

A round pod-like head atop a long, stout stem emerged from the ground, and in place of leaves, tentacles, far thicker than the vines that had attacked her earlier, flew out toward Ramya.

One grabbed her leg and threw her to the ground. Ramya screamed at the impact. She tried to push her stick into the ground to keep her from being dragged, but she couldn't hold on. She beat at the tentacles. When one withdrew, three others tossed her into the shrubs. In the next second they yanked her out again and threw her across the clearing. She was covered in moss and scratches, shaken to the core and every bone ached. She dug her fingers into the ground and desperately started crawling back toward the trees. A tentacle slithered up her back and around her neck and squeezed.

Ramya gasped for air. She clawed at the damp tentacle, the skin on her fingers tearing on its jagged surface. The world turned darker. And darker still. Her lungs were on fire. She heard a distant clang and a shout.

The hatch of the Berkari carrier had opened. Someone jumped out. He bounded over the floor of vines—dodging, ducking, skirting—until he reached Ramya. *Ross?* A boot landed on the tentacle holding her. Then again. A fist, a boot. They pounded on the monstrous appendage.

The choking hold around Ramya loosened slightly. Then

suddenly it fell off her and flew at Ross. It struck at his face. He yelped. It caught him by the leg and flicked him backward. Ross flew through the air, landing on the ground with a thud and a groan. He careened backward and hit the trunk of a tree. The pod jumped toward him, its tentacles hovering over Ross as if to make sure if he didn't have the strength to get back on his feet.

Ramya reached for her stick. Gripping the pole as tightly as she could, she stood up on shaky legs. The monstrous pod sensed her immediately and turned toward her again.

A tentacle shot out at her face. Ramya ducked. Another swung at her body. Ramya fell back and swiped with her stick. They swung away with ease.

"Damn it!" Ramya cursed under her breath. Her brain whirred in frenzy, trying to think of a solution. She couldn't break the monstrosity — it was far too strong and her stick was nearly useless — but she had to stop it somehow.

But how? All she had was the spiteful forest around her. Maybe she could use the forest. A fledgling plan raised its head — one with the trees and the branches — but it was going to be risky. A few paces from her, the tentacles regrouped around the pod. They flared like the hood of a many-headed snake and swayed. It was preparing to strike. Ramya's fists curled. It was now or never.

With a loud yowl, Ramya dashed toward the trees. She threw her stick to the right and hurled herself over a branch to the left. The tentacles followed. One jumped after the stick; another two stung at her legs. Ramya swung through the branches, gritting her teeth as rough bark and thorns cut into her already-bruised palms. The tentacles followed her.

Up, down, around, and over the branches she went.

They were nipping at her heels.

Ramya's legs ached and burned. She kept on swinging, scrambling, weaving back and forth through the branches and vines.

The tentacles mirrored her movements.

Her lungs screamed for air. Ramya didn't have time to breathe.

Up. Above. Under.

They kept coming.

On her fifth dash through the trees, Ramya noticed the tentacles slowing down. Her plan worked. They were entangled, just how she'd hoped they would. The pod was trying to pull its many arms out of the mesh but without much luck. It tugged, the branches groaned, but nothing budged.

Ramya picked up her stick and gripped it tight. The inside of her head was burning like wildfire, and Ramya knew that wasn't her own anger she was feeling. It was Temihula's rage at being trapped. Along with the fire came a smoky darkness that threatened to suffocate and blur her senses.

Now! Gritting her teeth, Ramya charged at the pod, hitting it at the center of its head just as the fire exploded like a grenade within her. The monster clutched at her hair, and Ramya fell to the ground, screaming in agony. This was the end, she knew. She had no regrets. She had done what she could. Now it was all over. Ramya collapsed in a heap at the feet of the monstrous pod as darkness poured over her.

For a never-ending minute or two, there was dead stillness everywhere—around Ramya and inside her. The quiet was calming yet terrifying. She didn't have the strength left in her to move a finger if she wanted, so she did the only thing she could: She closed her eyes and waited for death to come.

An unexpected light shone through instead, the dimness in her mind ebbing suddenly. There was no pain or death, but a breezy calmness sweeping through. Strength surged back into Ramya's limbs, hope made her heart flutter.

Temihula . . . had he relented? But he couldn't have. He had lost after all. Where was the anger? As Ramya caught her breath, the grove unfurled. Treetops straightened and light, dim as it was, streamed in and bathed Ramya. She blinked as her eyes adjusted to the change.

She saw Ross, propped up against a tree trunk, breathing heavily. Other than a few gashes on his face, he didn't seem hurt. The chief's carrier still stood like a rock, but the vines around it were slowly sliding off.

The monstrous pod lay in front of her, beaten and entangled. An unexpected sense of compassion flooded Ramya's mind as she watched the pod's miserable form. She had to untangle it. But what if it attacked again? It wouldn't, she was pretty sure. This battle was over.

Slowly, she kneeled next to the pod and tugged at its tentacles. They shivered at her touch. Fear, Ramya sensed. The forest had turned very still. She continued nonetheless, pulling the long tendrils out of the knot until they were all free.

Leaves rustled in relief. The pod pulled its tentacles near, flexing them slowly back and forth. Then it raised its head as if to look at Ramya. She scuttled back a little just to be safe, but the pod didn't move toward her. Instead, it opened up like a flower, unfurling in layer upon layer of color until its core lay exposed. The pod bowed a little, then a tentacle reached into its core, pulled out the dark center, and held it out for Ramya.

Ramya flashed a confused look at Ross. What was she supposed to do? Take the black center the pod was offering? A thought nudged her forward. It was Temihula again. He wanted her to accept this — a gift from his forest perhaps.

Ramya reached out, fearfully, hesitantly, until her fingers touched the dark stone and curled around it. The tentacles withdrew, and in the flash of colors, the pod closed back up. Then, as suddenly as the ground had parted to release the pod, it parted again and swallowed the pod back in. Ramya stared disbelievingly at the ground. It was untouched, as if it hadn't just split apart a second ago to release something dangerous.

The carrier's hatch opened with a clang and Ahool streaked out, waving his arms wildly, followed by the Berkari chief and his men.

The Mwandans rushed down the stairs and fell to the ground, touching it with their foreheads, over and over again and muttering something in Mwandan. Ramya put the black stone into her pocket and trudged over to Ross as the Mwandans continued their ritual.

She held out a hand for Ross and flashed a grateful smile at him. "Thanks for coming after me. You saved my life. Are you all right?"

Ross grabbed her arm and struggled to his feet. "I'm fine. I should've come out earlier," he said, nodding distractedly. "This mission is my responsibility, and I let you take the fall. That's not right."

"Hey! You didn't. I got myself into this hole when I challenged the forest god. I had to dig myself out of it."

Ross opened his mouth to reply but didn't get a chance to say a word. Chief Dal, a glittery-eyed Ahool in tow, strode up to them.

"Temihula has opened the road for us. Let's go to your ship and get your friends out."

"I'm all for that," Ramya said. "Let's go."

As soon as they had all stepped inside, the carrier started off again. Ahool, however, seated Ramya on a stool and inspected the mobility of her arms and legs. Then he busily examined her scratches and dabbed a clear liquid on her gashes. The cool medicine soothed the burning pain quite quickly. "You need some wraps," Ahool announced after he had attended to each wound.

Ramya raised a questioning brow. "A wrap?"

"Strong medicine. It helps you heal. I get you wraps when we reach Berkari colony." He walked away toward Ross but stopped midway and looked back at her curiously. "Keep your Drigganstone safe, all right?" he said, eyes glittering.

"Drigganstone?"

"The jewel Temihula gave you," Ahool said somberly. "Drigganstone is soul of ancients. Very powerful. Government steals Drigganstone from reliquary groves and makes weapons. That not good at all."

10

Ramya slipped a hand into her pocket and pulled out the stone the murderous pod had offered her. It was fairly large and looked nothing like a jewel. Dull, dark, almost a hexagon, it was not remotely attractive. How the Mwandan government made weapons out of it Ramya couldn't fathom, but the reverential look Ahool cast at the stone made her treat it with more gravitas.

"What do I do with it?" she asked.

"Keep safe," Ahool said simply. "Temihula blesses you with Drigganstone. You are lucky. You Temihula's chosen."

Ahool moved on to examine Ross after that. Ramya slipped the Drigganstone into an inner pocket of her jacket and joined the chief's behind the pilot's chair.

Chief Dal was watching the carrier zip through the forest. He turned to smile warmly at her. "Your ship is close. We just picked it up on our scanner."

Ramya breathed a sigh of relief, but even as hope surged in her heart, she couldn't ignore that tight knot of fear at the pit of her stomach that kept growing larger every second. Until she saw the entire crew of the *Endeavor* alive and well, Ramya wasn't going to have a moment of real peace.

11

The dull metallic gray of the *Endeavor* peeked through the trees ahead and Ramya's heart leaped. Then it sunk like a stone again. Who knew how the crew had fared until now? What had the grove done to the ship? Temihula didn't say he had caused damage to the ship, and that was the only thing that kept Ramya clinging to hope.

The carrier slowed as it neared the *Endeavor*, circling around until they reached the main entrance of the ship. Chief Dal barked orders and the carrier came to a stop some distance away from the *Endeavor's* hatch. The Berkari chief led his men out of the vehicle, and Ross followed. Ramya lingered at the rear of the procession, studying their surroundings as she stepped out.

The trees in the area looked strange. Ramya had seen trees on Morris II change shape, but this was more extreme than she had encountered so far. Here they had bent, forming a wrap of sorts over the *Endeavor*. The way the branches curved, curled, and elongated to enclose the *Endeavor* reminded Ramya of a large closed fist holding a fly. This was probably why the surface of the vegetation had shown a depression and why Ross had picked up the shape of the *Endeavor* from the mountaintop. This was also a problem. The Norgoran scout ship, if it was still circling the skies, could also just as easily notice the resemblance.

"I don't see critical damages to your ship. Nothing from where we stand," Chief Dal reported. Ramya had to agree.

The *Endeavor* looked as dated as it had looked the first time she had seen it in Nikoor, and while there were plenty more dents and scratches on it now from the assault of the Drednots, none looked bad enough to have crippled the ship entirely. She walked up and stood below the entry hatch, its outline in the shape of an upside-down trapezoid easily recognizable. It was tucked up and closed.

"Ross," Ramya called, looking askance at the commander. Ross had been poking at his wrist-mounted comm. His jabs had grown impatient swiftly and his frown turning deeper. Ramya had held back on the questions until now but it was time to find out. "Any luck?"

Ross pursed his lips and shook his head. "The main unit is still working." He pointed at the bright green light that indicated a working status of the communication channel.

"What's the problem then?" Chief Dal asked.

He threw a worried look at them. "No one's responding."

"Why wouldn't they?" Chief Dal asked.

Ross shook his head and shrugged listlessly. "I don't know. Anything could've happened since the Drednots attacked. Maybe the life-support module was damaged and they're all—"

"Or maybe the comm is damaged," Ramya cut him off desperately. "The *Endeavor's* comm system isn't the best in the universe. I've seen it fail before."

"I'm hoping that's the case," Ross replied. He kept jabbing at the buttons. "I'll keep on trying all the open channels."

"Is there any other way to hail them?" Chief Dal asked.

Ramya shook her head. "No, the *Endeavor's* system is too outmoded for the Stryker. Not that the Stryker's near or available anyway."

"Then we climb up there and pry the door open," Chief Dal said.

That had to be the next step. And not an easy thing to do. For starters, the hatch wasn't level with them; it hung about two stories above ground. The ship's surface didn't offer many niches or curves to climb up the side either.

Chief Dal hovered for a second or two longer before marching off into his carrier. He returned quickly. "I've summoned my engineers. They're on their way with equipment. I'll ask my people here to walk around and check the periphery of your ship. In case there's a visible breach somewhere..."

Chief Dal didn't complete his sentence, but he didn't have to.

Ramya clearly understood what he meant. A visible breach of the hull could mean life-threatening damage. Perhaps Flux had been the only survivor and now he too was . . . dead. Deflated like a pricked balloon, Ramya watched blankly as the chief's men started along the periphery of the *Endeavor*.

Chief Dal strode back to them. "Anything?" he asked Ross who replied with a hopeless shake of his head.

Tiredness swooped over Ramya, her lids suddenly too heavy to keep open. She wanted to curl up somewhere and sleep. This was all for nothing. They had fought with the behemoth Drednots, fought with Mwandan gods and reached the ship. They had overcome so much, but to what end?

"I'm going to sit down for a bit," Ramya declared sullenly and found a largish log to perch on. Her mind kept dawdling, like a blind person in a maze desperately seeking a way out but only finding dead ends.

If the *Endeavor* was crippled and its crew dead, how would they get out of Morris II? Yes, they still had the Stryker, but with the Confederacy and the Kiroff spies on their tail, how far could they go? If the Mwandans had spacecraft, they could've traded in the Stryker for a more normal craft. But Mwandans didn't believe in traveling out of their planets.

And then there was the biggest problem of all: the Locustan threat. How were they going to find out what was really going on with the Locustans and the missing Strykers? And how were they going to convince anyone of the impending invasion Dakrhaeth spoke about? Without Captain Milos, they were nothing. She was a pampered brat of an heiress whose best achievement in life was sneaking out of CAWStrat. And Ross? He was a nobody. The galaxy's fate was as good as written off.

Ramya jumped to her feet and shook the worrying thoughts away. She couldn't give up. The galaxy's fate was not a small thing to give up on so easily. She had to find a way out. She scanned the surrounding one more time, her eyes desperately seeking a means to access the hatch.

She was deep in thought when the shout drifted across the grove. It made Ramya jump. Instinctively she stepped closer to Ross and the chief.

"What the hell?" Ross said.

"It's my people," Chief Dal said breathlessly. Ahool and the rest of the Berkari burst into view from behind the trees, waving wildly as they ran. Chief Dal rushed toward them, as did Ross and Ramya.

Ahool frantically pointed toward the sky. "Look," he mouthed.

A shape—a dark torpedo with a rotating fish tail—glided into view.

"The Glasspointe," Ramya whispered. "It's still here."

"What has the world come to?" Chief Dal spat. "They're allowing Norgoran scout ships in now?"

"We think it's been sent by the Confederacy to find us. It's scanning for sign of life," Ross said.

"Stay under here," Chief Dal instructed as they scrambled under the flaring midsection of the *Endeavor*. "This will give us some shelter from their scans. I hope," he added.

"Can they see the *Endeavor* from up there?" Ramya asked. The canopy of branches over the ship was still in place, so she hoped they missed it.

"It's a Norgoran scout ship," Chief Dal replied. "What do you expect?"

Nothing escaped the eyes of a Norgoran scout ship. Nothing!

"They'd have dispatched the Confederacy already," Ramya said, releasing the breath she'd been holding. "We're running out of time."

"You've run out of time already," the chief said, his glittery eyes fixed on the scout ship hovering above. "You should leave now. Take my carrier, get back to your Stryker, and leave. Get yourselves out of Morris II while you can. I'll see if I can break into this ship when my engineers arrive. But you shouldn't linger. The Confederacy will block off escape routes as soon as they find out. Perhaps they already have."

Ross's gaze was dark with worry. "The Stryker's still offline," he said with a quick look at his watch. "So we're stuck here anyhow."

Ramya sighed. "And as long as we're stuck here and until the Confederacy forces arrive, we'll keep trying to get into the *Endeavor*."

If only the Glasspointe would leave them alone! But no matter how badly Ramya wished for it to go, the scout ship kept circling above. Most likely, the damage was already done. The Glasspointe had probably called the Confederacy, but if it spotted people milling around the *Endeavor*, the urgency of the situation would multiply in a heartbeat. Glaring at the scout ship, Ramya scooted backward into the *Endeavor's* shadows some more.

Chief Dal had rested his head against *Endeavor's* hulk and closed his eyes, perhaps trying to sense the forest. Quickly he opened them with a start and shook his head.

"The forest is trying to help us. It's shielding your ship."

"Then we have time," Ross said.

"No, we can't linger here," Chief Dal said with an air of finality. "We don't know the capability of the Norgoran ship. We don't know if they can look past the forest's shield. Let's keep our heads down until that scout ship leaves. But after that I will retreat. I don't trust the Confederacy. I can't risk my men's lives."

Ramya held her breath. She stole a glance at Ross who stared, rock-jawed at the chief.

"I can't command you, but I can advise," Chief Dal said. "My advice for you is to leave also. Just the two of you can't fight a Confederacy platoon. It's suicide."

Ross didn't say anything. He simply jabbed his comm a few more times. Ramya wanted to tell them both that she'd fight until the end, but looking at Ross's drawn face she held her tongue. He looked just as distraught as she felt herself, and truth be told, she didn't want to slight him. He had risked his life trying to save her from Temihula's clutches, and if she decided to fight the Confederacy he'd probably stay by her side again. And putting his life at risk wasn't fair.

Ramya drew a long breath and watched the Glasspointe disappear from sight.

Chief Dal sprang to his feet and gestured to his men. They filed up and rushed toward the carrier. Ahool lingered, hesitantly looking at Ramya and Ross, until the Berkari chief shouted, "Ahool Petta, fall back. Now."

As Ahool slinked away, Chief Dal nodded at Ross and Ramya. "We have to take cover until my reinforcements arrive. Waiting near the ship isn't safe anymore. The Confederacy can strike anytime."

Ross nodded back yet didn't follow. He simply stared at the comm on his wrist, and although Ramya waited, he didn't look up at her either. Ramya decided she'd wait for Ross to make a judgment call. No matter how difficult, she'd follow his orders.

Ross pounded the comm's buttons for the zillionth time. No sound came out of it. Ramya steeled herself as he turned at her.

"Your call, Commander," she said, forcing her voice to hold steady. "I'm with you."

She knew even before he said it what his answer was going to be. They had to leave.

Ross had just about opened his mouth when a terrifying clang sounded above their heads. Someone screeched, Ramya almost jumped, and the chief yelled, "Everyone, down."

A second of heart-stopping silence followed before the clang sounded again. Then Ross sprang to his feet and gave a whoop of joy. His eyes sparkled and a smile lit his face like a thousand stars. "That's the sound of the hatch opening, Rami," he shouted. "They're opening it. They're alive."

Ramya hadn't heard words sweeter than those. Her heart skipped a few beats before a wave of relief flooded her insides, almost like a Pax-induced surge of warmth. She forgot about the Glasspointe hovering above them, the Confederacy on their tail, and her father's unseen presence lurking behind her. She fell back against the

Endeavor's cold, hard hulk and closed her eyes. Finally! They were home.

12

Making the *Endeavor* space-worthy again was the critical task at hand. People rushed around the archaic battlecruiser-turned-freighter, buzzing like bees. Even the reunion of Ramya and Ross with the rest of the crew was hardly what it should've been under usual circumstances. But this was no usual circumstance. The captain simply patted Ross and Ramya's back. Wiz, the pilot, offered a fist bump or two and Fenny gave Ramya a quick hug, but that was all.

The Berkari chief posted a few of his men on watch for the scout ship. "They'll be back with reinforcements, I'm sure," Chief Dal commented when the Glasspointe glided away to the south a little after the *Endeavor* opened its hatch.

"We have to get out of Morris II before they do," Captain Milos said, running a finger over his bandaged forehead.

Flux was cooped up in Engineering Bay. The fuel store had taken a hit, and Flux along with a couple of Mwandan engineers worked frantically to get it patched. Since Flux was wrapped up in that work, Wiz was tasked with getting the communication channel up and running.

Fenny promptly pulled Ramya over to the COM where she'd been working on some blown fuses. "It was hell, Rami," she summed up the flight from Totori to Morris II. "Didn't think we'd make it. But we somehow did."

The captain had had what Fenny dubbed a minor accident with a dashboard during the battle with the Confederacy Drednots. Sosa, the medic, however, had termed it as a major concussion-inducing injury that needed proper treatment. The urgency of the situation nullified Sosa's dire indictments, so the miffed Norgoran medic had retreated to her chambers, Pax in hand and stayed there since..

"She's very upset," Fenny whispered to Ramya while the duo

worked on the wiring and short fuses in the COM. "The Stryker's pilot passed away right after you guys took off at Totori. Sosa took it iffin hard."

"It's not her fault," Ramya said, stretching out to reach the last broken wire under Fenny's control station. "He was sick to begin with. Then he got beaten up by those thugs."

"Yeah, well, tell Sosa that and she'll lecture you on a doctor's sacred duty and whatnot," Fenny said. She thumped a few buttons on the controls to check on the repairs.

"She can't work miracles," Ramya said. The last patch completed, she squirmed out from under the control station.

Fenny rolled her eyes. "I dare you, Rami, to tell that to Sosa's face."

Ramya sighed. That was a good dare that Ramya doubted she'd take Fenny up on. Sosa was a regal, even though totally obstinate, personality. She looked nice, spoke like a royal, but everyone who knew her thought a few times before entangling her in a debate.

Looking at Ramya's hesitant expression, Fenny chuckled loudly. "Told ya. Even the captain has stayed away. He said it's going to take her time to get over the pilot's death."

"Oh well. I'm just glad she's alive. That you're all alive," Ramya said. "I was scared to death thinking about what might've happened to you all."

Fenny had heard about everything Ramya and Ross had encountered on the way, and she nodded in an understanding sort of way. "We were pretty badly hit by cannon fire at Totori, but Flux managed to put some emergency patches on the hull. That kept the ship together, enough to get us here. The main trouble we had was with the pilot dying and Sosa getting all upset. And then we couldn't get out of the ship. It was like something had locked us in and none of the iffin hatches would budge."

Ramya wondered if the forest spirit had somehow locked the crew in.

"Anyway, all's good now. We're alive and well and we'll soon get out of here. No need to worry," Fenny said. Even though Ramya accepted the spirit of Fenny's words, she couldn't agree fully. There was still plenty to worry about, starting with the presence of the Glasspointe.

The sound of running feet came from outside and both Ramya and Fenny snapped toward the door. A gray head with glittering eyes peeked through it momentarily.

"Ahool, what's going on?" Ramya asked, recognizing the young Mwandan.

"Your captain asks you come," Ahool blurted. "Right away, he says."

Fenny raised an eyebrow at Ramya. "I have stuff to work on here. You go."

"Both need come," Ahool declared firmly. Another Mwandan — a female Ramya did not know — marched into the COM with a large toolbox in hand. She also had a deep brown coloring like Chief Dal, only her stripes were more gray than black.

"What the hell?" Fenny muttered. "Who're you?" she demanded of the new Mwandan.

"I'm Chief Dal's engineer," the Mwandan replied curtly. "Here to assist."

"Merin help with repairs," Ahool explained quickly. "You come to Captain."

Fenny handed Merin the list of pending repairs and followed Ramya out of the COM, throwing a fiery glare behind her and still muttering to herself. "I don't like random strangers twiddling with my equipment."

"Captain's orders, Fenny," Ramya reminded.

The reminder didn't stop Fenny's grumbling. "I'm thinking Sosa's right. The captain might've had a concussion after all."

Ramya held her tongue as they dashed down the corridor. The *Endeavor's* crew had been through hell. It was a miracle that they survived the Drednot attack and then even with the patched-up hull, managed to land in one piece on Morris II. They were all stressed out and pushed to the edge and behaving weirdly, concussion or no concussion.

Quite a few people were already in the captain's room when Ramya and Fenny reached it. The captain was seated in his favorite chair. Ross stood, cross-armed and frowning, leaning against the wall behind him. The Berkari chief sat in a chair across from the captain and another Mwandan—a female—sat in the chair flanking his. Ramya recalled seeing her briefly when she arrived with the engineers Chief Dal had summoned. A meeting was still in progress and Ramya, Fenny, and Ahool slinked inside and filed along the wall.

"Are you sure we'll have Mwandan support, Chief?" the captain asked.

Chief Dal gave him a thoughtful nod. "I can't assure you support of the Mwandan government, Captain. But from the report I received from Chief Mifek on Bucifer P9 and from what I've heard from you, it's easy to put the two and two together. I'm more than convinced about a new Locustan threat. We can't have another invasion, Captain Milos. The Berkari is willing do whatever it takes to help stop it. The Locustans can't be allowed to breach Anomaly Point again; there are no two ways about that."

Chief Dal extended his arms toward the captain, his palms open and spread upward. "On behalf of the Berkari on this planet, I pledge loyalty and life," he said. The way he said those words made Ramya shudder. A hush fell in the room, and Ramya could feel the taut anxiety rippling across. Every face was carved from stone, all eyes narrowed to slits. The captain extended his arms in the same way as Chief Dal until the tips of their fingers touched.

"May our covenant be blessed and may our mission fare well," the captain said, saying aloud ceremonial words that had been used for centuries to forge alliances in the galaxy.

A deal had been sealed. Stillness lingered a few more seconds until both the captain and Chief Dal drew their arms away.

"I will meet with Chief Mifek," the captain said. "But unfortunately, that won't be enough. To defend Anomaly Point we need space fighters. And right now — "

The female Mwandan who had been listening quietly until now rose to her feet. "I'll try to convince the Mwandan government, Captain Milos. And perhaps they can be prevailed on to speak to the Confederacy. Perhaps sway them. These reports of vanishing colonies in the Fringe are as real as you or me, and they need to be made to understand that."

The captain nodded again, rubbing his bandaged forehead tenderly as if it hurt. "Before it's too late."

"Yes, before it's too late," Chief Dal repeated.

The captain tapped his chin, muttering thoughtfully. "I'm hoping Chief Mifek will point us to some sort of recorded evidence of Locustan activity in the Fringe. If we can gather such evidence and show that to the Confederate Space Command . . . They have ignored my words and they'll never take the AI's words seriously, but they might not be able to shrug off recorded proof." He stopped, and flashed a sharp look at Ross. "We need to hurry and get to Mifek."

Dal rose to his feet. "We will start persuading our government, Captain. Maybe the two-pronged approach to prevail on the Confederacy will work. Before I leave, some of my people have volunteered to join you on the *Endeavor*, Captain. If you'll have them."

Next to Ramya, Fenny scrunched her nose. She clearly didn't like the prospect of Mwandan newcomers.

"I'd be honored, Chief. Some more hands will definitely help," Captain Milos replied. Fenny let out a long huffy breath. Ramya kept her face straight with a lot of effort. It was going to be interesting aboard the *Endeavor*.

Next to them Ahool twitched for a second and then scooted forward. "Chief," he said, bowing quickly at the Berkari chief. "May I be permitted to join *Endeavor*? Please?"

The Berkari chief frowned immediately. Ahool shriveled a little at his withering look, but held his gaze nonetheless.

"Ahool Petta, this is not the time to discuss —"

"I completed last mission honorably, Chief," Ahool interrupted. "I meet with Ross and Rami first. This mission happens because of me. I want to participate. Please allow, Chief."

"He's an iffin kid," Fenny muttered under her breath. "Can't even speak his words right." Ramya stole a glance at Fenny, whose nose had shot up again.

"He's plenty brave though," Ramya said. Ahool was indeed young, evident from the faded stripes on his neck and the mildly pampering way the chief and his men spoke to him. But it was no lie that Ahool had not only escaped prison himself but also aided Ross and her in their own search for the *Endeavor*. Ahool was right. This alliance to thwart the Locustans had happened because of him. Without him, Ross and Ramya would've been dead . . . killed by Temihula and the likes.

"You're far too young, Ahool Petta," the chief said in a steely voice. "Approving your first mission was a mistake and I cannot let you go on another. There's plenty of work to be done here. You can still help."

Ahool threw a beseeching look at Ramya and then at Ross. Ramya could see the yearning in those red eyes — they were pleading, begging for someone to come to his aid. She badly wanted to help, to take Ahool's side, but she was also aware of her own position. She was the youngest, newest recruit on the *Endeavor*. She had hidden her identity and she was sure Ross still remembered. Now, in the presence of Captain Milos and Commander Ross, saying a word against the Berkari chief would be a terrible mistake. She bit the inside of her cheek to keep the words from spilling out.

"Let's go, Ahool Petta," Chief Dal said. He nodded toward the female Mwandan. "You heard Officer Noko. We have work to do."

Ahool spun around to look at her again and Ramya's fists curled.

This was wrong. Ahool deserved better. She couldn't simply stay quiet and ignore his pleas. The chief could turn her down, but she had to say something.

"I don't mean to offend you, Chief," Ross spoke before she did, taking everyone in the room by surprise. Ramya stiffened; her eyes and ears glued on the commander. "But even though Ahool Petta is young, he's a remarkable soldier. We would have died without him. If you can spare him, and if Captain Milos would allow it, he'd be a great addition on the *Endeavor*."

Ramya sighed in relief and flashed a grateful look at Ross. He didn't seem to notice, but Ramya kept thanking him silently for backing Ahool.

"Great, just great," Fenny said through gritted teeth. "Now Ross has to poke his long nose into this."

Fenny was clearly infuriated but Ramya was happy for Ahool. Given how loyal Ahool was, she was glad to have someone like him on the *Endeavor*, particularly on a mission as dangerous as this.

"Well, Chief Dal, I put a lot of faith in my commander's judgment," Captain Milos said. "Ahool Petta is welcome aboard my ship. Pending your approval, of course."

Ahool fixed his glittery eyes on the chief who looked away with a sigh.

"I worry because he's a little young, Captain," the Berkari chief said after a second's silence. "Actually, he's the youngest of the Berkari on this planet. Ahool's not had his second birthday yet."

Fenny scoffed under her breath. "An iffin toddler," she hissed. "We're gonna have an iffin toddler on our hands now."

Ramya stifled a sigh. Fenny was not handling this well, which was a little weird considering how eager Fenny had been in taking her in. So it wasn't that Fenny was totally opposed to getting new members. Then what was it? Something to do with Mwandans? Or was she opposed to having so many newcomers at once? Before Ramya could come to a conclusion, Ross spoke.

"He works very well with Rami. Maybe she could be his mentor. Ahool would be in good hands," Ross said. Ramya's eyes grew wide and her mouth fell open in an instant. Did Ross just . . . sort of praise her? What the heck was wrong with the commander?

Chief Dal looked from Ross to Ramya and then to Ahool. He shrugged and nodded slowly at Captain Milos. "Well then. He's all yours, Captain."

A sound of running feet came from the corridor outside and Flux's disheveled face peeked through the door. He stiffened a little, seeing the crowd inside.

"Yes, Flux," Captain Milos. "You have good news, I hope."

Flux flashed a wide grin and nodded vigorously. "The fuel leakage situation is under control, Captain. We'll need significant repairs soon, but we're ready to take off now."

"How are the communicators?"

"Near fixed."

Captain Milos left his chair and strode forward. "Good. Rami, you're going to pick up the Stryker. Ahool, can you assist? Chief Dal will drop you off near the ridge."

Ramya replied with a sharp nod, but Ahool nodded so vigorously it seemed like his head would fall off. Suppressing a chuckle at Ahool's enthusiasm, Ramya looked at her watch. It was almost four hours since they'd left the Stryker. Dakrhaeth was close to complete with his repairs. He better be or they'd be in trouble. They had spent a long time on Morris II and somehow, by some stroke of luck, the Confederacy hadn't showed up yet. But this was pushing it, and at one point or another, luck was sure to run out.

13

A whole day had passed since the *Endeavor* left Morris II. Ramya sat in the tiny entryway of the Stryker interviewing Dakrhaeth. She had been at it for two hours straight. She was tired, exhausted rather, both mentally and physically. But Ramya kept at it.

Her task was critical. The captain needed to find out as much as they could about the Locustans and their history, and Dakrhaeth, being a Locustan combatant in his previous life, was obviously the best source. Progress was slow however. Dakrhaeth's memory of his life prior to crashing on Kyo-Sedra-5 was foggy at best. But Ramya persisted with as much diligence as she could muster. Tiredness creeped around the edges of her senses though, and every now and then Ramya was completely swept away by it.

There had been no other incident during the journey out of the Mwandan sanctuary, nothing dramatic in nature. The ship lifted off, mostly thanks to the help from the Berkari engineers. A couple of them—Namaan, Azzi, and Merin—along with some other non-engineers had joined the *Endeavor's* crew.

Ramya, along with Ahool, had retrieved the Stryker without trouble. Dakrhaeth had been waiting, repairs completed and anxious about Ramya and Ross. On hearing Ramya's account, Dakrhaeth made some snide comments about excessive recklessness but thankfully, lack of time cut his lecture short. After a rushed introduction between the AI and Ahool, they were airborne, and not too long afterward, safely docked inside the *Endeavor*.

Ramya had slept like a baby through the next twelve hours as the *Endeavor* cruised toward its destination, the remote space station of Torsus-Mele. They were actually on their way to the Mwandan sanctuary on Bucifer P9 in the inner Fringe from where Chief Mifek had transmitted the news of vanishing colonies in the area. In a normal situation, the *Endeavor* could've done without stopping at the space station, but with the damaged hull and fuel cell leakage issue from the Drednot attack, a refueling and repairing stop at Torsus-Mele — the closest space station to Bucifer — had become a necessity.

"So, all you remember is being ordered to follow this directive you call the One Path?" Ramya asked Dakrhaeth for the third time in a row. His foggy memories, her tiredness, and the enormous complex mystery that was Anomaly Point, made for exhausting conversation. "And that path led you to the Fringe?"

"Yes, Mihaal," Dakrhaeth replied in a bored voice. "I shall search my memories, but they are distant. I apologize."

"But you crashed on KS5 in Sector 22. How did you get from the Fringe all the way to Sector 22?"

"I don't know. There had to be another directive. I cannot recall."

Kyo-Sedra-5, and its entire system for that matter, was a barren expanse. There were no settlements, no planets with minerals of any value. Why did a Locustan squadron go there?

Ramya would've asked a few more questions but the light atop her newly-bequeathed comm unit blinked a bright green. Ramya sat up and pressed the large button below. Wiz's voice crackled immediately, "Rami? All hands at the med-bay. Come over right now." Just as abruptly as it had come, his voice clipped and ended.

Ramya packed up her notepad and took leave of Dakrhaeth.

"Good luck, Mihaal," he said, making Ramya frown with his choice of words.

"Why do you say that?" she couldn't help asking.

Dakrhaeth took unusually long to reply. "Just a thought, Mihaal," he said finally.

Ramya slowed a little to ponder. That was a strange reply and her gut said there was little truth to it. But she didn't have time to press Dakrhaeth, so with a casual smile at the orb at the center of the Stryker's entryway, she climbed out.

"You can shut down, Dakrhaeth," she shouted before closing the door.

The hold was lighted brightly, but Ramya's fingers curled over the blaster at her hip as she strode across its length. Since the Pterostrich attack she luckily survived, Ramya couldn't shake the tingly fear off her spine each time she entered the hold. Now, the lone Pterostrich was secure in a large and sturdy cage, but she still wasn't taking any chances.

Ramya had crossed halfway when a loud clang made her freeze. Tucking her notepad into a pocket, she pulled the blaster out. Her heart was thudding away in wild frenzy; the cold hand of fear had gripped the base of her spine. Ramya tried to focus on everything but her trembling fingers. She scanned around her slowly, her senses on the alert for the slightest movement, the softest sound. None came.

Blaster raised, Ramya stepped forward stealthily. She had taken two more steps when the clang, louder this time, sounded again. It almost made her jump. She took a second to compose herself, breathing deeply to ease her panicked mind. She wanted to run. The entrance of the hold was not too far, but if it was the Pterostrich, running would be useless. The bird would catch up in no time and tear her to pieces before she could turn. Then again, maybe it wasn't the Pterostrich at all. In that case, it would be better to find out what was making the noise. Holding the blaster tighter, Ramya walked in the direction of the sound.

Five steps down, the noise came again. This time, along with the clang was a low clucking and something else . . . a voice. Was that a human voice?

Ramya hurried forward, ears holding on to the low whispers. She skirted a few boxes and crossed a large stack of mining equipment. The sounds grew louder as she walked. She had neared the final turn around an enormous screen-like structure the Mwandan engineers had put in place overnight when Ramya finally recognized the voice.

"Fenny?" she yelled incredulously. The woman had been kneeling outside the Pterostrich cage, speaking to the lone chick who sat facing her with its outsized head bowed. At Ramya's call, Fenny jumped to her feet, as did the chick. "What are you doing?" Ramya asked.

Fenny shrugged and smiled rather awkwardly. "Just talking."

"To that murderous chick?"

"Vittoria. Her name's Vittoria," Fenny corrected fervently. "And Vi's not the one who attacked you. She's not murderous, Rami. Never has been."

Ramya sighed and sheathed her blaster. She wanted to roll her eyes at Fenny. Pterostriches were universally vicious and everyone knew that. No one had ever known a Pterostrich that practiced non-violence. But pointless as Fenny's idea was, seeing her indignant expression, Ramya didn't have the heart to taunt her. She decided to change the conversation instead.

"Captain's called us all. Did you hear that?" she asked.

"Yes, I know," Fenny replied, and walked away from the cage. "I was just wrapping up with Vi. Come on, let's go."

Ramya threw a quick glance backward at Vittoria as she walked toward the exit with Fenny. The chick had trotted up to the front end of its cage to look wistfully at them. It raised its head and let out a sad coo when Fenny closed the door of the hold as if it were missing her. Fenny sighed noisily. "Vi's a nice girl. She's no murderer."

"Fenny, a Pterostrich chick can't be your pet," Ramya said once they were inside the elevator. "They're ferocious."

"They're trained to run races, Rami," Fenny said. "They can be trained."

"You know nothing about training them," Ramya countered.

Fenny's eyebrows danced. "I do. I read a bunch of articles on training them." She leaned closer and whispered, "I've already started giving her lessons. She's good."

"Fenny . . ." Ramya couldn't say what she wanted to. It was a stupid enterprise. The Komilahns who trained Pterostriches for a living had done that for generations. They knew their business. Fenny, on the other hand, was a navigator on a freighter who knew nothing about Pterostriches. Heck, she probably didn't even have a lizard to play pets with. Playing with a Pterostrich was risky. One mistake and Fenny could be dead. But looking at Fenny's shining eyes, Ramya knew, advice would be lost on her. "Call me when you go about training her. I'd like to watch."

Fenny smirked. "Watch over me, huh, kid?"

"Maybe," Ramya said. "Just call me, all right?"

"All right, all right," Fenny said. "Why do you think the captain called us?"

That was a nice deflection. She didn't say it aloud though, simply chuckled a little. "To discuss our plans?"

"We already know our plans. Get to Torsus-Mele, get the fuel store fixed, and then get to Bucifer P9 and meet Mifek. What's there to discuss?"

She was right. They knew those plans already. What else was there to talk about? A worry came quickly to the surface, one she had been forcing down heavy-handedly for a day. This could be about her, about her identity to be precise. She didn't have too much to worry about since the captain already knew, as did Fenny. Still, Sosa might and definitely react to her duplicity, if not Wiz or Flux. Her gut tightened at the thought and Fenny nudged her elbow right away.

"You coming?" she asked playfully. The elevator doors were already open and Ramya hadn't noticed. Fenny threw a meaningful look at her as she trudged out.

"I think it's something to do with Sosa," Fenny said worriedly. "That woman's been quiet as a rock since her patient died."

Sosa's patient, the pilot of the Stryker, had been laid to rest in a quick ceremony at the Reliquary grove. That was the only time Sosa had emerged from her quarters and the only time Ramya had seen her since coming back to the *Endeavor*. The Norgoran had looked drained, her usually bright green skin pale and splotchy. She had barely spoken to Ramya.

"You think she's unwell?" Ramya asked.

"We'll find out," Fenny said, pushing open the green painted door of the med-bay.

They were all gathered inside. Sosa sat in her chair backed by the bottle-filled alcove, Captain Milos next to her, and Ross, Wiz, and Flux on the other side of the table. Everyone looked as Ramya and Fenny entered, but Ramya was sure Ross stared particularly keenly at her. Ramya's heart picked up pace as she found a spot to stand along the wall. This was about her, she was sure.

"Now that we're all here, let's get started," Captain Milos said. Ramya tucked her icy fingers into her pockets and held her breath. "You can see I've only called the old crew together. That's for a reason. First of all, I wanted to raise a glass in a toast to all of you and our survival."

He held up a glass of Pax. Everyone—Ross, Wiz, and Sosa—who had glasses in their hand raised them in response. The captain smiled and continued in a grave voice. "But there's more to it than cheer. You all know, we have a difficult task ahead of us. We have to find allies, convince the Confederacy that an invasion might be looming. I hope Chief Mifek can lead us to the evidence we need to get the Confederacy to act. And I hope we aren't too late already." He paused to let out a long, labored breath. "I don't know where our path leads us, but it sure isn't a pretty path. If any of you want to leave, I'd be happy to let you go."

As soon as the captain paused, swift glances flew around the room. A hushed murmur rose before dying down quickly.

"We're in this together, Captain," Wiz said assertively. "I don't think any of us thinks otherwise."

The captain looked around the room and nodded gravely before speaking again. "I'm proud of you all. If what we've heard until now is true, the galaxy is under siege. But people who should be defending it are unwilling to accept the weight of the situation. They'd rather be mired in their petty politics."

The captain stopped and ran his fingers over the bandage on his forehead the way he had been doing for the past day. Ramya squinted. He had to be in considerable pain. She was about to tear her eyes away when she noticed Sosa. She, too, was looking at the captain, her gaze worried as it scanned him. Ramya inhaled sharply, her insides tightening. Something was wrong, she was sure of it.

"We are the only ones who are in a position to do something to stop an invasion if it happens. But we're just a few and believe me . . . we're nothing in front of a Locustan invasion. We need people — friends, allies, anyone who's willing to fight with us. We have to do whatever it takes to recruit people to this cause."

He paused again and took a long breath. And once again Ramya noted how Sosa's eyes narrowed.

"The Mwandans are our first allies. So, I want all of you to be extra courteous to our friends on this ship." He looked around the room, his gaze lingering on Fenny before moving on. "We need them. Remember, we need everyone — thieves, mercenaries, outlaws — anyone who'd fight for the galaxy and the survival of our races."

Captain Milos pause and gestured at Ross. "That's all I had to say. Your turn, Commander."

"Ah, yes. There's something I wanted to talk about. Something you all need to know," Ross said. He paused and twiddled his thumbs for a moment, then quickly looked at the captain and Sosa. "I wouldn't have known this if I hadn't gone out on the Stryker."

Ramya sucked in a lungful of air and held it. He was going call her out. Ross looked around the room, his gaze icy as it came to rest on Ramya. He might've stared for merely a second, but it felt like an eternity in hell. Ramya realized she was not ready to see their faith in her shatter and definitely not prepared to be called out so publicly as a liar. But ready or not, it was about to happen.

Ross tore his gaze off her and looked around the room again. "I realized . . . how important all of you guys are to me. You're family. All of you." He flashed an awkward smile and shrugged. "That's all."

That's all? What the hell? Ramya let go of the breath she'd been holding and gulped instead. Wasn't he going to tell them who she really was?

"That's the sweetest thing you've ever said, Ross," Fenny said, breaking into a loud cackle. "But it totally doesn't suit that grumpy thing you've got going."

Wiz and Flux joined in her as well and soon the whole room reverberated with laughter and chuckles.

"All right, if that's all then that's all," the captain said after a while. "Let's get back to work, everyone."

No, this wasn't all. Why Ross chose to not disclose her secret, Ramya didn't understand, but she did understand clearly what she wanted. Or what she didn't want. Perhaps Ross was simply giving her a pass, but she didn't, not even for a second, want him to turn her secret into a weapon against her. She *had* to tell them. She trusted all of them enough.

"I have something to say, Captain," she declared. "If I may," she quickly added.

"Of course, Rami," Captain Milos said.

Ross, along with Flux, Wiz, and Fenny, had already headed for the door. They turned around curiously. Ramya's fists turned into balls, nails biting sharply into her palms, the pain grounding her flitting intentions. It was now or never.

"There's something you need to know about me," she blurted.

Wiz guffawed. "That you kicked that Mwandan forest spirit's hind? Ross told us all about it."

He did? Why? He wasn't shy about his resentment toward her on the Stryker. He had even called her a Kiroff spy.

"No, it's not that," Ramya said, shaking her head to push the distracting questions away. "When I came aboard, I didn't tell you my real name. I couldn't. I was running away from my home, my parents, my . . . my real name. From everything I've ever known, actually."

Sosa seemed remarkably calm, as if she had already known what

Ramya was saying. Wiz crossed his arms and frowned.

"You in some kind of trouble, Rami?" Flux asked.

"Maybe I am, but I don't care. There's far more to worry about," Ramya said. She really didn't care as much anymore. The fear of Trysten Kiroff catching her had sunk into some distant corner of her mind, and even though it surfaced from time to time, the instances were far from often.

"What's your name anyway?" Wiz asked.

"Ramya. I'm Ramya Kiroff, daughter of Trysten Kiroff of House Kiroff," Ramya said slowly and deliberately. A weight had lifted off her by the time she finished speaking.

"That's iffin cool," Flux said, chuckling. "A runaway heiress, fancy that."

Wiz blinked a few times. "You're nasty Kiroff's daughter? Oh, wait, forget I said that, all right? I won't again . . . I promise. I won't call him names."

"It's all right, Wiz," Ramya said. "It's not like I'm going to report to him. I don't hope to meet him anytime soon anyway."

"Besides, Trysten Kiroff deserves every name we've ever called him," Fenny said.

Fenny, Wiz, and Flux broke into an animated discussion about Trysten Kiroff's many virtues, but Ross broke away from the group.

"That's all, right?" he asked Ramya. "I've got a million diagnostics to run, so if you're done, I'll get going."

He stepped out of the med-bay as soon as Ramya nodded. For a second Ramya stood there, thinking, and then she hurried after him. He was nearly ten paces away from the door when she rushed out.

"Ross," she called. He stopped and turned around slowly. A small frown rippled on his forehead and his eyes were stony behind his eyeglasses. "Commander Ross," she corrected herself quickly.

He shook his head. "You don't need to call me that. What is it?"

"Why didn't you tell them about me?" Ramya blurted. "You wanted to. It needed to be said."

His face softened as looked away at the distance. "Because you deserved a second chance," Ross said. He tucked a long strand of hair behind his ear before looking steadfastly into her eyes. "You're not your father. You are Rami, a worthy crewmate I trust. I chose to remember that."

"Thank you." Ramya could barely manage to push those words out of her choking throat.

Ross gave her a curt nod. He turned to leave but then turned back. "You didn't have to tell them. Why did you?"

Ramya didn't have to think to find an answer for him. "They deserved to know. I care about them too."

A grin broke the taut lines of his face. It made him look so much younger. "I know, Rami. I know."

He hesitated for a second, then reached out to pat her shoulder. "Off to work," he said before striding away.

Ramya watched him walk down the corridor, a silly, happy smile making her face stretch. *Finally!* She had made peace with Ross. The happiness and the relief were unexpected, and for a while it made her forget the precarious situation they were all in and the danger that was closing in on them from all sides.

14

Long before the *Endeavor* approached the space station for refueling and repairs, Captain Milos had assigned two teams: the first team Flux would lead to get the spares for repairs, and the other team would be led by Fenny to pick up provisions. Ramya was happy when she was asked to assist Fenny. Along with Fenny, she scoured the hold to check on food supplies and other sundries, making a list of things to acquire during the pit stop.

They were checking off the final — quite long — list in the mess hall when Fenny's comm blinked.

"What now?" Fenny said grumpily. Wiz's voice crackled with urgency as soon as she pressed the button.

"Fenny, course change coming up. Need you at the COM."

Fenny sat up immediately. "What? Why?"

"They've tagged us, Fenny. We've been put on the Confederate Space Command's Rogue Ship list."

Fenny dropped the list she had been holding on the worn steel table and grabbed the sides of her forehead. "What?"

"What did you expect after the shit we pulled at Totori?"

Fenny closed her eyes and let out a long sigh. "So . . . we can't go to Torsus-Mele? But we need the iffin repairs done before we start for the Fringe to meet Mifek."

"You think the captain doesn't know that?" Wiz chuckled, and Fenny rolled her eyes.

"So there's another plan?" Ramya asked.

"Yes, kiddo. There is another plan. We are going to Nebeca 21."

Why Fenny slumped back in her seat and sighed exasperatedly, Ramya didn't quite get, but she could assume Nebeca 21 wasn't a place on top of Fenny's "to visit" list.

"Guess we have to cloak up as well?" Fenny asked.

"Of course," Wiz replied. "Can't just walk into that den of rats with a wanted tag on our back."

"Fun never stops. I'm on my way, Wiz," Fenny said into the comm. After she'd slapped the comm off, Fenny looked up at Ramya.

"'Cloak up'? What does that mean?" Ramya demanded to know.

"We hide the identity of the ship. Give them false creds when we dock."

Ramya frowned. She had never heard of that before, but she guessed it was a fairly common thing. "Cloaking is easy?"

Fenny shrugged. "Flux and I can pull it off quite well. Haven't needed it much lately. But . . ." Fenny let her words trail off. She tapped the table and shook her head.

"Something else worrying you?" Ramya asked.

"Everything's worrying me. Like a noose is getting tighter around our necks," Fenny said. "Nebeca 21 is an iffin crap-hole. Octus Laurden the Sixth runs it. It's like a nest of the shadiest people in the galaxy. Mercenaries, gangsters, traffickers, you name it, they're swarming on Nebeca. But if the iffin Confederacy tagged us as rogue, that's the only place we can get in and out of without being spotted right away."

"We can carry weapons, right?" Most space stations in the galaxy did not allow visitors to carry arms, but Nebeca sounded lawless enough to have different rules.

"Yes, we can," Fenny replied with a dour shake of her head. "But weapons only go so far, kid."

On that uplifting note, Fenny left. Ramya sat with the final list of things they needed to acquire, hoping they'd all make it out of the space station in one piece. Whatever she had heard so far, the prospect of visiting Nebeca 21 did not sound good . . . at all.

***

Captain Milos was at the gate, his hands on his hips and foot tapping as he watched the teams pack up. "Be careful out there. Get in and out as fast as you can."

Ross stood with his back to the wall, also watching intently. Between Ross and the captain, Ahool bobbed back and forth. The young Mwandan had asked the captain permission to join one of the teams, but the captain had refused coldly. Azzi, one of the Mwandan engineers, was placed in Flux's group and another Mwandan — a stout and gruff fellow named Rei — was coming with Ramya and Fenny. Since Mwandans were hardly seen outside of their sanctuaries and would attract instant attention, both Azzi and Rei were covered from head to foot in clothing to hide their Mwandan heritage. The captain didn't want to send them out in the first place, but with so much that needed to be done in so little time, there was no other choice.

The captain stayed firm in his refusal to let Ahool venture out though. Ramya was sure it was because of his age. She had tried to explain that to the Mwandan boy, but not with much success. Ahool fretted and fumed and complained and . . . bobbed around.

With a final shake of her head at the fidgety Ahool, Ramya looked away. She pulled out her blaster and turned it back and forth to make sure it was all right. She patted her pocket to ensure the list was in place. She tugged at her visor, pulling it low to cover her face. She was ready when Fenny nodded at her.

Their team set out first, and Flux and Azzi followed in their heels. Ramya's heart thudded like a war hammer on steroids, even more as they walked into the security area just outside the docks. Shabby-looking security screens lined the exit pathways, but they didn't seem functional at all. The place was also remarkably empty. Ramya had been to quite a few space stations with her family. Most of them were in the prime sectors and most were gaudy affairs. People — security personnel mostly — thronged them. None was as deserted or as unkempt as this.

And then there were the massive paintings of an Octus. Ramya assumed it was Octus Laurden the Sixth, the owner of Nebeca 21.

They were hung on every wall, hulking things that seemed to glare at anyone passing through the corridors. Laurden the Sixth was an impressive specimen of an Octus — his honey-colored eyes bulging out of his fiery orange shell, eight thick arms typical of a Crustoid spread out like a halo behind him. They could tear apart an enemy in a heartbeat. That glint of insanity in Laurden's eyes and the cruel smirk that twisted his thick lips clearly corroborated that like every Octus before him, and she had no doubt that he would also enjoy the act of tearing someone to shreds.

Ramya shuddered thinking of the stories she had heard of the Octus. The galaxy was not settled peacefully and the humans had to fight the Octus for ages before things settled into the current state of apparent balance. Ramya tore her eyes away from the nearest painting just in time to notice Fenny slow down.

"All right, guys. Now we go in," Fenny announced. "The Souk is on the first floor, three levels down from here. That's where we're headed." She paused a while, her keen gaze scanning Ramya and Rei from head to foot. "Keep eye contacts to a minimum, all right? Let's not attract attention."

With that she pushed the door open and walked into the main deck of the space station. Ramya followed, trying her best to keep from ogling at the milling crowd. Nebeca 21 was different from any other space station, and the people here were different too. Everyone seemed eager to keep to themselves, and seeing the many scars that most faces sported, they had reason to keep away. Most also sported large weapons, and those who seemed to carry no weapons actually had them concealed under their clothes.

"Keep moving, Rei," Fenny barked, and Ramya realized their Mwandan mate had slowed down considerably. That was understandable. To a Mwandan, seeing as many people from all races would be a shock of sorts. Ramya had to praise the captain's wisdom in keeping the boy on the ship as she imagined how Ahool would've reacted to being here.

There were shops all around and Ramya's eyes scoured the eateries longingly. Quite a while had passed since she had eaten a freshly cooked meal and her stomach twitched at the sight of the steaming fresh food displayed in shop windows. But there was no time to yearn for food or to stop for a bite, so Ramya forced her eyes away.

"Two more floors," Fenny declared as they weaved through the crowd in search of elevators. It wasn't too difficult to get to the Souk, a dingy floor with less than optimal lighting. Strange smells — from spicy aromas to the stink of dried fish — hit Ramya's nose as soon as she stepped off the elevator. This floor was considerably less crowded. People turned to look at them more, particularly at Rei, which Ramya assumed was because of his attire.

Fenny hurried them on, stopping or slowing nowhere until they reached a largish shop with a paint-stripped door and grimy windows to match. The proprietor was a buxom woman with faded yellow hair and eyes as blue as the seas.

"Hello," she greeted in a scratchy voice as soon as the trio marched in, her eyes lingering on Rei.

"Hello," Fenny said, nodding at Ramya to hand the shopkeeper their list. "Need to push off quickly. Can you put a rush on this?"

The woman scanned the list and grunted. "Well, I have everything, but a few customers are in line so . . ."

A few customers? There was no one else in the shop. Ramya frowned, but Fenny was clearly not about to argue. She dropped a wad of money on the table and gestured at it. "That's an extra thousand lieres. Perhaps your other customers can wait?"

The woman snatched the money off the table and passed it into a drawer. "I'll put a rush on it," she said before waddling off into the back of the store.

"That she will," Fenny muttered. She threw a meaningful look at Ramya and Rei. "In places like this, we let money do the talking."

The money did talk quite well. A shifty-eyed Norgoran soon

pulled a cartful of supplies in front of the shop. The buxom woman waddled out after him.

"There's everything you wanted," the woman said to Fenny.

Fenny chuckled. "That was quick," she said. In another few minutes she had paid the woman and the trio marched back to the docking area.

Ahool and Wiz met them at the entrance.

"Where's the captain?" Ramya asked, glancing around. Since docking at Nebeca 21, either Captain Milos or Ross was always at the gate. But now neither was present. "And the commander?"

"They're in a meeting," Ahool informed. He pointed at the cart laden with supplies. "Can I help with those?"

Wiz dug into the topmost bag and pulled out a bar of chocolate. "Ah, you got my favorite kind, Fenny. Dark with fennel and pepper. Perfect."

Fenny scoffed and shook her head. "You're welcome. Hey, is Flux and Azzi back yet?"

Ahool shook his head. "They just called us. Said they need another fifteen minutes or so."

Another fifteen minutes? It was a pity they couldn't grab a bite to eat. Ramya couldn't stop the sigh from coursing out of her. Fenny's brows shot up right away.

"Can you guys inventory all the stuff?" she asked. Ahool nodded eagerly and Wiz mumbled something back. As soon as Rei wheeled the cart away, Fenny crossed her arms and cocked her head at Ramya. "What's going on? What's that look on your face?"

Ramya flushed as Fenny's eyes bored into her. "It's nothing," she said.

Fenny was having none of it. Tapping her chin, she took a step closer and frowned. "Come on, kid. You have a funny look on your face. I haven't seen that one before."

To hell with it! "I'm just craving for some fresh grub, that's all," Ramya explained. "It's silly," she added hastily.

"That's it?" Fenny made a face and thumped Ramya's back. "Come on, let's go. There's a saloon right outside the docking area. We'll be done before Flux gets his lazy hind back to the ship."

Ramya marched back into the space station, matching strides with Fenny. Her steps were light and brisk as they trooped into the saloon. The eatery was large and fairly clean. A waitress with dark braids and a heavily made-up face showed them to a table almost at the center of the room. Ramya and Fenny ordered right away, Ramya settling for a meat-and-dough soup. It was right after the waitress set the steaming bowl in front of her that a strange feeling tingled Ramya's spine and made her stiffen. It was the odd sense of being watched.

"What's it now?" Fenny said, munching on a thick five-layered sandwich. It was uncanny how Fenny quickly picked up on her expression, almost like an elder sister.

Ramya shrugged. She was worrying needlessly. Putting another spoonful of soup into her mouth, Ramya looked around. Nothing seemed out of place, and no one was looking at them.

"You sure it's nothing?" Fenny asked.

"It's just a funny feeling," Ramya confessed. "Like someone's watching us."

Fenny looked around furtively. "I don't see anything odd."

"I know," Ramya said. Trying to shake off the feeling, she forced a few more spoons of soup. The meat was succulent and the nuggets of dough were soft and melty. But far from being swept away by the delicious food, Ramya fought the nervous jitters that kept on growing.

She spotted the man in the muted-green uniform of the Confederate Troopers on her third scan. She was far too late. By then Fenny's comm had started blinking frenziedly.

"Fenny, where are you?" Ross said in a low, guttural voice as soon as Fenny enabled the channel.

"We're at the Outpost Saloon," Fenny replied casually. "It's close to the docking ports."

"Get back to the ship right now. Flux spotted a squad of

Confederate Troopers inside."

"I see one right across from us," Ramya whispered as soon as Fenny turned off the comm. "He's watching us."

Fenny took a large bite off her sandwich and slowly placed it back on her plate. "All right. Act normal."

That was easier said than done. Ramya's stomach churned and she wanted to run out of the eatery in that instant. Somehow she kept from bolting and stayed put in her seat.

Fenny continued in a calm, low voice. "So they're outside the front door, right? We can't use that door. There's an exit on the other side. Should lead us to the back of the eatery. With me, Rami?"

Ramya nodded. Three other men in similar green uniforms had joined the first trooper. One of them had stripes on his collar that signified the rank of an officer. They spoke animatedly among themselves. Ramya's glanced askance at the heavyset, square-jawed officer. He looked extremely familiar yet Ramya couldn't quite place him.

"Got to move, Rami." Fenny placed some lieres on the table and rose swiftly to her feet. Ramya set her spoon down and followed. From the corner of her eye, she saw the troopers spread out along the front of the eatery.

By the time Ramya and Fenny were halfway to the back exit, the officer had marched into the saloon, three of his men in tow.

"Halt," the officer shouted.

"Keep walking, Rami," Fenny said. Her hand hovered over the blaster at her thigh.

"You two," the officer shouted again. Ramya could sense the fingers pointed at their backs, then she heard the telltale sound of weapons being drawn.

"Rami, duck." Fenny's urgent whisper had barely reached Ramya's ear when blaster fire roared behind her. Ramya threw herself at the exit. Her body bumped into the door, flinging it open. She crashed shoulder first onto the grimy floor on the other side. Fenny careened through it a moment later and rolled away from the opening. In the next second the sound of blaster fire filled the air, and the door riddled with blaster holes looked like Erocondian cheese. Something more potent than a blaster fire hit the door right after, ripping the edges and setting it ablaze. Ramya shielded her head and scrambled to one side, away from the flaming skeleton of the door.

The moment she caught her breath, Ramya spun around and took stock. They were not out of the saloon but had ended up in a back hallway. There were doors along the wall, so they weren't trapped . . . yet. They had to find a way out.

But first she had to get to Fenny. They had both rolled away from the door after crashing through it, but to opposite sides. Fenny was now on the right side of gaping hole in the wall that had been the door. Ramya pulled her blaster out and stood with her back against the wall, straining her ears to find out what the troopers were doing inside. There were muffled voices, sound of running feet. Fenny was barely ten paces away on the other side of a belt of smoke, fire, and debris, listening intently as well. Holding the blaster tightly to her chest, Ramya took a long breath. She could do it. She had to reach Fenny. Another breath. Then Ramya sprinted.

Just then, a big chunky block flew through the broken door, crossed Ramya's path, and hit the wall. Ramya didn't know what it was, but she was sure it was an explosive. A couple of balls—Ramya identified them instantly as concussion devices—came bouncing through the door right after. Ramya desperately tried to stop but she was running too fast and her feet slipped on the debris. She toppled backward, the blaster flying from her hand. Not too far away, the big blocky device hissed menacingly, releasing copious green fumes.

"Fall back, Rami," Fenny screamed. "Fall back."

Ramya scuttled backward as fast as she could, but it wasn't going to be enough. The block hissed louder. Someone grabbed her by the arm and pulled. The hissing block receded. Then the room exploded in a shower of heat, flames, flying debris, and an ear-splitting ruckus.

Ramya covered her ears and head and kept scrambling away. A door opened and she crawled through it. It was dark on the other side, but at least the air was cleaner.

Ramya breathed as if she had not breathed in ages. Her ears rang, the jarring sound reverberating through her bones and shaking her core. For a few unending seconds, the whole world turned blurry. Ramya blinked furiously, but the haze refused to lift. The grip on her arm stayed firm. Whoever had saved her from the troopers' raid was still with her. She could tell it was a human male, and he wore blue.

"Thanks," Ramya whispered to the unknown blur next to her.

He nodded in response. "My privilege, Lady Ramya," he said.

Strange how a few words could clear her senses like a magic wand had been flicked. Ramya's thoughts, murky since the blast, turned as clear as the ocean waters off Somenvaar in an instant. He had called her Lady Ramya. He knew who she really was. Her vision cleared slower than her mind, but it cleared nonetheless, and she had no trouble recognizing the man in the sharp blue uniform of the GSO, who was shooting at the smoking mess with a sleek, state-of-the-art Nihilator field gun.

He was Trysten Kiroff's man in the GSO, Lieutenant Gael Arlington. She remembered the name clearly. He was the one she had danced her last dance at CAWStrat. But what was he doing here? Trying to catch her, or was he trying to get to the Stryker? Was he here alone or did all of the GSO know the *Endeavor* had docked at Nebeca 21?

The more her mind raced with questions, the more Ramya's heart turned into an icy blob of fear until she could barely think any more. Only a constant monotone: "Get away," it kept saying. "Run!" But there was no way out of this battlefield.

Someone shouted. Loud voices sounded in the smoke-filled saloon. Footsteps. Orders. Yells. The grip on her arm grew tighter. Gael Arlington was pulling her away again. Every fiber of her being came together, cut through the fog of fear, and rose up in protest.

14

"What are you doing?" Ramya shouted, trying without a smidgeon of success to wrench her arm free of his vice-like grip.

"Isn't it obvious?" he said through gritted teeth, shooting in the direction of the blaster-fire. "I'm trying to keep you alive."

Maybe he was, but he was not a friend. He was Trysten Kiroff's flunkey, and Ramya didn't need to be saved by any of her father's minions. Besides, he was dragging her away from the saloon and away from Fenny.

"I have to get back to my ship," Ramya yelled. "And that's the other way."

Gael shoved her through a door and dragged her across the storage room behind it.

"The other way? The other way's through a firefight, Lady Ramya," he said. "You've lost your weapon and I don't think you're impervious to blaster-fire. Tell me how you'll get through there."

Maybe he was right. Hell, he *was* right. But she couldn't just trust him, could she?

"Run," Gael yelled suddenly. Ramya sprinted, running blindly after Gael, noting the faint plop behind her.

Gael dashed through another door and Ramya followed. Seconds later the room they'd just left behind turned into a ball of fire. Gael fell to the ground and rolled sideways and Ramya dove after him. Tongues of fire leaped out of the doorway behind them. The world shook again, a momentary blackness spreading in front of Ramya's eyes like a thick, suffocating curtain.

15

Ramya stumbled through a smoke-filled corridor, her ears still ringing and her vision barely normal. Ahead of her, Gael edged forward stealthily. Ramya wished she were back in the *Endeavor*, that she'd never wanted a trip to the saloon, but wishing didn't help any. The only thing she could do was trudge ahead through the smoke and the debris. And keep following Gael. She had to admit, she was in a pretty bad situation. She'd lost her weapon. She'd lost Fenny. Heck, she didn't even have a map of this place.

A thought that hadn't struck her suddenly numbed her heart. Had Fenny survived? She had last seen Fenny duck when the explosives set off, but what happened after that?

A desperate need to find out swamped her. Coming back into the space station and visiting the saloon was her idea. And now Fenny was . . . Ramya couldn't think any further. She *had* to get back and make sure Fenny was all right. But how could she get back? The only way was along this corridor that took her further away from the saloon and her crewmates.

A chance came moments after. They had reached a crossroads of sorts. Eight walkways merged at a central hallway like the hub of wheel, each corridor just as deserted as the other. Ramya's mind picked up pace. The corridor on the right was in the direction of the saloon's entrance. Sure, the Confederate Troopers could still be lurking, but Fenny had to be there as well. She had to try to get back and this was her chance.

Gael's hand clamped on Ramya's arm even before she'd taken the first step. "Don't even think about it," he said, tugging her into one of the other walkways. He was taking her away from the path back to the saloon, away from Fenny.

"That's the way back to my crewmate," Ramya yelled. "Don't you get it? I have to find her. Help her."

"You can't, Lady Ramya," he said. "You're not in a position to help anyone. Now, keep moving."

The more she tried to fight him off, the more his grip tightened on her arm. Where the hell was he taking her? Not back to the *Endeavor*, that she was certain. To her father? She was certain her father had sent the troopers. She had to get away, but she had to be careful. She couldn't lead him into finding the *Endeavor*. If her father got the Stryker back that'd be even worse. Without Dakrhaeth's account, who would believe the Locustans could be coming? The Confederacy would throw Captain Milos into prison. Then there'd be more politics, more deflection, and more waste of time. Meanwhile the Locustans would come and the galaxy would fall.

A projectile flew past them and hit the wall ahead. Gael pushed her behind a column and threw himself over her. An explosion rocked the hallways a split second later, debris—crumbly tiny pieces thankfully—showered over them.

She pushed him off herself the moment the sound died down. He didn't seem to notice as she checked the corridor on both sides. He was busily inspecting a holo-map of some sort, possibly of this sector of the star base. Ramya mulled her options. She could make a run for it. All she needed was get into that partially open doorway down the corridor. It looked like a room of sorts, and she could lock herself in there. *Twenty paces, that's all there is to it.*

Ramya stole a glance at Gael. His eyes were still glued on the map. It was now or never. She had to escape Gael Arlington at any cost. She couldn't let him drag her over to her father. Not now. Not ever.

She was about to make a run for it when she noticed the movement around the corner. Ramya blinked at the tiny black spot in the distance. It was the muzzle of a weapon aimed directly at them.

There goes my last chance!

She grabbed Gael by the scruff of his coat and sprang forward, hoping to reach the other side. Before she could blink, a blast of light flew through the spot they had been in. Gael shot back in the direction of the blast and ran to the opposite side, and Ramya ollowed. Skidding over the debris, they dashed toward the next bend in the corridor.

Turning the corner, Gael threw himself into a sizeable depression on the wall before yanking Ramya into it. They were pressing against a doorway, Ramya realized. The door was locked with a large, state-of-the-art keypad lock embedded into it.

"I can't leave Fenny behind," Ramya blurted. "I just can't. I have to go back."

"Why do you keep wanting to go back? Are you suicidal or something?" Gael hissed, his right brow arched quizzically. "Did you recognize that Confederate officer? That was Melroon Danukis back there. Those men were his, all loyal to House Danukis."

No wonder the officer had looked familiar. He was the uncle of her ex-classmate Armand, that arrogant, annoying pig.

Gael continued his lecture. "Those bastards would love to catch you. And here you are, hell-bent on running into their arms."

Ramya took a bracing breath. "I can't leave my crewmate behind."

"She'll be fine. She looks like the kind who can take care of herself," Gael shot back.

He was right. Fenny was more than capable of defending herself. But Fenny wasn't all Ramya worried about. "I would rather die than get hauled back to Somenvaar."

"Really? You'd rather give up your life?"

"Yes, I would."

"Oh, well. Then you should really stay away from Melroon's people," he said simply. "Melroon wouldn't kill you. He'd simply keep you as hostage so he can negotiate a deal with your father."

He was right again. Melroon Danukis would like nothing better than a means to humiliate business rival Trysten Kiroff, but her father was never going to negotiate for her. She wasn't worth enough. No, that was wrong. He would. Because to Trysten Kiroff, even though Ramya's life wouldn't be a stake high enough, the honor of House Kiroff certainly would.

Gael's fingers danced on the keypad on the door and within a second or two, the panel beeped and the doorway parted. A small dimly lit room was on the other side. "Step inside please, Lady Ramya," he instructed curtly.

Ramya did as he asked, but she seethed inside. Not just because he called her Lady Ramya, *again*, but also because she had no other choice but to follow his bidding.

"Do not call me that," she snapped as soon as the door closed behind Gael.

He looked a little surprised at her vehemence, his narrowed eyes settling on her face. "What should I call you then? Lady Isbet?"

Ramya stiffened. He still remembered? That was the false name Ramya had given him when they had met at the CAWStrat. She flushed a little, but she was not going to let him embarrass her. He had lied to her as well. She crossed her arms and tilted her chin defiantly at him. "You can call me Rami, CSA Stevan Helves."

Why Gael grinned so stupidly at her reply, Ramya had no idea, but it irked her endlessly. "Hear something funny?"

Gael shook his head. "Um, no. You're just . . . unexpected."

She was about to ask him what he meant, but then that would be engaging him too much. Gael Arlington was annoying as heck and the last thing Ramya wanted was to make him feel important. So instead Ramya studied the small room they were in. It was bare, with another closed door on the backside. "What the hell is this place?" she muttered, mostly to herself.

"A place that's not exploding on us," Gael replied.

Ramya rolled her eyes. As if she needed to hear his smug quips! Resolving to keep her mutterings under her breath next time, she kept on probing. The walls sounded unusually dense when she tapped, and the way trusses crisscrossed meant that this room was deliberately reinforced. Space stations had built-in shelters strong enough to withstand everything short of a nuclear explosion, everyone knew that. Had Gael found one of those? The lieutenant was resourceful, she had to give him that.

Something crackled and Ramya turned to look. Gael dug up a sharp-looking communicator from his pocket, a model Ramya had not seen before. If this was a safe room, it was odd that any signal could penetrate its walls at all. That device had to be pretty cutting edge.

Gael shot her a quick look with a funny expression on his face that Ramya couldn't quickly identify. He pressed a couple of buttons on the communicator and a familiar voice filled the tiny room at once.

"Lieutenant Arlington, I hope you're all right," Trysten Kiroff. "There are reports of a firefight on Nebeca 21, so I thought of checking on you."

Ramya froze at the sound of her father's voice. Even though they were only speaking over a communicator, it felt as if he could see her, as if he was standing right there, frowning dismissively at her. It had been weeks since she'd last seen her father, days since she'd heard his voice. She had moved past her dread of him, she'd thought.

Not so much!

Anger coiled at the pit of Ramya's stomach. She hated herself for being so weak. Biting the inside of her cheek, she breathed with all her might. She had to grow out of it, she *had* to. Ramya's fists tightened with resolve.

"Please tell me you're well," her father said, his voice pliant with concern.

Ramya shifted on her feet, discomfort welling inside her. He was checking on Gael. Her father, the heartless Trysten Kiroff, was checking on a worthless minion? That was new.

Gael chuckled. "I'm well, Lord Paramount. I might be missing a few hairs on my head, but I still have ten fingers and just as many toes, I think. Haven't counted them in a while though."

Ramya's eyes widened at the casual way Gael spoke to her father. She braced for her father to snap back, to put Gael in place.

"I'm quite glad to hear that," her father replied. *Was that relief in his voice? No, it couldn't be.* "Please stay safe, Gael."

Ramya frowned. *Stay safe, Gael?* It almost sounded like her father cared for the lieutenant like a father would care for a child. A pang of jealousy welled up inside her. That was how he should've cared for her. But did he? She'd never heard that tone, not once in seventeen years.

"I will," Gael replied. "I have news for you."

Her father let out a long breath. "You've secured the Stryker. Thank you."

Gael shook his head and shifted uncomfortably. "Not yet, Lord Paramount. The Stryker's here, but I haven't secured it . . . yet."

A tight silence hung in the room. Gael shot a look at her across the room and Ramya knew what he was about to tell her father. She inhaled long and deep and held the breath inside her, too afraid to let it go, afraid that she'd never find the strength to take another breath again.

"What other news then?"

"I found your daughter."

This time around, the quiet stretched longer. Ramya didn't know when cold had invaded her body, but she suddenly realized her fingers had turned into chunks of ice.

"On Nebeca 21? What was she doing there? Scrubbing the floors for Octus Laurden?"

A startled look came over Gael while Ramya cringed at her father's cutting words. She fell back a step, and then another, until the cold metal walls of the safe room pushed back at her.

"Not really, Lord Paramount. She was with Captain Milos."

Another sliver of quiet. Ramya could see her father's face clearly in her mind, lips stretched into lines, eyes flashing like fire.

"How so?"

Gael looked up at her, and Ramya held his questioning gaze steadily. Was that hesitation in his eyes? Ramya couldn't be sure.

"She's been with them since she left CAWStrat," Gael said.

Her father scoffed. "So she's been scrubbing the floors of that junk ship of his."

"Perhaps," Gael replied jauntily. Ramya wanted to smash that stupid grin off his face. She wrapped her arms tightly around her body, fearing that she might really take a swing at him. Gael totally ignored her glare and continued to speak. "Mostly though, she's been flying the Stryker. She's the one to blame . . . or credit for the spectacle at Totori. Space Command still won't release the extent of damage there, but I can guess it's pretty massive. I'd steer clear of your daughter when she's anywhere near the Stryker."

Did he just praise her?

Ramya studied Gael intently. The grin was still twisting one corner of his mouth, a roguish gleam making his dark eyes shine. She couldn't tell what he was up to. Not yet.

On the other end of the communication channel, her father sighed. "What a mess," he said after a while. "Gael, I don't need the Confederacy knowing this, all right? Let's keep this quiet. Can you secure everything?"

"Yes, of course."

"You don't sound so sure, Gael," her father said. "If you like I can send someone else."

"No, I'm fine."

"All right, then."

"Lord Paramount . . ." Gael paused hesitantly for a bit. "Lady Ramya is here with me. Do you wish to speak to her?"

"No." There was no uncertainty in that refusal. His vehemence stung Ramya like a backhanded slap across her face. "Good luck on your mission, Lieutenant."

The line clicked to an end. Ramya glared across the room at Gael, silently daring him to begin a conversation. He didn't.

"So, you're going to take me back to Somenvaar?" Ramya said when she couldn't hold it any longer.

Gael stared back at her with an inscrutable expression.

"Lost your tongue or something?" Ramya snapped. "Is that the plan? The all-powerful puppet master expects you to deliver the Stryker and me to him."

Gael's brows came together. "Is that how you always speak of your father?"

"Yes, I do. Did you hear how my father speaks of me? You could've asked him why he does that," Ramya retorted. "Oh no, wait! You're a minion he keeps to do his bidding. How will you question him?"

"Minion?" Gael said, an amused expression swamping his face. "Did you just call me a minion?"

"Why . . . you don't like it?" Ramya tapped her chin and studied the roof. "Let's see, what else can we call you? Stooge? Flunkey? Henchman? Or maybe, Trysten Kiroff's newest pet?"

The sound of blaster-fire trickled in. Gael stilled and listened to it intently for a bit before turning back to Ramya.

"Remember me saving your life just about five minutes ago?" he said in a teasing, slightly arrogant voice. "You should be thanking me. But all I get is hate." He strolled closer to Ramya's end of the room and circled her like he was hunting down a prey. "Why? Just because I can take you back home? Or because your father is nice to me?"

Somenvaar was no home. And why would she care if Trysten Kiroff was nice to Gael?

Ramya scoffed and rolled her eyes. "Who cares if he likes you or roasts you for dinner? Incidentally, how much did he pay you to make you betray House Arlington? You must've made quite a fortune to forget all that enmity your house has for the Kiroffs?"

Not too long ago, the Arlingtons would've spat on the ground a Kiroff walked on. Clearly not anymore. Tucker Arlington, Gael's father, had to be furious at his son's disloyalty.

Gael, however, simply cocked his head at her and flashed that infuriating all-knowing smile of his. "Yes, I was offered a fortune, but I didn't have to betray House Arlington. This is an arrangement between the houses, between Trysten and Tucker. Hate me if you will, but I'm just a pawn, only a strategic piece in a game of galactic power play."

His words stirred another memory from their last conversation at CAWStrat. What had he said exactly? Something about lives being swept away in galactic politics, into strategic marriages . . . Ramya's thoughts crashed to a halt. The room seemed to close on her, the air turned too thick to breathe. She forced her lungs to pull in the heavy air and forced the words out of her parched throat.

"What exactly did my father promise House Arlington?" she asked, running her tongue over her rapidly drying lips. "What's your stake in this? And why do you keep following me around?"

He didn't reply as fast as he usually did. Instead he seemed to be mulling his answer.

"I'm *not* following you around," he said finally, with unusual deliberation, taking time to utter each word as if he were weighing each of them. "And I'm not at liberty to discuss what was promised."

He didn't have to tell her. She knew already. The thought had struck her like lightning—sudden, intense, and clear as clear could be.

"He promised you my hand in marriage, didn't he?"

He blinked. That was enough for Ramya. He didn't have to say another word.

Anger simmered along the edges of her head. This man was a lieutenant of the GSO, an accomplishment anyone could be proud of. How could he have sold his fate to the wiles of Trysten Kiroff?

"What kind of a man are you?" she yelled. "Don't you have any self-respect? You wear the blues, for stars' sake. You're supposed to have pride in yourself, in building your own destiny. How can you allow anyone to trade your life for the rights of a planet or two?"

Gael's eyes narrowed some and his jaw hardened. He didn't say a word, but Ramya was on a roll anyway.

"Or maybe you're just that desperate. House Arlington must be tired of coming in second all the time. So why not pimp yourself out? That Kiroff girl looks quite fetching anyway. Not a bad deal to get to the top tier."

Ramya paused to take a breath, suddenly realizing how quiet Gael was. His shoulders had slumped a little and a deep frown had formed on his forehead. Ramya opened her mouth to spout some more rebuke, but she closed it, noting the vacant, faraway look in Gael's eyes. For seconds that seemed like forever, they stood, staring blankly at each other.

"Are you done?" Gael broke the uncomfortable silence.

"Yes, I'm done," she snapped, striding past him to the door. "We need to get out of here. I don't know what your plan is, but I have to get back to my ship."

Shooting a blistering glare at Gael, Ramya turned her attention to the door. She pressed her ear to the panel. It was quiet outside, nice and peaceful. Perhaps the firefight had stopped.

Gael simply stood at the middle of the room, watching her. "Are you going to help or what?" she asked irritably.

"We can't go outside with just this," he replied, raising his Nihilator. He had a point. Melroon's fighters had some serious weapons on them and all they had was one Nihilator. But they couldn't just sit in this room forever either.

"How long will we wait?"

"As long as it takes."

"What?" Ramya spat. Anger, unjustifiable fury spewed out of her. "Just so you know, holding me in this room won't make me fall head over heels in love with you. The last thing I'll ever do is marry you, Arlington. So let me out."

He crossed his arms and shook his head. "No wonder your father doesn't have faith in you. You are absolutely, utterly . . . irrational. No, I'm *not* opening the door, Kiroff. Like it or not, this is where you'll stay until I decide it's safe to get out."

His scornful expression set Ramya's head on fire. "I don't take orders from you, Arlington," Ramya retorted.

"The hell you do. Right now, you don't have a choice," he snapped back. His intense, dark gaze bore a hole through her. "And just to make things clear, I'm no more interested in you than you are in me. But not everyone can just run away when things don't go their way. Some of us stick around and face hell, even after seeing the only person they care about ripped out of their lives. That's called surviving, Kiroff. I survive."

His words had hardly sunk in when a commotion grew outside.

"Stand back," Gael ordered, pushing her away and facing the door, his Nihilator raised.

"This is it," someone shouted. The voice was faded but familiar. "Move back, I got the codes."

Ramya caught the clicking sound of fingers punching on the panel lock. Someone was about to walk into the room.

"They're coming in," she whispered. "What do we do?"

"We fight back, Kiroff," he said. "What else can we do?"

"Fight back? With what?"

"I don't know," he replied through gritted teeth as he aimed his Nihilator at the door. "Think of something."

There wasn't much time to think. The door was starting to part. Ramya patted her pockets. She found nothing. She made a mental note of hiding a dagger on herself the next time . . . if there would be a next time.

Just then, her heart leapt with joy. *The hair pins!* They were small, but at least they were something. She could stab a couple of people with them. If she were fast enough she could bring an attacker down.

One tug and she had two sharp and long needles in her hands. The problem was that she could only use them at close range. Ramya darted from behind Gael to the side of the door. Gael twitched, but his tight jaw relaxed just a bit on seeing the pins. Ramya couldn't be sure, but she thought she saw the ghost of a smile on his face.

The door kept parting. The voices grew louder.

"Rami," someone called.

"Fenny?" Ramya yelled incredulously.

"She's in there," Fenny shouted. "How many hostiles with you, Rami?"

Hostiles? Ramya looked at Gael. He wasn't really a hostile. He had saved her life. But then . . . given a chance he would drag her back to Somenvaar, to her father, and into a loveless marriage.

"One," she shouted. "But he's going to put his weapon down." Holding Gael's gaze, she ordered, her fists tightening over the hairpins, "Put it down. Now, Lieutenant Arlington."

"Lower your weapon," Fenny shouted from outside the room. "You're outnumbered four to one, Lieutenant," she added. "Do the smart thing. Put that gun down."

"You like surviving, remember?" Ramya said. "Put it down and step away."

He smirked at her like he had won the fight, and for a fleeting second, Ramya was puzzled. She grabbed his Nihilator the moment he set it down on the floor and fell back to the far wall.

"All clear, Fenny," she shouted, taking a steady aim at the lieutenant.

In the next second, Fenny was by her side, cradling a humongous Meson cannon. Behind her came Flux, as well as another man and a woman Ramya did not know, all of them armed generously. Fenny shot a quick glance at Ramya. "Are you all right, Rami?"

Ramya nodded. "All good."

"Let's get out of here then," Flux said. "What do we do with this GSO guy?"

"Leave him here," Ramya said. "I'm sure Lieutenant Arlington can find his way out of the space station."

She followed the rest of the team out. The new man and woman led the way. Flux followed and Fenny brought up the rear with

Ramya. Ramya slowed at the doorway and turned to look Gael in the eye.

"I'm glad you didn't fight back. Would've had to kill you otherwise."

"I don't fight battles I can't win."

"Ah, yes. You like surviving."

He flashed a careless smile. "You got that right."

Fenny prodded. "Come on, Rami. We gotta hurry."

Ramya nodded at Fenny, then turned to Gael. She couldn't leave without a few more words. "Tell your master today just wasn't his lucky day."

"We'll see about that," Gael replied. A mocking smile twisted his lips. In a voice so low only Ramya could hear, he added, "Run and hide, Kiroff. Run and hide while you still can."

There was something about the way he said it, something ominous in his tone. The words rang in Ramya's ears as she sprinted with her crewmates through deserted corridors and darkened staircases to the gate where the *Endeavor* was docked.

16

Ross was waiting at the gates when Fenny and the rest of her team reached the docking port with Ramya. As soon as Ross saw them he spoke urgently into his comm. "They're here, Captain. All accounted for." He didn't wait for a reply but simply gave them a quick once-over and barked orders. "To your stations, everyone. Fenny, we leave right now."

The crew dispersed in the blink of an eye, but Ramya hesitated a second at the doorway. Ross noticed it immediately.

"Check in with the medic, Rami," he instructed. "The captain will see you in his quarters in thirty."

"How are we going to get away from the space station? If the troopers were in here, they must have battleships around too."

Ross shook his head. "We're lucky. There's just one, an old and clunky Merlin 5 that's much slower than us. Besides, it's docked in the fueling port. If we can get out quickly, we have a chance."

"We ran into some GSO as well. The Cutlass has to be here. That'll be—"

"Go to med-bay, Rami," Ross cut her off. "The captain will see you soon."

With that, he hurried away. Ramya stood there for another second or two before starting toward med-bay. She felt the telltale movement of the *Endeavor* leaving the space station as she clambered down the ladder to the level of the med-bay. She had barely taken a step or two when a loud squeal made her stop and turn around.

Ahool rushed down the corridor, waving his arms wildly. "You back, Rami."

"Yes, I am."

"I am glad. They say you lost in firefight. I pray. A lot."

"Thank you, Ahool," Ramya said, patting the young Mwandan's

shoulder.

"I decide, I stay with you always from now," Ahool declared.

"That's kind of you, Ahool. But it's not necessary," Ramya tried to calm him, but her effort was likely lost on Ahool, who simply stared, glittery-eyed at her. Ramya knew that expression—it meant he had made up his mind and nothing could budge him. She decided to let the debate rest, at least for the moment. She had to meet the captain soon. "I have to see the medic. I'll talk to you later, all right?"

"Can I come to medic?" Ahool asked. "I want to see her, but she does not talk." Even though Ramya wanted to visit Sosa alone, she also knew shaking off Ahool now was next to impossible. The Mwandan was stubborn, to say the least.

"All right, let's go," she said. Ahool grinned happily as they strode toward Sosa's lair.

The med-bay door was ajar. Ramya rapped the panel as she entered. "Domina Sosa," she called. The door was open and that was odd. Sosa was usually fiercely protective of her dominion and selective about allowing people in.

"Rami," Sosa's voice came from somewhere deep inside the bay. She emerged soon after seemingly from within one of the cabinets on the far side.

"Why she inside cupboard, Rami?" Ahool muttered. Ramya shook her head. She didn't know. To be entirely honest she had a sneaking suspicion. Perhaps Sosa had yet another hidden room behind that closet just like the one she had stashed away the Stryker's injured pilot Habardein and Ramya in when the SLH troopers came aboard.

"Are you all right?" Sosa almost pounced on Ramya, patting her cheeks and squeezing her fingers and arms to make sure she was still alive.

Ramya extricated her arm from Sosa's grasp. "I'm fine. Absolutely fine."

"They told me you got separated in a firefight. What happened?"

Gael Arlington happened. Long, tiresome arguments happened.

"Rami!" Sosa patted her cheek, pulling her out of her thoughts. "You look shaken, child. Let me give you some Pax. It'll help."

That she couldn't dispute. Soon Sosa had handed her a large goblet filled to the brim with her signature blue-and-red concoction. Ramya sipped at it as if her life depended on it. As expected, a warm, soothing calmness spread over her as soon as the Pax coursed down her throat.

"Thanks, Sosa," Ramya said with a long sigh. "I needed this."

"Of course you did," Sosa said. "I made a special mix for you as soon as Terenze told me about the new plans. I thought—"

"Can I have Pax too?" a glittery-eyed Ahool cut Sosa off.

Sosa frowned at the Mwandan, while Ramya's thoughts lingered Sosa's unfinished sentence. New plans? What did she mean by that? She couldn't get to ask the medic because Sosa and Ahool had embarked on a fierce verbal battle over Pax.

"I'm enough old," Ahool declared to a finger-wagging Sosa. "I drink Gommo extract at home."

Sosa's brows shot up. "Gommo extract? What's that?"

"It's drink. Like this Pax."

Sosa waved dismissively at Ahool. "I have never had a Mwandan drink my Pax, let alone one so young. I don't know enough of your physiology to predict what the effects will be. So, no."

Ahool wasn't giving up just yet. "I'm doctor-in-training. I explain to you Mwandan physiology," he started. As the duo animatedly discussed Mwandan organ functions, Ramya settled down into a chair and watched and sipped at her Pax. Ahool, she realized, would make a good assistant for Sosa. Ahool was not only training to be a doctor, but he matched Sosa well in temperament as well—stubborn, curious, and loyal to a fault.

Her thoughts drifted right away. Gael matched her father in a way too. Like a playful foil to Trysten Kiroff's cold cunning. Jealousy twisted inside Ramya once again. What did Gael have that she didn't?

He had pluck. He had the nerve to make light of a situation even when Trysten Kiroff was breathing down his neck. Like the time he praised her skills with the Stryker.

Ramya's anger at Gael abated a little at the thought. It wasn't his fault that her father hated her. He was as much a victim of galactic politics as she was. Maybe even worse things happened to him. Didn't he say something about someone he lost? Maybe he loved someone, but they forced him into this arrangement with her instead. Oh well, such was the state of things everywhere.

Her father's words came back and lingered painfully. *Scrubbing floors,* was what he had said. Ramya's fists clenched. How dare he? She shifted uncomfortably in her chair. How in the stars was she ever going to prove her worth to him? She had started with a plan of sorts, but that plan was all but lost in this affair with the Locustans and the Stryker. When, if at all, she could get to find the Moanus and wrest the Kiroff hearth back from them, Ramya had no idea.

Ramya took another sip of her Pax, suddenly realizing something new. How much had she thought of the Moanus since boarding the *Endeavor*? Not much. Not much at all. To be honest, she didn't care about the Moanus as much anymore. The cause she was fighting for now was far bigger than her own little life. How did it matter what her father thought of her when the fate of the entire galaxy was at risk?

Ramya's fingers curled determinedly around the stem of her goblet. She had to remember that there were greater things at stake than her value in her father's eyes. She *had* to remember. Ramya sucked in a lungful of air and held on to it, repeating the pledge. Next time she came across Trysten Kiroff she had to take it in stride.

Ahool's jubilant voice broke Ramya thoughts for a second. "See, we have thing like your enzyme also. It helps us handle Pax," he said. Sosa had pulled out a drawing pad now and Ahool was scribbling enthusiastically all over it. Ramya checked her watch. The captain had asked her to stop by his room and it was almost time to get going.

"I've to go see the captain," she announced. Sosa and Ahool were now in a deep conversation about molecular structure of Pax. They both looked up at her. Sosa nodded distractedly and Ahool flashed an acknowledging smile.

Perhaps the Pax Sosa had given her was extra potent since it took Ramya a lot of strength and focus to walk out of the med-bay. She reached the captain's room after a relaxed walk along the ship's corridor, lost in thoughts.

She turned the final bend in the corridor not a moment too early. Captain Milos stood at his doorway, watching curiously as she approached. "There you are, Rami. Come in. We have much to discuss."

As soon as she stepped inside the room, he said, "Sit." The place looked messy as usual and a fat flask of blood-red noja sat next to the captain's favorite couch. He settled into his couch while Ramya slid into a seat across from him. "We have a slight change of plans."

Plans had been changing around her like a chameleon's skin and Ramya had gotten used to it. Intriguing was the fact that Captain Milos called her to his chambers to discuss a change. She was not as high up in the hierarchy to talk strategy with the captain unless she'd accidentally became part of it somehow. Like after the Stryker's pilot had spoken to her and later the Stryker itself both resulted in her being pulled into discussions with the captain. Without those, she was a regular entity on the *Endeavor*.

What had she stumbled into now? Ramya couldn't figure. She grabbed the cup of noja he offered and took a long sip. Bitter and biting, the noja jolted her senses, as always. That was pretty timely since it cleared the mist of Pax from her mind in an instant.

"We're going to make a brief stop at Posci and then go to meet Chief Mifek," the captain said. He looked expectantly at Ramya.

She didn't know what to say. For all Ramya knew, Posci was a rogue planet. Some called it a wandering planet. Others called it a starless planet. Posci didn't belong to a particular star or a planetary system. Instead it orbited the galaxy itself. Mostly unclaimed by the Houses and the Corporations, such planets were free of settlements and were often used as transient bases along freight routes.

"Aren't you wondering why I'm telling you this?" the captain asked.

"You must have a reason," she said. "You always have a good reason."

The captain chuckled. "Do I? Well, I'm meeting with Trysten on Posci. What do you think of that?"

For a second or two, Ramya's heart thudded. There was no denying that she wished what the captain had just said was her imagination and only that. That she was afraid. But Ramya didn't let the fear get hold of her. She forced another gulp of noja down her throat and soon the distracting buzz in her ears faded.

"Like I said, you must have a good enough reason to want to meet him," she replied as calmly as she could.

"I do," Captain Milos said. "I wouldn't have called you to explain why, but you're a valued member of this team and I have not forgotten what brought you to my ship."

He paused to take a sip at his noja. Ramya's mind was sprinting at a furious pace. One question burned on the top of her head: When did the captain talk to her father and decide to meet?

"I've known your father for a long time, Rami. Your grandfather and I were friends, so I heard a lot about Trysten from him even before I met him." Captain Milos stopped and looked around the room, his eyes narrowed as if they were looking at some distant point in the past. "Trysten and I have seldom looked eye-to-eye. I would've avoided this meeting if I could. But there's no way forward without this."

Captain Milos leaned over and tapped a button on the side of the center table. Ramya heard a creaking sound before a holographic image formed above the table. It was the image of space—three stars hung in the distance and right in front was the hulking shape of an enormous starbase.

"That's Anomaly Point," Ramya exclaimed, recognizing the distinctive horseshoe shape of Starbase Zeta that the Confederacy had put in place after the Locustan invasion.

"It is indeed," the captain said. "That's where the wormhole had opened the last time and let the Locustans in. That's also the likely point where they'd come in again. We need to guard the place like it's the last thing worth saving in the galaxy."

"Space Command has squadrons stationed in Zeta. Don't they?"

"They should. I'm not sure how many." Captain Milos leaned back into his couch and exhaled noisily. "I don't know if they're prepared for another invasion. I'd tell them but they aren't prepared to hear me. They're more worried about us than the Locustans."

"I know," Ramya said, recalling the zeal with which Admiral Kanaa had attacked them. "They might think we're imagining an invasion."

"They definitely will," the captain said. "And if they're not ready, that starbase will fall in a matter of hours, if not minutes, when the Locustans come in."

Ramya's fingertips had long turned cold. Now she felt the chill all over. "It'll be like the last time. We'll have to scramble."

"It will be worse than last time," the captain pronounced direly. "If Zeta falls, and if Space Command has as many squadrons homed there as originally planned, that's the end of a third of our squadrons. We'll be even more outnumbered. And then, if what Mifek told us is true, I worry that the missing Strykers are already raising a Locustan army somewhere."

Ramya placed the cup back on the table. She didn't trust her cold fingers to keep holding it for long.

"An army? How? Why?" she whispered.

"I don't know. But remember what Chief Dal told us? According to reports from Chief Mifek, people are disappearing from the Fringe. What's happening to them? I think . . . I think they're being captured and turned into a Locustan army. Why else would colonies full of people vanish overnight?"

"The Confederacy needs to know that." Ramya barely managed to get those words out of her parched throat. "And . . . act."

"I would meet them and explain to them, Rami, but they'll throw us in prison before they hear a word from me. I thought of sending them a message, but that'll help them track us down and come after us. So I've sending information in roundabout ways. Haven't got one response back."

"But you're forming an alliance. The Mwandans are with us."

"Trying to," the captain replied. "The Mwandans—at least the Berkari faction—is on our side. But we can't fight the Locustans on foot. We need space fighters. That's where your father comes in."

The Kiroff factories could easily manufacture space fighters and every other craft that was needed to prepare for an invasion. The captain was right—her father could be a valuable ally. But first, he had to agree to be one.

"You think he'll accept your proposal?"

"He might," the captain said with a hesitant smile. "Knowing Trysten, I have to pitch him the right way. Provide him with the right incentive."

Ramya chuckled. The captain couldn't be any more correct. Her father would need a powerful incentive beyond the lofty goal of saving the galaxy to get into this. Ramya held Captain Milos in very high esteem, but she still had serious doubts that the captain could entice Trysten Kiroff into backing this cause. But he had gotten him to agree to a meeting, and that was something.

The thought brought on another thought that had slipped through the cracks of her mind. "My father hardly goes out of his way to meet people. And he's coming all the way to Posci? How did you get him to do that?"

The captain took a long sip at his noja and shook his head. "I can't take credit for that. That's all Gael's expertise. He's the one arranging the rendezvous."

"Gael?" Ramya had to struggle to get the name out of her mouth. "Gael Arlington of the GSO?"

The captain's eyebrows crinkled. "Yes, the same. He stopped by when we were docked at Nebeca. This was partly his idea."

A million questions bombarded Ramya's brain but she could only get one out quickly enough. "You trust him?"

"Gael is an honest man," the captain said. "Something I won't say about his father Tuck."

"I see," Ramya muttered. She hardly saw at all. Things could get real messy from here, but was there another way? No. Not one she could see anyway.

The captain's eyes had turned to slit, his gaze piercing as it scanned Ramya's face. "You don't approve of Gael?"

Approve of that self-serving, greedy spawn of the Arlingtons? Hell no!

"He seemed concerned when he heard you got in trouble at Nebeca," the captain continued, all the while studying her face.

Ramya held her breath. He knew? Had he come looking for her . . . to help her escape Melroon and his Confederate Troopers?

"Anyway, that's beside the point." The captain switched off the holo image and leaned forward to look into Ramya's eyes. "So, I wanted you to know that you might come across your father at Posci and there's a chance your flight will end."

Ramya shrugged. "Well, guess we'll see when we get there."

The captain rubbed his chin as his eyes narrowed. "You don't seem very afraid of your father anymore."

Ramya shifted in her seat. "I won't lie, Captain. I am. I'm terrified of facing him. But I'm trying not to be. And I'm getting better at that."

Captain Milos raised a curious eyebrow. "So you're simply going to tell Trysten to go to hell as far as your future is concerned?"

That was the plan. Not in those exact words, but close. "I think so. I've thought about it a lot. I don't need to be so afraid. I'm a quasi-adult, I can choose what I want to do, right? I mean, really, what has he got on me? The lure of money? What if I don't want it? What if I'm perfectly happy here?"

"Are you?"

Ramya nodded without a second thought. "Absolutely."

"Good for you," the captain said. There was no derision in his voice, and Ramya was happy for that. "But, Rami, that's not the kind of money you pass over completely without thinking."

Ramya sat up. What was Captain Milos trying to do? One second he was pleased at her happiness and the next he was making her rethink her priorities.

"Why not?"

"Life on a freighter is a hard life, Rami. You know that now. When you leave a life much more comfortable, you have to be absolutely certain you won't regret the decision."

"Do you regret yours?"

For a second his face stayed frozen, then a bemused expression softened it and made it crinkly. "You have the Kiroff snap, no doubt about that," he said, chuckling. "You remind me of Abelei so much. And no, I don't. But I've seen plenty who do. So, dear girl, think it through. Trysten isn't going anywhere. There's no rush."

There was a rush. The moment her father set his eyes on her, he'd try to browbeat her into submission like he'd always done. She'd have to fight back, hold strong. How would she do it if she didn't refuse the power he wielded?

"May I leave now?" she asked, eager to have a few moments to herself.

Captain Milos nodded. "You may."

She had reached the door when he called her back. "Remember this, Rami. Everyone in the universe has needs, wants, hopes, and dreams, but powerful people hardly ever show their need to anyone. That's how they hang on to their power."

Ramya's mind stumbled to a halt. Who was he talking about? She would've asked for an explanation, but the captain waved a curt dismissal. "Go now. Get something out of Dakrhaeth if you can. He just might hold the key to our survival."

The captain's words stayed with Ramya even after she had returned to her room, picked up her notepad, and set off to interrogate Dakrhaeth.

17

Ramya marched into the cargo hold the next day to find Fenny was back at the Pterostrich cage. Even though her task was interrogating Dakrhaeth, Ramya insisted on staying with Fenny. But Fenny refused steadfastly, her pitch rising when the Mwandan engineers sauntered in to work on the large screen-like object they'd been constructing.

"You worry for no reason, Rami," Fenny said, shaking her head, making her displeasure clear. She cast a proud look at the chick before continuing. "Vittoria is extremely well behaved. Besides, our Mwandan friends are right next to me. They can help in case anything happens. Now go, just go!"

Fenny almost shooed Ramya away. The Stryker was at the far end of the hold and it took what seemed like forever to reach. Not that the distance had changed but Ramya was distracted and worried. She dragged herself into the Stryker, and her mind was swirling around the upcoming meeting with her father. Trysten Kiroff was dangerous as an adversary and Ramya was not sure her father had friendship on his agenda.

The captain seemed to trust Gael, but he was the other thing Ramya was worried about. He was Trysten Kiroff's minion after all. And she had seen such people all her life—all eager to please and none with a shred of honor. How could Gael be different? What stopped Gael into luring the captain into a trap?

She wished she could speak to Captain Milos about her concerns, but the captain was busy. Besides, he had said he trusted Gael. Ramya couldn't ask again and insult his judgment. So instead she lumbered on, trying to keep her mind on the tasks assigned to her. At the moment, it was speaking to Dakrhaeth again.

"Hello, Dakrhaeth," she greeted as she settled down in one corner of the Stryker's entryway.

The ball atop the column that was the only physical manifestation of Dakrhaeth bobbed up and down. "Good to see you, Mihaal. You seem unhappy. Someone snipe your Pax?"

Dakrhaeth was observant, no doubt. He had even found out about her liking for Sosa's Pax. Sometimes though, his intense perception and subsequent probing comments were annoying. As it was for Ramya at the moment. She bit the inside of her cheek and tried to ignore the needling.

"No. No one sniped anything," Ramya replied impatiently.

"What is it then?" Dakrhaeth asked. "Is the commander feeling too grouchy?"

What did the commander being grouchy have anything to do with her? Anyway, she hadn't seen Ross since leaving Nebeca. He, along with the captain and Lefrasi, the leader of the twenty-one Mwandans aboard, was in closed-door discussions in the captain's chamber. No one was allowed in, and no one knew what was brewing in there.

"No one's grouchy," Ramya said irritably. "Forget about all that. Let's get some work done, all right?"

"I am always ready, Mihaal," Dakrhaeth replied. "And I have some—"

A wild cheer erupted outside, interrupted Dakrhaeth. Curious, Ramya leaned out of the Stryker's hatch and listened. It was indeed a cheer, but the language was not one she understood. The Mwandans! It had to be them. But what were they cheering?

"The Mwandans sure sound excited," Dakrhaeth commented. "They must've found something to rejoice. You should join them. It'll make you feel better."

Ramya stifled a sigh. With all the worries swimming in her mind, Ramya was not in the mood for enjoying Dakrhaeth's all-knowing commentary. Anyway, she had to go check out the reason behind the continuing cheers, and that was a timely and valid excuse to get away from the Stryker. Grabbing her gear hastily, Ramya jumped off the fighter.

"Shut down, Dakrhaeth," she instructed. Dakrhaeth had the habit of staying in a light Sleep Mode, a state which let him pick up activity—conversations even—on the *Endeavor*. Ramya didn't quite appreciate the behavior so she repeated the instruction. "Did you hear? Shut down. I'll be back later."

"Shut down? But I cannot do that. I'm working on the faded star scenario."

Ramya turned around. "Faded star? What's that?"

"That's when we started on our mission to your world, Mihaal," Dakrhaeth informed. "Our leaders would always remind us of the faded star. I remember that."

That was hopeful. The faded star could be a marker.

"I can't remember anything more unfortunately," Dakrhaeth said, crushing Ramya's little hope for some answers.

"It's something at least," Ramya said, forcing cheer into her voice.

"I agree. I'm scanning the constellations in the area around Anomaly Point. Perhaps I'll find something."

"All right. Finish your work. Then you shut down. No eavesdropping on everyone. That's an order," Ramya yelled, then she strode toward the entrance of the hold.

Almost all the Mwandans were assembled in front of the semicircular screen-like structure they had been erecting in the past days. Their eyes glittered like gems as they smiled and talked incessantly in a Mwandan tongue. On the other side of the chattering cluster of Mwandans, Fenny stood with arms on her hips, scowling and muttering. Ramya walked over.

Fenny scrunched her nose as soon as Ramya was within earshot. "The grays are driving me nuts," she said with a vehement shake of her head. Ramya winced at the dismissive way Fenny spoke of the Mwandans. Until now, she had not thought much of it. At the moment though, seeing Fenny snarl at the Mwandans made her insides twitch with unease. This wasn't right. The Mwandans didn't deserve such disdain. Besides, they were on a mission together, so, like it or not, they *had* to be respectful toward each other.

"Why do you hate them so much?" Ramya asked.

Fenny's eyes turned into perfect circles. "Hate them?" she balked. "I don't hate them. I'm just"—Fenny's voice dropped a couple of notches—"I'm just weirded out by them. And I don't trust them much either. That's all."

"Weirded out? How so?"

Fenny closed her eyes and sighed. "Have you seen what they've done to the upper deck? It's full of these funny plants now. And the grays take turns soaking in starlight. It's never ever empty."

The Mwandans needed to soak up starlight because of their genetic makeup, much like the plants they were descended from that needed to photosynthesize to make food. Mwandan also ate food, but they had to "charge up from time to time," as Ahool explained. The upper deck, with its domed glass top, was the best place to find starlight on the *Endeavor*. Ramya still couldn't understand why Fenny was mad about that.

"What's wrong with that?"

Fenny shrugged. "I don't know. It's like they're doing this weird ritual I don't understand. And . . . it makes me uneasy."

"They might think we're weird, Fenny," Ramya said with a chuckle.

Fenny stared at her for a second before tilting her chin stubbornly at Ramya. "What's wrong with me? I'm perfectly normal."

"You're raising a Pterostrich chick as a pet, Fenny," Ramya said. "You're not normal. You're nowhere near normal."

A deep flush flooded Fenny's face and she busily studied her nails for a while. "Well, I guess you have a point," she said finally. "In a way I'm weird too." She cast a sidelong look at the Mwandans who were still talking among themselves, seemingly oblivious of Ramya and Fenny's presence. "But admit it, Rami, they're weirder than I am."

Ramya chuckled. A lighthearted Fenny was what she needed. She was about to ask Fenny about Vi when the door of the hold screeched open.

Captain Milos marched in, flanked by Ross and Lefrasi. Behind them were two people Ramya didn't recognize right away. Then she recalled — they were the man and the woman Fenny had found to help at Nebeca.

"Those two are with us?" Ramya leaned toward Fenny and whispered.

"Who?" Fenny asked. Then she followed Ramya's gaze. "Oh, Bo and Lolo? Yes, they were looking for a ride to the Fringe so . . ."

So the captain offered them a ride. Given they saved her life, a free trip wasn't asking too much. But something about them was odd. Their eyes never settled on anything or anyone but continuously shifted and slipped and slithered from one thing to another. Their faces were rigid as if they were ready to walk into a war, and their mouths drawn into thin lines.

"Don't stare at them, Rami," Fenny cautioned. "They're mercenaries. They don't like it when people stare."

Ramya tore her gaze off the woman's thickly muscled biceps.

"You got mercenaries into the *Endeavor*?" Ramya blurted. "You didn't find *them* weird?"

Fenny shrugged. "What could I do? I had to get you back, kid."

While Ramya appreciated the thought, she couldn't shake off the niggling bit in her head. The wary way Bo and Lolo looked around, as if evaluating how much everything in the *Endeavor* was worth, made her worry. Perhaps she was overreacting just the way Fenny had to the Mwandans.

Fenny nudged her elbow. "Come on. Let's see what the grays are so excited about."

The Mwandans, except Merin, the engineer, had stepped away from the giant screen. She stood facing the screen, her eyes closed.

"What is she doing?" Fenny muttered.

"Praying," Ramya offered. But to whom? There were no forest

spirits around.

"Come on." Fenny grabbed Ramya's arm and scooted over to Ross. "Hey, Commander," she whispered.

Ross frowned even before he turned to look at them. Grouchy . . . just like Dakrhaeth had said. Ramya slid back a bit, just enough for some cover behind Fenny. She had had enough confrontations with Ross already, and this one she could do without.

"What's the circus about?" Fenny asked.

"This isn't a circus," Ross snapped. "Merin's an Uminato. She's trying to set up a communication channel to Chief Dal and Chief Mifek. The Berkari can't use official Confederacy channels so they have to invent these mind-projection decks. It seems they got through briefly to Chief Dal."

An *Uminato*. On Morris II, Ross had used that word to describe Chief Dal. In the rush of events, Ramya had forgotten to ask him what it meant. She didn't want to have a conversation with grouchy Ross and had hoped Fenny would ask what an Uminato was. But Fenny decided to stare open-mouthed at Merin and the projection deck, oblivious of anyone else's presence.

"What's an Uminato?" Ramya asked.

Ross didn't frown. Or snap. Or reply in a miffed voice. "All Mwandans have strong extra-sensory powers. An Uminatos are stronger than most."

"You mean they can read minds and stuff?"

Ross walked over to her side. "No, they can't read minds, but they can sense emotions."

"Ah, yes. I remember now. Chief Dal said that when he was asking us about what brought us to Morris II."

Ross flashed a smile. "You could call them empaths. If you lie to them, they'll pick it up right away."

"So . . . an Uminato is colored different?"

"Yes. Remember Chief Dal?"

Ramya nodded. She remembered vividly. Instead of the deathly gray of most other Mwandan, he was the exact shade of brown as Merin, only the stripes were a bit different.

"I guess you'd need an Uminato's mind power to set up an interstellar communication channel," she added.

"You guessed right," Ross replied. His lighthearted tone was unexpected and strangely charming.

"That's pretty powerful," she said, ignoring the peculiar blips in her stomach.

"I've read books that say Mwandans know psychokinesis. Back in ancient times, long before the galaxy was settled, they had wars. All fought with mind power. Later, they gave it all up and went into seclusion."

"Why?" Ramya asked.

Ross shrugged. "No idea. There's very little information on Mwandans out there."

"You still know a lot about them. Where did you manage to find out so much?"

Ross gave out a small sigh and Ramya sensed a pall of sadness fall on him. But it lifted almost instantly. "I used to be a bookworm. Loved studying history. Used to scour the nets digging up information on ancient lore. Wrote fat volumes of theses." He paused for a second and looked up at the rafters. "Useless enterprise, if you ask me."

It was far from useless. Ross had dreamed of going to the university and then Trysten Kiroff's greed had snatched that dream away.

"No, it's not," Ramya blurted, immediately regretting saying it aloud. Ross gave her a sidelong glance before turning away to stare fixedly at Merin and the screen, his jaw hardening. "I'm sorry," Ramya hastened to apologize. "I have no right to comment on—"

"It's all right," Ross cut her off. "I appreciate your thought. I really do." He turned to hold her gaze. "I might have said otherwise earlier, but what happened on Halperion is not your fault."

It was kind of him to say that, but Ramya couldn't stop feeling responsible for what happened to Ross and all the people on Halperion. If there was a way to fix it, she would.

A flicker on the screen brought an abrupt end to her thoughts. As a grainy image of Chief Dal formed on it, the hold erupted into cheer. Seconds later, Chief Dal enthusiastically spoke about the advance they had made in the past days—reaching out to their government and setting up an assembly to discuss the Locustan threat.

Even though Ramya listened to the chief's updates, her mind lingered on the conversation with Ross that was left dangling. And oddly, Ramya kept on wishing she could talk some more with Ross. But she didn't get a chance. The captain asked everyone except Ross and Lefrasi to leave the hold, obviously to discuss strategic matters with Chief Dal. Ramya hung around the COM for a while with Wiz and Fenny before retiring to her room to pore over her notes.

18

An awful, gut-clenching, bone-rattling tremor awoke Ramya in the middle of the night. For a moment or two, Ramya couldn't recall when she had dozed off, still in her regular clothes and her notes strewn over the cot. The ship groaned and shook again. Ramya sat up with a start and then scrambled for the M-gun she always kept under her lumpy mattress. Her fingers curled around the sleek grip of the weapon far before her eyes adjusted to the dimness in the room. The panic in her brain took longer to subside. It was far too dark, way darker than when she had gone to bed. The sleep light had turned off, Ramya realized. She pressed her wristwatch awake to check on the time. It was, as she had expected, night hours still.

Ramya pressed on the button of her comm next. Nothing but a dull buzz came out of it.

"Not again," Ramya muttered under her breath. The ship's communication channels had been a nightmare since she'd set foot on the *Endeavor*. After the Mwandan engineers worked on it, Ramya had hoped it'd stay trouble-free. No such luck obviously. She pressed the buttons a few more times only to be greeted by the same buzz.

Annoyed, Ramya looked around, her heart freezing the moment her eyes fell on the sole dirt-encrusted window in the room.

Two bright lights — one white and the other reddish — shone in the darkness outside. This wasn't right. They were supposed to be in the SLH and the fake scenery screens were supposed to be on every window. That was how it had been when she had slept — the standard bright picture of a mountainside covered with flowers had flashed on. But now she could see the stars outside, which meant that they had fallen out of the SLH. That couldn't have been according to plan. The plan was to go all the way to the system nearest to Posci and then jump out. They couldn't have reached near Posci so soon.

Gripping the M-gun tighter, Ramya rolled out of bed, her legs a tad unsteady under her as she slowly walked to the door. She slinked outside without much noise, the M-gun ready in her hand. Ramya had never seen the main lights in the corridors turned down so low. Something was definitely wrong. Heart thudding, she scanned the corridor, which was dimly lit by the standby light. She placed her back flat against the wall and tried to think.

That was easier said than done. Her heart was thrashing against her ribs as if hell-bent on jumping out of her body, and thoughts zoomed past in a wild rush before she could pause on one and vet it thoroughly. She tried as hard as she could, breathing in with all her might, until the slight metallic air settled in her lungs and weighed her heart down.

Ahool's room was the nearest place from here, but Ahool would be of no help. He was too young and he didn't know the *Endeavor* well enough. She had to get to the COM or find one of the original crew. All of the old crew had quarters on the port side of the ship, on the other side of the COM.

The COM was where she had to go. Fenny had to be there, as well as Wiz. They had to have answers. Clutching her gun with both hands, she tiptoed along the cold, dark corridor, pausing every now and then to check around her before starting again. Her fingers were as cold as ice and her forehead was covered with sweat when she finally reached the entrance of the COM.

The door was open and shadows flitted across the entrance. People were talking inside, but Ramya couldn't recognize the voices. She pressed against the wall and tried to listen.

"We came out far too soon," a woman's voice said. "You should've waited. I told you to wait."

A man scoffed in response. "This is an iffin ancient ship, Lolo. I don't know what half of these shitty controls do."

Lolo! She was one of the mercenaries Fenny had sought help from at Nebeca. Which probably meant the other voice was of the man, Bo.

Her heart dropped at the realization. Whatever these two were up to couldn't be good.

"That's why you should've forced the pilot to work for us," the woman, Lolo, hissed. "Not conk him out cold."

The pit of Ramya's stomach fell out. They hurt Wiz. Did they kill him? She had to find out.

Ramya whispered a quick prayer and braced for a quick peek.

"Please, let them be looking away from the door," she muttered a few times. Ramya inhaled deep. She was just about to lean forward when she saw the shadows turn darker behind her. Ramya froze for an endless second before whirling around. She knew it was too late already, but she swung anyway, the M-gun in her trembling hands pointed into the dark.

"Rami, stop, it's me." The whisper was urgent, fearful, and familiar. Ramya's arm dropped.

"Fenny?"

Fenny scooted to her side. "What's going on?" she asked in a rushed whisper. Ramya told her what she had found out and Fenny gave out a low anguished cry. "It's my iffin fault. I should've never —"

"We have to fix this," Ramya cut her off. "That's all that matters."

Fenny nodded ruefully. "We've got to find better weapons," she said, waving the blaster in her hands. "I'm sure those iffers have cannons."

Ramya raised an arm to shush Fenny. Someone was speaking again in the COM. They had to find out what Bo and Lolo were planning. Ramya couldn't catch what Lolo said, but she heard every word Bo said.

"Stop freaking out," Bo snapped. "We're just one system off our original plan. They'll take a little more time to find us, but they will find us. They'll come. We just have to keep this piece of junk under control until then. It's that simple."

Ramya exchanged a quick look with Fenny, panic raising a swift head in her guts. Who was Bo talking about? Someone was coming to meet them? But who? And why were they coming after the *Endeavor*?

"What in the hell do they want with this bag of bolts?" Lolo said. "If I were settling scores, I'd just blast it off the face of the universe."

"There must be something valuable on it," Bo replied. "I would've found it out, too, if that shriveled old captain didn't throw us out of the hold during the meeting."

"You're right, there has to be something important in here. They're paying us far too well to just take over the ship. I didn't get half us much when I killed a shop full of people on Coroni."

Terror and realization hit Ramya like a flash of lightning, sending a stream of shivers up her spine. The Stryker! Someone . . . whoever had sent these thugs had their sights set on the Stryker.

But who could've sent this pair of cold-blooded killers? Her father? Could Trysten Kiroff be double-crossing Captain Milos?

Fenny nudged her elbow. "Come on, Rami. Let's move," she said. "We need weapons to put up a fight."

Fenny fell back a few steps and Ramya followed. They tiptoed back to the ladder and clambered down to the lower level. They reached the weapons hold without incident.

"I hope they haven't changed the locks," Fenny muttered as she keyed in the code on the door, exhaling with relief when the door slid open.

A shadow leaped across the room even before Ramya could blink. A Stunner gun, its barrel the size of an oversized human arm, was thrust into their faces. Ramya would've screamed but she recognized the man behind the weapon quickly enough. So did Fenny.

"Ross?" Fenny croaked.

"You?" Ross blurted at the same time. He gestured at them frantically. "Get in here, quick."

Barely had the door closed behind them before all three started speaking in unison. Ross had been at the engineering bay with Flux when the *Endeavor* fell out of the SLH. He had asked Flux to stay put while he checked out the COM. There he found out the two mercenaries had taken over. Unarmed and unequipped to do anything, he had come to the weapons store.

"I was at the hold with . . . Vi," Fenny said. "What about the rest of the crew? The captain?"

"I'm sure those thugs locked them in."

"My door wasn't locked," Ramya said.

"I don't think they considered anyone on the starboard side to be of any threat," Ross said. The idea made sense even though it was a little demeaning. All of the older crew, including the captain, had quarters on the port side, and the rooms on the opposite side had been allotted to newcomers. Ramya and all the Mwandans boarded there.

"That's a problem," Ramya said. "What if one of the Mwandans come out of their room like me? They'd get killed."

"We have to warn them," Ross said. Pressing on the buttons of his comm, he frowned. "I think they've shut down our communicators."

"We'll have to get the captain out," Fenny added.

"Let's grab some weapons and split up," Ross suggested. "I'll go check on the Mwandans. You and Rami talk to the captain. We have to get out of here before their back-up arrives."

Ramya and Fenny strapped on body armor quickly. Fenny picked up a Meson cannon from the shelf. "Bo has one of these." She gave a disgusted shake of her head. "I should've never trusted those iffin pieces of filth."

"You sure have judgment issues," Ross said sourly before turning to Ramya. He pointed at the M-gun in her hand and frowned. "Where did you get that?"

That he'd notice the gun or recognize it as not one from the *Endeavor's* store surprised Ramya, but guilt came before answers. The M-gun was yet another thing she had quietly brought aboard the *Endeavor* and hidden from its crew.

"I-I had it when I got on the ship," she explained, barely able to hold on to his questioning gaze.

"Get something bigger," Ross said simply. He didn't seem to care about the M-gun, or maybe he was too angry to talk about it. Either way, this wasn't the time to linger on the issue. Making a mental note to speak to Ross about it once they had the situation under control, Ramya tucked the M-gun into the holster strapped to her leg. It would make a good sidearm. She scanned the shelves and settled on an Oori, a rifle she had carried on her first trip to the cargo hold. Ross shook his head right away.

"That's useless against these people," Ross said. He picked a large assault rifle and handed it to Ramya. "This should be good."

The rifle was heavy, much heavier than the Oori. But Ross was right — Bo and Lolo and whoever was coming were likely armed to the teeth. She had to have something just as effective.

"All set?" Ross asked after they'd checked the weapons and filled their pockets with extra clips.

As soon as they nodded Ross pressed on the door switch. The panel slid open slowly. The corridor outside was just as quiet and dark as it had been a few minutes ago. But the quiet lasted for just a second. Lolo's sniveling face swung into view, her muscled arms cradling a Stunner rifle that she aimed squarely at them.

"Oh, hello," she said in a bone-chilling voice, baring a set of yellow, pointy teeth. "Going somewhere?"

19

A crackling sound out of the Stunner tore the stunned silence into shreds, discharging a wave of electricity into the weapons store. From the size of the Stunner, they'd be incapacitated for ten minutes at least if hit, Ramya guessed. Ross ducked and Ramya threw herself to the ground behind him. The air above them hummed.

A blast ripped out of Fenny's cannon even before Ramya hit the floor. Lolo flew backward. She hit the wall and crumpled in a heap to the floor, her shoulder spewing blood. Undaunted, Lolo whipped her sidearm out and raised it, but Fenny was quicker.

"Take this, you iffin rat," she hissed before unloading another round of cannon fire on the woman's torso. Lolo's armor would have held up against the fire for a bit, but one shot found its mark on the woman's neck, tearing it apart. Blood sprayed on the wall behind her and the woman collapsed.

"She's dead," Ramya whispered, trying to keep her body from shaking. She'd never witnessed anyone getting killed. It had happened too quickly, but as she stared at the woman's remains, a buzz grew in her ears, and for a second or two she could barely feel her limbs.

"Rami!" Fenny called. "What's wrong? Are you hit?"

"She dead," Ramya repeated.

"Yes, she's dead," Ross snapped. "If Fenny hadn't got her, you or I would be dead instead. Would you prefer that?"

No, but all that blood, pieces of flesh stuck on the wall, the suffocating smell of gunpowder and burning flesh . . . they didn't make for an easy situation to handle.

"Lolo?" a voice crackled out of the dead mercenary's armor, probably out of a built-in communicator. Ramya recognized the voice — it was her partner, Bo. "Where the hell are you, Lolo?" he growled.

Ross rose to his feet stealthily and gestured at Ramya and Fenny to head toward the captain's room. Weapons ready, they crept forward along the long cold corridor. Ross went the other way to round up the Mwandans. Not more than twenty steps later, a loud clanging noise made Ramya jump.

"What's that iffin noise?" Fenny muttered, falling back toward Ramya. They saw Ross in the distance, frozen in his tracks.

They might've stood there for mere seconds but to Ramya it felt like an eternity had passed before Fenny whispered in a rush, "I know what it is. Come on, Rami," she said, and broke into a sprint toward Ross.

Ramya followed. She had no clue what Fenny had suddenly realized, but Fenny knew the *Endeavor* more than she did. Right now, Fenny, after having killed that mercenary, was the undisputed leader. Fenny skirted the blood-spattered floor around Lolo and ran up to Ross. As Ramya joined the duo, careful to keep her eyes off Lolo's battered corpse, the clanging sound came again. This time, it seemed louder.

"That's the sound of the main hatch opening, Ross," Fenny said in a breathless voice. "What is he trying to do? Throw all of us out?"

Ross stared at Fenny, worry in his eyes swiftly turning to fear. Then he shook his head. "If that's what they wanted, they would've done that sooner," he said. "Anyway, no point talking about it. Let's go up to the main deck and check out the hatch."

Endeavor's hatch, like most all spacecraft, was a double-layered system. The inner door opened into a small cabin — an airlock — the other end of which opened to the outside. If anyone went outside when the ship was in space, they had to walk into the hatch in a spacesuit, and follow a strict pressurization protocol before they could come back in. Ross had to go out once to fix a capacitor box, the only time Ramya had seen *Endeavor's* hatch opened out in space.

What the hell did Bo have in mind?

Dread rising like an acrid surge in her throat, Ramya followed Fenny and Ross. Why would anyone open the hatch in the middle of dead, cold space?

Ross led them to the main deck up the ladder. He peered down the corridor on both sides before signaling them to follow. They went up another ladder to a catwalk that ringed the hallway around the main hatch. This was a maintenance path, not the direct road leading up to the hatch that Ramya had always used. She had seen Flux tinker around with the heater units up here. Now they walked around bulky equipment until they reached the end of the elevated walkway. Ross dropped to one knee next to a staircase that led down to the main level and raised a fist, signaling them to stop.

Ramya and Fenny kneeled behind Ross and peered. The deck below was empty, but the clanging—now louder because of their proximity to the hatch—continued from time to time.

"What's going on?" Ramya asked.

"Bo's opening the hatch remotely from the COM," Ross replied. "They're fitting a boarding bridge on the other side, I'm sure. "

The thumping of Ramya's heart rose to a mad beat. A boarding bridge—a simple, short tube connecting one craft to another through an air locked interior—was just as ominous as it was effective. Pirates used them to storm disabled ships, Ramya knew that, but even the thought of it happening to *Endeavor* was gut-churning.

Fenny thumbed at something behind them. "There's a porthole back there. I'm gonna take a look outside." She crept away as Ross and Ramya hunkered. Fenny was back in a second; her face was carved out of stone. "You're right. There are three ships outside. One's trying to dock."

"Pirate ships?" Ross asked. "What faction?"

Fenny shrugged. "I didn't see any marks, but they're all Scuttlers for sure."

Scuttlers were medium-sized spacecraft favored by space pirates. They were cheap because they could be purchased as a bare-bones craft, which could then be customized. Scuttlers were often fitted with boarders—tubes that would attach directly to a ship's hatch—that were used to enter a spacecraft they had attacked and disabled.

"Damn!" Ross said under his breath. "Who knows how many are in that ship."

"What's the plan?" Ramya asked. She wasn't sure if having a plan would help given the odds stacked against them. Even if they could stop one ship, what about the others?

"Scuttlers usually carry ten to fifteen, so let's think fifteen. We'll pick them off one by one as they enter. I'm going to do that," Ross said. "They're going to spot us soon. Then they'll rush us. You two will cut them down. Understood?"

Fenny nodded and moved to the right side. Ramya scurried to the left and found a spot near the mouth of the staircase, forming a rough semicircle along with Ross and Fenny. She scrunched low, making her body as small as she could.

She noticed movement in the airlock a second before Ross muttered, "Here they come." A sharp clang and a hiss sounded, and a man with a bright orange hair and leather shorts walked out of the hatch. He was huge, carved entirely out of muscles. Ross pulled his rifle up and nuzzled his eye against the scope. He was fast. Even before Ramya could blink a report rang out and the orange-haired man collapsed on the deck, blood spurting out of the hole on his temple.

Ramya crouched lower as the pirates returned fire. Ross cursed, and Ramya quickly saw the reason. Four pirates charged forward, all of them heavily built and clad in armor. Ross fired, catching the foremost pirate in the chest. He toppled backward, the gunfire impinging on his chest plate, possibly just knocked out of breath. His mates kept charging on until Fenny started shooting.

The deafening blasts from her Meson cannon caught one of the leading pirates in the head and the other in the neck. The third one lunged at the stairs, swiveling around the metal banisters as he leaped upward like a giant ape. Within seconds, he had reached the rails in front of Ramya, his chunky gloved hand landing with a thud on the metal.

Ramya scooted backward. Someone shouted, "Just pull the trigger, Rami!"

She would, if she could keep her hand from shaking.

The pirate swung upward, raising his sidearm as he came into view.

"Rami! Now!"

Ramya clenched her teeth and squeezed the trigger. The bullets got him in the face, and he flew backward, spewing blood as he toppled down the stairs.

"Damn, they're getting through," Ross shouted as Ramya heaved to catch her breath. The air was thick with the smell of gunpowder, her vision blurry from the acrid smoke. "Cover me, Fenny. I'm going to chase them down. Can't have them reach the COM," Ross shouted, bounding over Ramya and hurtling down the stairs. Fenny sprinted behind him.

Two pirates darted out of the hatch, guns blazing, when Ross and Fenny were halfway down.

"Fall back," Ross yelled. They fired back at the pirates as they rushed back up the stairs. There was little to shield them on the stairs. The pirates kept advancing.

"Oh no, you don't," Ramya muttered angrily. Gritting her teeth and pulling her assault rifle close, she flicked a switch that turned the weapon to full auto mode. She pressed the trigger with all her might, spraying the two pirates with a shower of hot metal. She kept on pressing until both went down.

Fenny crawled up next to her. "Well done, kid," she said between heavy breaths.

"Thanks," Ross said. Blood was oozing out of his arm, but he managed a smile nonetheless. "That's the last one I guess," he said, thumbing at a pirate clad in dark-green armor who'd just dropped out of the hatch.

"I'll give him what they want," Fenny said. Snapping around, she fired her cannon, its earsplitting boom echoing across the hallway. The pirate answered fire and ducked behind the hatch.

"Wait," Ross raised his uninjured arm. He listened intently for a second. "Did you just hear shots?"

"Of course I hear shots, Brainy," Fenny snapped and loosed another round of cannon fire on the pirate who ducked behind a column. "We're in the middle of a firefight. What do you expect to hear? Music?"

"No . . . I meant shots fired far inside somewhere," Ross explained, his face darkening immediately. Ramya didn't want to think about it because it wasn't a good thought. They had let three pirates escape into the ship, and if Ross heard gunfire elsewhere in the ship, it could only mean the thugs were rampantly killing the crew.

Anger snipped at Ramya's fingertips. She hunched over her rifle again. They were going to pay for this. The lone pirate opened fire. Ramya ducked and pressed the trigger, spewing another round of hot fire. The man fell back behind the hatch again. Ramya heaved.

The ship groaned, then it moved. Ramya stumbled at the sudden movement, grabbing the rails in front of her to regain balance. She brought the stock of her rifle back to her shoulder and aimed at the hatch, waiting for him to emerge out of his shelter. Instead of charging, the pirate bolted back into the airlock. A loud clang sounded in the next moment.

Grabbing his bleeding arm, Ross leaned forward to look. "They disengaged?" he asked in an incredulous voice.

"What the iffin hell?" Fenny said. She darted to the porthole and immediately started yelling. "We're moving." There was a bright flash outside and Fenny yelled again. "Someone . . . we . . . just shot at one of the Scuttlers. The other one's . . ." Another flash. "Oooh! The other one's history, folks."

Ross gave out a loud chuckle and scrambled to his feet. "You know what this means? One of our crewmates has taken the COM back from Bo. Told you I heard shots."

"What are you waiting for then?" Fenny asked. "Let's go find out."

They found their way down from their perch, their progress slow and cautious as they headed to the COM. At the final turn in the corridor, Fenny stopped suddenly. Her drained face made Ramya rush forward and peer. Bodies were strewn on the deck, and blood had turned the floor red. Ramya felt her stomach turn at the sight of the three pirates among the dead, but there were far more bodies.

Ramya trudged forward, wincing at the sight of their fallen comrades. Four Mwandans—Ramya recognized Namaan, one of the engineers—had died. But their death wasn't in vain. In the COM, gracing the captain's seat, was its rightful owner—Captain Terenze Milos. He cradled the largest assault rifle there was, a PKM-44, in his arms and shouted orders at Merin and Azzi who steered the *Endeavor* away. Between the captain's chair and an obviously dead Bo on the floor, Lefrasi stood with a blaster.

As soon as Ramya entered with Fenny and Ross, the captain turned and nodded. "Good job out there. We shook the bastards off." He'd obviously been watching the firefight at the hatch. The captain's eyes narrowed as they fell on Ross's bleeding arm. "Get that checked, Commander."

"Yes, sir," Ross replied before nodding at Bo's body. "Who were these guys?"

The captain's face turned grim. "Laurden's thugs. Found this on our dead friend here." The captain pulled out a silver hexagon emblazoned with Laurden's sigil, a black spider. Everyone knew that hexagon—commonly called a mark—was exchanged when a death contract was signed. Bo had obviously accepted one from Nebeca's overlord.

"Why did Laurden want us?" Fenny said. "What the hell have we done to him?"

The captain slipped the mark back into his pocket and shrugged. "Don't know. The Octus are hard to read."

"How did you get out of your room? Didn't they lock you in?"

"Blasted the door off," Captain Milos said, brandishing the PKM. "No one locks Terenze Milos in. And no one steals my ship while I'm watching."

Ross smiled and nodded wisely. He turned to leave, then shot a quick look backward. "Where's Wiz?"

"He's badly hurt, but he'll survive," Lefrasi replied. "I lost four of my people though."

The captain placed an arm on Lefrasi's shoulder and shook his head morosely. "We lost four of our own, Lefrasi," he said gravely.

A thick silence crept into the room. It would've lingered longer had it not been for Merin. She turned around to look at the captain.

"The SLH's coming up, Captain," she announced.

"Take us in, Merin.

A slight shake later, the *Endeavor* cruised into the Super Luminal Highway.

20

The fight with Octus Laurden's goons had taken a hefty toll. Broken limbs, wounds, and other trauma were matters people could take in stride, but casualty was not. Death of the four Mwandans sat heavily in everyone's hearts. It was hard to keep in mind that the count of deceased among the *Endeavor's* crew was exceptionally low, especially considering most of them were rookies facing a seasoned bunch of killers.

The *Endeavor's* interior, particularly the main level, bore marks — broken, bullet-ridden walls, blood-spattered decks, the acrid smell of blood hanging in the air — of the ambush and kept reminding everyone of the bloody battle. Ramya and Fenny, as well as every Mwandan who was relatively uninjured in the battle, had taken up mops and brooms to clean up evidence of the firefight.

The captain and Ross — his arm decorated by a gaudy orange bandage — barged out of the elevator when they were halfway done with the task.

"Damn it! We're late," the captain's growl reverberated across the corridors. It made Ramya stop sweeping a large and stubborn patch of blood off the deck and turn around to look curiously. She had not seen Captain Milos so grouchy in all the time she'd been on the ship. Seeing that crack, however thin, in his calm façade was weird. And unsettling to some extent.

Fenny propped her mop against the wall and strode up to him. "It's just a few hours, Captain," she said reassuringly.

The captain's brows arched immediately. "Why aren't you at the COM?"

Fenny eyed the freshly scrubbed deck and scratched her arm. "Merin and Azzi wanted to help. Since we're on autoflight inside the SLH anyway, I thought they could take over for a bit while I help

Rami out here. Trust me, Captain, Merin and Azzi are good at the controls."

The captain gave her a stern look. "That's heartening to know. But they're new at this, and this meeting at Posci is important. I want at least one experienced hand at the COM, Fenny. Others can take care of scrubbing the deck, don't you think?"

"Yes, Captain, sir," Fenny said. Clicking her heels, she touched her forehead with her fingertips in a hasty, rather artless, salute at the captain and dashed away.

Captain Milos fixed a frown on Ramya next. "Do you want to be at the meeting?"

She did not. Seeing her father was not on the agenda. No matter how much she had steeled herself—and she had, no doubt—she wasn't looking to facing Trysten Kiroff anytime soon, and certainly not now.

"No, I don't," she said.

The captain nodded and left without another word, Ross in tow. Ramya scoured the marks on the deck with extra vigor while pondering about the meeting with her father. There was a chance—a big fat chance—that she'd have to face him regardless of her refusal. If he asked for her, that is.

A bright blink on her wrist pulled Ramya out of her thoughts. From the flashing ID code, she realized it was Sosa calling.

"Yes, Domina Sosa," Ramya said, tapping the device on. "You need me?"

"Come to med-bay, please," Sosa said. "I need more hands."

The comm. clicked off. There was no mistaking the urgency in Sosa's request. Ramya dropped her mop and announced her departure to the rest of the provisional cleaning crew, and rushed to the med-bay.

As expected, the med-bay was full of people, mostly wounded Mwandans. Wiz was sporting a huge bandage around his head. Sosa was hunkered in one corner applying swaths of bandage around a

Mwandan's arm. Ramya looked around the room and spotted Ahool in the far corner of the room riffling through a cabinet.

"Hey, Rami," Wiz said groggily, waving.

"How you feeling, Wiz?" Ramya asked the pilot. They had all been worried seeing the wound on the back of his head. Sosa had later declared that it was lucky that the blow hadn't killed him on the spot.

"They were real mad at me," Wiz explained his encounter with the mercenaries. "They wanted me to follow their orders and get them out at the next system. I told them they could go to hell. That's when that hairless wrestler type crashed his cannon's butt on me."

"Wiz, stop talking. Rest," Sosa yelled, gesturing at Ramya to leave the pilot alone. "Rami, we need help," she said, and pointed at a Mwandan female hunched in a chair. "Her right foot needs to be looked at."

Never in her life had Ramya shown any interest in the medical sciences. When she was hired on the *Endeavor* as the medic's assistant, it was a temporary solution, a means to an end. Mercifully so far, she hadn't been asked to perform a task that needed medical skills or understanding. But now she faced the Mwandan and her foot. Ramya gritted her teeth. What was she doing here? What if she hurt the patient while trying to help? This was a person, not a piece of equipment she could tinker with.

Sosa must've sensed Ramya's hesitation because she yelled, "There was a piece of shrapnel stuck on her foot. Gave her a nasty gash."

Shrapnel? Did Sosa expect her to perform surgery on this poor Mwandan? Did she realize Ramya could kill the patient?

"Sosa, I can't—"

"I took the piece out, Rami. And I also put a small dressing on," Sosa said, and Ramya sighed in relief. "All I need you for is to put a sturdier bandage over it. Can you do that?"

That she could do. "All right. Yes, I can do that," she shouted back.

"Rami can do anything," Ahool declared. He was busily tending to Wiz but took a second to flash an adoring smile at her.

"To you, I can do no wrong," Ramya muttered with an indulging shake of her head.

She completed the first task Sosa had assigned soon after, but there was no dearth of work in the med-bay. After escorting Wiz back to his quarters, Ramya assisted Sosa some more until all of the injured crew had been tended to. Then, together with Ahool, she tidied up the med-bay. Sosa retired into making some fresh Pax for the trio, an incentive that drove both Ramya and Ahool to work as fast as they could.

They had finally made it around the table in Sosa's alcove when Ramya felt the telltale shake of the *Endeavor* leaving the SLH.

"What's going on?" she asked to no one in particular. Had they come near Posci already? So soon?

"We've arrived," Sosa said, nonchalantly pouring the shiny globule-filled mixture into three goblets. "Terenze is going to meet with that . . ." Sosa let the rest of her words trail off, and Ramya had no trouble imagining the colorful adjectives that had halted at the tip of Sosa's tongue.

Ahool, however, was uninformed about the situation. "Meet with the leader of House Kiroff, you mean. He is much powerful man."

Sosa started inspecting the rafters all of a sudden. Ramya nodded but Ahool wasn't satisfied with just a nod. "Why speak of him badly?"

Sosa might've realized there was no skirting the issue, so she finished her task on the rafters and crinkled a nose at Ahool. "You'll find out soon enough. Now, would you like some Pax?"

Ramya's arm shot forward. She needed the drink. Tired, aching all over, and heart heavy with dread at the upcoming meeting with her father, she was desperate for a diversion.

Sosa pulled out a black box from underneath her table and placed it at the center. Ramya recognized the box; it was the eavesdropping device she had seen Sosa use before.

"Have to keep up with the latest news," Sosa said, smiling at a curious Ahool. "This is how we do it, young apprentice."

She flicked a switch and a dull humming noise trickled out.

"Captain," Fenny's sharp voice drifted out a moment later. "There's a ship approaching us. I can't read its creds. Should we get back in the SLH?"

The captain's voice was steady. "No, hold course. Merin, slow down." Ramya set the goblet down on the table and sat up. What ship could it be? After a devastating encounter with Laurden's mercenaries that they barely scraped through, the *Endeavor* and its crew didn't have the energy to fight another battle so soon. "I see it. Zoom on the hull, Fenny."

Ramya held her breath. *Let it not be a Confederacy ship,* she prayed silently.

"That's the Kiroff colors," the captain announced, and Ramya finally let go of the breath she'd be refusing to slip out of her. She took a long sip of the Pax and leaned back into her chair.

"There, I see their sigil too," Ross added.

"I see it now," Fenny said, then chuckled loudly. "It perfectly suits Trysten Kiroff's sunny personality."

Ramya felt a flush creep up her cheek. The Kiroff sigil was a spiral of thorns meant to signify the plights the house had to survive over the ages. Now it was a butt of joke. Only no one dared say it out loud in front of her father.

"What kind of a ship is this anyway? Looks like a Cutlass but . . . look at those cannons up top."

He had brought the Kinvari. Of course. It was a ship custom designed for Trysten Kiroff, armed like a Drednot but nimble like a Cutlass.

"The ship's the least of our worries, Ross," the captain said. "The bigger question is: Why is it here? We were supposed to meet on Posci."

"I think you'll get an answer soon, Captain," Fenny said. "They're hailing us."

A clicking sound that meant Fenny enabling the communication channel was followed by a familiar voice.

"Captain Milos, we meet again," her father sounded positively gleeful. Ramya felt sick to her stomach.

"Yes, we do," the captain's voice was guarded. "I thought we were meeting at Posci. This isn't Posci."

Her father chuckled. "I thought we were meeting two hours ago," he said, not holding off the mockery in his words.

"We got held up," the captain said.

"So I heard," her father replied. "Laurden has sent note to the Confederacy. They're on their way to Posci already."

The captain let out a guttural sigh. "That Laurden is—"

"Despicable, I know," her father remarked. "But very effective. I'd suggest you get out of here before Admiral Kanaa arrives."

A faint metallic creak drifted out. The captain must've got off his chair.

"We need to talk, Lord Paramount Kiroff. We can't put this off. Time is running out." It was not just the slight rush behind the captain's words or the terse tone of his voice, but the fact that he addressed her father as Lord Paramount clearly showed the urgency of the situation. The captain was showing his hands to her father and that wasn't a good thing.

"We'll talk," her father said calmly. "I'll come to your ship. And we'll talk."

There was a moment's silence before Captain Milos spoke again. "All right, come aboard my ship."

Sosa sat up like a whip had been flicked at her. "No, no, no, Terenze. You do not invite a snake into your home. No!"

Captain Terenze Milos wasn't listening. "Lower the shields, Fenny," he said.

"Why in the stars is he lowering the shields?" Sosa said, breathing heavily.

"To allow him to teleport," Ramya said, remembering how the GSO had tried to use that outlawed technology to break into the *Endeavor*. It was strange how lucid her brain was at the moment. She could hardly find a shred of fear in her bones. She was not afraid of her father anymore. Well, almost.

Sosa cradled her head, shaking it from time to time, muttering, "No, Terenze! This is a mistake."

Ramya didn't think it was a mistake. She understood—the captain was risking it all to find a chance to save the galaxy. To him, it was a gamble worth risking his life and his home.

"Commander," the captain's voice boomed. "I'll meet Lord Paramount Kiroff in the War Room. Other than emergencies, I do not wish to be disturbed."

"Oh no, not that room," Sosa said, falling back into her chair with a loud sigh.

"What's problem?" Ahool asked.

Sosa confirmed what Ramya suspected already. "I don't have eavesdropping arrangements in every room of the ship. Although, I should have considered wiring the War Room, but it is rarely used under normal circumstances," she said. Obviously. The room was so seldom used that Ramya did not even know where it was. Sosa grunted. "Now we won't know what that snake has to say."

While Ahool nodded in understanding, Ramya took a long sip of her Pax and slid out of her chair. Ahool gave her a questioning look, but Sosa didn't stay silent. "Where are you off to?"

She didn't know where exactly, but staying at the med-bay was not of much use.

"I'll go to my room," she said. "I'm tired." It wasn't a lie. She did want to lie down and rest a bit.

She had just crashed into her bed when her wrist comm lit up. Ramya sat up in a hurry and turned the device on.

"Rami, where are you?" Fenny asked.

"My room. Any updates?"

"Well, we're back in the SLH. Heading to Bucifer P9 to meet Mifek. And . . . your father is on the ship talking to the captain." Fenny clearly didn't know that Ramya already knew.

"And?"

"And . . . according to Ross, it's not going well. Apparently, he laughed at the captain. Said a second invasion is simply not true, that it's horseshit. His words, Rami."

So much for risking everything. Trysten Kiroff was just here to get his Stryker back. Perhaps Gael had known that. He definitely knew the captain would fall for this chance to forge an alliance. Ramya's fists curled. *The dog!*

"Hey, Rami," Fenny's voice cut through the furious thoughts. "Before the captain left, he asked you to stay put. Wherever you are, stay put."

"Will do," Ramya replied, eager to end the conversation. Tiredness caught up suddenly, swooping over her with the weight of a mountain.

"I'll try to swing by your room," Fenny offered in a goodhearted way, but Ramya's mind had already drifted. Barely noticing when the comm clicked off, Ramya fell back into her lumpy cold bed and curled into a cocoon.

20

21

Ramya sat up at the sharp rap on her door. She didn't remember when she had drifted into sleep. For a moment or two she couldn't recall where she was, but then memories trickled in.

The fight with the mercenaries . . . the meeting with her father at Posci . . . Fenny's instruction to stay put. Fenny! *That must be Fenny knocking*, Ramya thought. Didn't she promise to stop by?

Ramya took a second to compose her thoughts before she pulled the door open. She could not have expected the person on the other side in her wildest dreams. Her father, the indomitable Trysten Kiroff, stood with his arms crossed, his face carved in stone. Behind him were four buff guards in Kiroff colors, armored and armed as if they were walking into a warzone.

Before Ramya could utter a word, her father stepped into the room, making a path for himself as he edged past her. If Trysten Kiroff wanted to be somewhere, there was no stopping him. So she had heard since childhood. *This was how it is done*, Ramya mused. A few nervous jitters raised their heads at the pit of her stomach but Ramya crushed them with a strong hand. Closing the grunting door behind her, she observed her father. He stood, stiff and resolute, scanning the barren room, his nose crinkled with disdain.

"This is where you live," he said finally, his tone as icy as it was full of scorn. He pointed contemptuously at the sparse furnishings. "This . . . you prefer *this* over Somenvaar. Really?"

"I do," Ramya replied, keeping her answer as short and as pointed as she could. There was no winning a winded conversation with her father so she was not getting into a conversation at all.

His eyes narrowed to slits. He had possibly caught on to her plan already.

"Where did I go wrong with you?" he said, spitting out the words like blaster fire.

Every word stung and burned and ate into her heart, but she wasn't going to let him shame her into submission. She had done nothing wrong. She had a right to live her life. She had found a purpose, happiness. Ramya was not going to let Trysten Kiroff snatch it away from her. Biting the inside of her cheek, Ramya willed herself to stay quiet. But her father was not going to let her.

"You're a Kiroff," he snarled. "How can you put yourself among a bunch of nobodies? Where's your pride?"

Captain Milos and his crew weren't nobodies. They were the only ones smart enough to understand the Locustan threat. It was an honor to be on the *Endeavor,* and serving Captain Milos made her prouder than she'd ever been before. Her father couldn't understand that, and she wasn't even going to try and make him understand. He could hold on to his misplaced beliefs for all she cared.

"What's this?" her father asked suddenly in a voice that had suddenly lost its bite. He was looking at something behind her. A frown still remained, but barely. Instead, a look of surprise had taken hold. He walked — no, glided over like someone in a trance — to the cabinet that flanked the door. He looked into the paper bowl on top that held the stone Temihula had given her. "Is this Drigganstone?"

The hint of a tremble in his voice and his gaping eyes surprised Ramya. Her father was the last person to wear his emotions on his sleeve, and seeing such childish wonderment on his face was almost unreal. With much difficulty, Ramya tore her eyes off her father and squinted at the Drigganstone. Ahool had said it was rare and used by the Mwandan government to make weapons, but to have enthralled her cold and impassive father as much, the Drigganstone had to be quite out of the ordinary.

"Yes, it is," Ramya replied simply.

He spun around to look at her incredulously. "Where did you get it? Who gave you a Drigganstone?" he said, words gushing out of him at a furious pace. This was odd behavior, no doubt.

Ramya shrugged. "I got it on Morris II. It's a Mwandan sanctuary where—"

"I know what Morris II is," he father cut her off abruptly. "How did you get that stone?"

Ramya took a breath. "Temihula gave it to me. Guess you already know who Temihula is." She couldn't help the jab at the end even though it was as good as asking for a snub.

Her father scoffed. "Temihula? He gave you that?" His brows rose as if she had just told him the most fantastic thing ever. If she had told him a fairy had arrived on a unicorn and presented her with the stone it would be far more believable.

Anger glowered around the edges of Ramya's head. Her fists curled. Just like always, her father couldn't imagine she could be capable enough.

"Yes, he did. After I defeated him in a duel, he presented me with that." Ramya stopped. The anger inside of her grew on seeing the disbelieving look on his face. "Since you find it hard to believe my account, I could line up a few witnesses for you. Ross was there, as was Chief Dal and quite a few of his men. Ask them if you like."

Her father waved at her distractedly and turned back to the stone. "That's not needed." He gazed at the stone almost lovingly. "This is truly exceptional. The granules are so dense. I've never seen such an excellent specimen before."

Ramya stepped to his side. "You mean you've seen Drigganstones before?" She regretted saying that right away. Of course he had seen Drigganstones. Was there anything Trysten Kiroff didn't see or know of? How stupid did she have to be to expose her naivety and invite her father's ridicule?

"Yes, we've experimented with a few," her father replied. Odd that there was no mockery in his voice. "The Mwandan government uses these stones in their explosives. They're said to cut through force fields. We did a few experiments, but these stones are hard to find."

Something he said stirred a question she had long overlooked . . .

about the Mwandan projectiles that had cut through the Stryker's shield on Morris II. If Drigganstone weapons were known to cut through force fields, could that have been why the Mwandan offensive damaged the Stryker's wing even when its shield was up?

Before Ramya got a chance to complete her chain of thoughts, her father was back to being his usual stony self. "So, what is your grand plan?" He fixed a mirthless stare on her face. "Haven't thought it through, I presume," he said, a jeering smile twisting his lips. His questions were erratic, talking about Drigganstone in one moment and her future in another.

"You're wrong," Ramya retorted. "I have a plan. But why do you need to know my plans anyway? You don't need me. Why can't you let me be?"

He drew a long, unnecessarily long breath . "House Kiroff needs you."

"House Kiroff has you."

"I won't live forever."

That sounded too mushy, too unlike Trysten Kiroff. All part of a game, Ramya was sure.

"You'll live long enough. By then Ryon will have grown up."

"You're the heir. Ryon is not."

If she were gone for long enough, she'd lose the claim as an heir — galactic laws were clear on that. Ryon, her much younger brother, would be the next in line. It was that simple. Why was her father making it sound like it wasn't?

"The galactic laws are—"

"This is not up for debate," her father cut her off icily. "You are the only heir of House Kiroff. You have a blood oath to the house to serve when time comes. You're not free to walk away from it."

She knew that. Every firstborn had a blood oath to serve the house they were born into. But her brother Ryon could take her place if her claim was lost. Unless her father died before Ryon turned fifteen, but that wasn't likely.

Before Ramya could say another word, her comm crackled. Fenny's voice drifted out when Ramya accepted the incoming.

"Rami, the captain wants you at the hold right away," she said.

Her voice was rushed and Ramya couldn't contain her curiosity. "What's going on?"

"It's Chief Mifek. He sent an urgent message," Fenny explained. "I gotta go, Rami. Need to locate that bad-tempered father of yours."

Ramya held her breath at Fenny's snide reference. Her father inhaled sharply, a violent flush swirling into his face.

"Fenny, he's right here," Ramya blurted. "With me."

A moment of silence. Then Fenny's unabashed voice trickled out. "Oh. Bring him along as well, will ya?"

The comm cut off with a sharp click and Ramya had a feeling Fenny was too eager to jump off. Ramya was eager as well. She needed Trysten Kiroff out of her room and out of this senseless, frustrating conversation.

"That was our navigator, Fenny," she said, tucking her M-gun into the leg-mounted holster. He was watching every movement intently, but Ramya ignored him. "The captain needs us at the cargo hold."

"What are you waiting for? Lead the way," he snapped.

Not a polite bone in his body, Ramya mused. Suppressing a sigh, she walked out of the room, her father following. The buff bodyguards followed them all the way to the cargo hold. Her father asked them to wait outside, thankfully without Ramya having to ask him. She didn't want to spend time in meaningless bickering, especially when the universe was falling apart so fast.

22

Merin, the Uminato, stood in front of the projection screen with her eyes closed, trying to set up the communication channel. The captain, Ross, and Lefrasi, along with eight of his Mwandan lieutenants, stood behind her. They were looking intently at it when Ramya and her father walked into the hold. Captain Milos nodded curtly.

"Two hours to Bucifer P9, Captain," Wiz's voice came over the captain's communicator. "Should we hold course?"

"Yes," Captain Milos replied. "Fenny, keep scanning the system. All the neighboring planets. We're waiting for Chief Mifek to come online."

Ramya inhaled deep to counter the rising chill inside her. Just a few hours ago they had an update from Mifek. All had been well on Bucifer then. What was the sudden urgency?

Captain Milos walked over to Ramya and her father. "You should get back to your ship, Trysten," the captain said, and her father frowned in response.

"Why do you say that?"

"Because, as you've said many times already, this is not your fight," the captain said. Ramya noted how Captain Milos kept his voice low, as if to provide a shield of privacy to her father. "You should get away while you still can."

Her father crossed his arms and gave the captain an icy look. "I can't just walk out empty-handed. You have my Stryker. You have the heir to my house. Give them back and I'll go."

A long forgotten rage leaped to life inside Ramya. He talked about her as if she was another object he owned. Would it have hurt to show her a tiny bit of respect? But that was too much to expect. Some things could never change.

The captain sighed. "I don't think you realize the problem here.

Our galaxy is about to be made extinct. Someone needs to save it. Or
at least try. I'm going to try. I'd hoped you'd join, but I see you're not
interested." He paused a second to breathe and rubbed his bandaged
forehead. Ramya squinted at the captain's face. He didn't look sick
and Sosa hadn't raised hue and cry over his health lately, but Captain
Milos had been bothered by the injury. "The Stryker can help us
figure out the Locustan plan. So, I need it. We also need your
daughter since she's the one the Stryker has sworn to serve. But you
don't need to risk your life or waste your time here."

Ramya sniggered inside. *In other words, you're non-essential, Lord
Paramount Kiroff.* Her father's lips twisted and eyes took on a glacial
veneer. He had clearly picked the captain's intent.

"I will leave when I decide to leave," he said.

No one spoke for a moment or two, and anyone who paid the
slightest attention could pick up the unmistakable chill in the air.
Thankfully, Ross stepped near and cleared his throat.

"Captain," he called, nodding in the direction of the screen.

A grainy picture of Chief Mifek had formed on the screen. Mifek
was also an Uminato and of a rich coloring. His skin was a deep, shiny
brown and the stripes on his neck dark as a starless night. But today,
he was as pale as pale could be. If someone met him for the first time,
it would be difficult for them to imagine the real Mifek.

His sudden and utter paleness was alarming. If Ramya could take
a wild guess, it was because Mifek was scared. Scattered behind him
were other Mwandans, both male and female, all with equally dull
eyes.

"Chief Mifek," Captain Milos walked closer to the screen. "You
summoned?"

"Yes, I did," Mifek whispered. "We're under siege, Captain."

"Siege?" Captain Milos sounded just as incredulous as everyone
else in the room felt. "By whom? The Confederacy?"

Mifek shook his head. "No, Captain. It's *them*." He threw a quick
nervous glance over his shoulder. "They're here, Captain Milos.

They've taken people." He blinked rapidly, and Ramya could've sworn he paled even more as he spoke. "They've taken our settlements. I'll show you."

As Mifek led them through dense, dark shrubbery, the captain tapped Ross on the shoulder. "You have the recorders on?" he asked.

Ross nodded. "Yes, Captain. Always."

About after twenty paces through the shrubbery, Mifek slowed. Carefully he parted the foliage in front of him and gestured at a gully beyond. Ramya stepped forward and squinted. Mifek was showing them a small settlement with about ten houses. They were shaped like upside-down saucers, all painted white.

It wasn't the houses that were important, but the people who were walking about around them. Ramya gulped before running her tongue over her dry lips. Those people . . . they weren't the kind Ramya was used to seeing. It was a race she had only seen pictures of and studied in illustrations. They had been part of her nightmares for years, and every person in the galaxy near her age would say the same. She was looking at Locustans, alive and walking on Bucifer P9.

Ramya fell back a step and breathed with all her might. Her childhood nightmares had turned real. She wished them away, but they didn't vanish. They lingered, terrifying abominations on the giant screen.

Simply described, they were insects. They were tall, towering insects with two huge, powerful wings and muscular, clawed legs. Two bulbous eyes implied excellent vision, which in turn made them superior hunters. Mifek didn't have to tell them who was in charge of that settlement on Bucifer, as it was clear from the way the Locustans patrolled the buildings.

"They dropped from the skies in the morning, Captain," Mifek said, the tremor in his voice unmistakable. "Then they took over my settlement and captured the entire population. I was out patrolling the northern ridge when the ambush happened."

Ramya shuddered. Captured the entire population . . . that meant they were growing even more Locustan soldiers. She recalled the terrifying sentence from her history book—they only had to pump their DNA in and the host would metamorphose into a Locustan within days.

"Do you have anyone left to fight back?"

"It's me and eighteen of my morning patrol. But fight those things?" Mifek gave a dry chuckle and walked away from the viewing point. "We don't have weapons strong enough to pierce their exoskeleton."

Was Bucifer P9 as good as lost then? What about the Mwandan government? One of their weapons had torn through the Stryker's defense shield on Morris II. They had to have something similar on Bucifer P9.

"Doesn't the government have better weapons?" Ramya said desperately, ignoring her place in the conversation.

Mifek shook his head in a hopeless sort of way. "They definitely do, but I don't have the means to contact them. These pests have destroyed our radio installation and the nearest squad outpost is a long way from here. We didn't take our rambler out for our morning patrol so all we can do is walk."

Ramya's shoulders sagged. The chief's chances of surviving this didn't seem very high. Chief Mifek knew that also. No wonder he had lost his coloring. She stole a quick look at her father. He was staring stony-faced at the screen, not a trace of emotion evident in his stiff posture.

"What's your battle plan, Chief?" Captain Milos asked.

"Start walking to the outpost. Get the word to the government. But I don't have high hopes."

"We'll get there soon, Chief. We'll get you out of there."

"Forget about us, Captain," Mifek said. "This area is infested by these things. You can't help us anymore. But you can help the rest of the galaxy. Save them. If you can."

The blurriness of the image grew some more. The projection was withering away.

"Wait, Chief," Captain Milos shouted. "Find a safe spot and evade them for a couple of hours. We'll get you out of there."

Mifek's gray face filled the screen. "There's a shelter . . . a cave at Yobeta Point. We'll hide there as long as we can. If you see the top blown, don't risk coming any closer, Captain."

His face faded but his last words lingered like a bad dream. No one moved; it almost seemed like no one even breathed. The captain slapped his comm on. "Wiz, how much longer to Bucifer P9?"

"One hour and forty-three minutes, Captain."

The captain nodded gravely. "Get us there as fast as you can, Wiz. Mifek and his people's lives depend on it." He looked at Ramya questioningly. "How about flying the Stryker down there and getting these people out? What do you think?"

Ramya nodded. "I can do it, Captain," she said.

"I'll go with her," Ross volunteered.

"Can I come with you?" Lefrasi said. Ramya had not noticed when the tall Mwandan had quietly joined the huddle. "These are my people. I want to help them."

The captain placed a hand on Lefrasi's shoulder. "The Stryker doesn't have too much room, I'm afraid. Rami and Ross will do their best to retrieve Mifek. They're our people too."

"You might need a hand," he said, nodding at Ross's bandaged arm. "The commander is wounded."

The captain pondered a bit before replying. "All right."

Lefrasi let out a sigh and shook his head. "This is unbelievable. They've taken over planets and . . . no one notices." Behind him, the other Mwandans had gathered, all their faces pale and lifeless. "I will check on Yobeta Point. Get the coordinates for you," Lefrasi said before leading the group of Mwandans out of the hold.

Ramya was about to excuse herself and head to the Stryker when her father spoke. "This is a suicide mission. You shouldn't be going anywhere near Bucifer P9, let alone send someone on a rescue job. A trip to P9 can only end one way, Captain Milos, and it's not something I'll let my daughter walk into."

"Well, that's her choice, isn't it?" Ross snapped even before Ramya could think of a suitable reply.

Her father's lips thinned but he didn't spare Ross one look. Instead he spoke to Captain Milos again. "I will speak to the Confederacy. We'll have to quarantine Bucifer P9 right away. We cannot have people going in there."

"This is all your fault," Ross said, pointing an accusing finger at Trysten. "You couldn't contain your experiments — experiments that you had no business performing in the first place. Now they've taken over entire planets and they'll do worse. You should be the one flying in and rescuing those poor Mwandans."

Trysten flicked a cold stare up and down Ross. "Your insolence amazes me. But it shouldn't. How can I expect any more from someone with clearly no decent upbringing?"

Ross flushed a vivid crimson and anger turned his eyes hard but before he could get another word out, the captain intervened. "Commander, can you plan your gear, please? Make sure you carry enough weapons with you. You'll need them."

With a quick salute at the captain and a curt nod at Ramya, Ross marched out of the hold. Ramya watched mutely, fists curled, anger ripping her insides. How Ross got his temper in check so fast, Ramya couldn't imagine, but he did. She wasn't so sure of herself. Thankfully, the captain spoke.

"I have questions for you, Trysten," he said, tapping his chin thoughtfully. "Those things we saw in Mifek's projection . . . they're full-grown Locustans. I don't understand how they got here. We killed all of them, every single bastard. How could they have come back?"

Ramya could tell by the way his gaze drifted off from the captain's face and hugged a distant corner that he knew the answer. Did her father have something to do with resurrecting the Locustans?

Could he have done it on purpose?

"What exactly did you do in Sector 22, Trysten? Did you bring the Locustans back to life somehow?" the captain grilled him in a pitiless voice that Ramya had never heard before. "Answer me, Trysten."

"No, we didn't do that," her father protested. It was funny how his arrogant tone had been so quickly and completely swept away. He looked like a young ward caught in the act by his mentor, uncomfortable and remorseful. Ashamed even. Ramya stared at her father's face, thoroughly stunned.

The captain didn't relent. "But? There has to be one inconsistency lurking somewhere."

"The pilots," her father blurted. "They were not bonding with the Strykers so we enhanced their genetics a little."

"With Locustan DNA?" the captain asked in a spent voice. He looked every bit as exhausted as he sounded.

Her father nodded. "Yes," he whispered. He looked up at Captain Milos and held his gaze. "But it was a controlled experiment. We only used benign traces to enhance their psychometrics. This wasn't supposed to happen."

"They somehow mutated," Captain Milos muttered distractedly. "Four pilots have now built an army of Locustans. If they weren't such a deadly species intent on wiping us out, I'd be pretty damn impressed."

"The pilots were perfectly fine for years," her father said in a rushed voice. It seemed to Ramya that he was trying hard just to justify his actions to himself. "Then suddenly . . ."

The captain exhaled noisily and shook his head. "Something triggered a change. Of course. You don't know half of their physiology and there you were, tinkering, playing god. What were you thinking Trysten? Ambition . . . you were always blinded by ambition. Always. Now look at what you've done."

Ramya didn't exactly know what came over her at that moment or why. Perhaps it was seeing the clash of pride and humiliation in her father's face, or perhaps it was just a pressing need to bring some hope into the conversation that made her speak out.

"We'll fix this," she said to Captain Milos. "Captain, we'll find a way. We have to." Ramya paused a second to push down the throbbing lump in her throat. She could've stopped there, but she went on, rolling toward some unknown end. "This was a mistake, Captain. I don't think anyone meant it. And maybe . . . if we all work together . . . we'll make this right."

She looked hopefully at her father, but there was no warmth in that face and none of the kindness she was hoping for. There was no reconciliation coming from Trysten Kiroff.

Ramya's insides shriveled. What was she thinking? *Stupid, stupid, Rami!* The ache in Ramya's throat gushed up, embarrassment at having exposed her naiveté to her uncaring father once again making her face burn.

"I'll prep Dakrhaeth, Captain," she managed to push the words out before her voice choked completely.

As soon as Captain Milos nodded, Ramya dashed away as quickly as her legs would carry her to her sanctuary within the Stryker.

23

Dakrhaeth was in a fairly agitated state when Ramya entered the Stryker. He greeted Ramya chirpily and announced his awareness of the mission.

"Yes, Mihaal, I know," he said as soon as Ramya brought up the subject. "By the way, I met your father."

"So you did," Ramya said in the most off-putting way she could muster.

Dakrhaeth chose not to be weighed down by her dismissive handling of the topic. "Yes, I did. He's . . ." Dakrhaeth lingered before passing a judgment on Trysten Kiroff, and as aloof as Ramya pretended to be, she was quite curious about the AI's opinion. "He's not you," he said finally. His calculated and non-committal reply made her smile.

"Good to know," Ramya said. Who knew if that was a compliment or otherwise, but at least he didn't openly start worshipping her father. "Listen, Dakrhaeth, this is a simple extraction mission. We'll swoop in, pick them up, and get our tails out of there," Ramya explained. She took a long bracing breath to steady her voice. "Run a check on your systems. Make sure everything is working well."

"I already have, Mihaal," Dakrhaeth said. Of course. He had heard the conversation and prepped right away.

"We're short on weapons, right? No torpedoes left." They had spent all of the Stryker's torpedoes in the battle at Totori.

"We have two. I regenerated them during our repair time on Morris II," Dakrhaeth informed.

"Oh!" Ramya blurted. She had never heard of a craft being able to regenerate weapons, but this was a hybrid super craft built in a Kiroff factory, so who could imagine what else it could do?

"The commander will join us again, I suppose?" Dakrhaeth asked.

"Yes, he will. And Lefrasi will come too," Ramya said. Since Dakrhaeth was already set, there was no point spending time chatting. There was other work to be done. She swung out of the door and dropped to the deck. "Any progress on the faded star thing?" she asked before leaving.

"No, Mihaal," Dakrhaeth replied simply, just like Ramya had expected. They were at a dead end. Even after questioning Dakrhaeth for days, she had found no new clues about the imminent invasion. Ramya's steps were dragging when she walked out of the hold, dark thoughts making her heart leaden with worry.

However, as soon as she picked up some chores, time passed at a furious pace. Along with Lefrasi, she helped Ross pick out weapons for the mission. After hauling the stash to the Stryker, she visited the dining hall. It was better to not start on an empty stomach, she reasoned. Who could predict when she'd get the next meal? Recalling the near-starved condition she'd been in when they'd landed on Morris II, she also filled a bag of food packets to stock up the Stryker.

The chores kept the dread from piling too high inside her, but it was far from gone. Ramya tried to think otherwise, but the truth was just like her father had said it—this was a suicide mission. What did she know of Locustans, what did she know of fighting them? She was an untrained, inexperienced dud, who had had a lucky break or two. Luck never lasted, not as long as courage did anyway. Ramya only hoped she'd not run out of courage, but even hope was hard to come by.

There was only one saving grace in those final hours; there was no sign of her father or his guards anywhere she went. On that front at least, Ramya spent the time before the mission in relative peace.

***

Bucifer P9 was as dim a planet as Morris II had been, Ramya realized as the Stryker sunk lower into the planet's atmosphere. The difference though was twofold. P9 was mostly oceans with only three small continents and its skies were almost purple. As soon as the craft dropped below the sheet of clouds, Ramya gasped in surprise. They had entered right, their destination — the smallest continent of P9 — was directly below. But the element of surprise was the vegetation, dark and thick just as it had been on Morris II.

Ross raised a curious eyebrow at her, so Ramya decided to share her observation. "It's sort of weird. This place is just as dim and covered just as densely with possibly the same plants we saw on Morris II. Suddenly felt like we're living in a time loop."

Ross chuckled. "I had the same thought."

"That's because all our planets are chosen for a reason," Lefrasi explained. He had been assigned a seat near the entrance of the Stryker. "The flora you see is special. We call it the Manoko. It only thrives on planets with a certain level of illumination."

"So you settled only on planets that had the Manoko?" Ross asked, turning slightly to look at Lefrasi.

Lefrasi chuckled. "No, no. It's the other way around. We found planets suitable for the Manoko and then went to live there," he explained.

"I didn't know that," Ross said.

"Manoko is the native flora of Taymen, our original home," Lefrasi added. "Taymen is no more, but we believe pieces of it still exist since all of our sanctuaries are built in its image."

That was an interesting way of doing things. Probably to a traveler leaving for the unknown it was a common thing to carry the essence of their home world with him. Probably the only way to keep sane in the vast and terrifying odds he faced. The humans did it too. Old Terra, the distant planet many galaxies away from which humans evolved, had been an image for the early human settlements. But the humans sure didn't take it to the level of the Mwandans.

Ramya's thoughts were cut short by a bright red spot on the Stryker's console displaying a map of the terrain below. A second after it appeared, the spot started blinking.

"That's Yobeta Point, Mihaal," Dakrhaeth announced. "I see the peak, but there's nowhere I can land."

"You're not landing anywhere." The crisp voice of Captain Milos boomed across the Stryker's tight interior, startling Ramya a little.

This—a working communication channel—was new. A little help from the Mwandan engineers, some parts from Nebeca, and the *Endeavor's* radio system was now at par with the Stryker's. Or maybe not at par according to Dakrhaeth's objective assessment, but they were able to synchronize just fine. But now it meant anyone at the *Endeavor's* COM was able to listen in and join them in conversation.

"You are going to circle the peak, check if they're present, and set the ladder down so they can climb in. Then get out of there. Understood?"

"Yes, captain," Ross replied promptly.

The captain continued. "We're trying to get through to the Mwandan HQ down south so we'll have to switch channels on you. We'll be right back."

"Assuming there's still time to help them," Ramya said.

"Can't give up on hope, Rami," the captain said. "Godspeed."

That was a nice thing to hear but the reality was quite different. If the Locustans had found an obscure Berkari settlement, would it be hard for them to find and attack the HQ? Or maybe she was looking at it wrong. Maybe obscure little settlements were easier targets.

"What did Chief Mifek mean by top blown?" Ross asked. They had discussed that earlier, but no one could draw any clear conclusions. Now that they were nearing their destination, they had to find a solution to the riddle.

"I think we'll know when we get near Yobeta Point," Lefrasi said, hovering behind the cockpit. "He said there was a cave. So . . ."

Pointing the Stryker's nose toward the roughly triangular peak ahead, Ramya pushed hard on the throttle. Time was not on their side and every second could make a difference. Squinting at the landform didn't help much, so Ramya twiddled with the display a bit.

"There's nothing," Ross said, peering all around and down.

"I'll circle the peak once," Ramya said, tugging the flight stick. The Stryker turned smoothly and quickly around Yobeta Point.

"Look there." Lefrasi pointed toward the side of the peak. A large chunk of the rock had fallen off, revealing the dark inside of the hollow within. "That must be the top. It's blown." Lefrasi let out a long sigh. "We're too late."

Depressing silence fell swiftly in the cockpit. Ramya let her thumb off the throttle some. The mission had failed. They had lost. She turned around a little and positioned the Stryker above the open pit. If Ramya was hoping to spot survivors, she was not in luck. Nothing moved and nothing made a sound.

"Let's just leave," Ross said after a while and Ramya nodded. She tugged lightly on the flight stick, nudging the Stryker around. Her eyes were still scanning the ground below, eager to find a sign of life.

"Mihaal, I detect movement below," Dakrhaeth said suddenly. "It's coming toward us and closing in fast."

Gritting her teeth, Ramya pressed on the throttle and twisted the flight stick to move away from the spot they were hovering. *Better not be the Mwandan missiles again,* she hoped. Those had left them stuck for hours of repair on Morris II.

"What are those?" Lefrasi exclaimed. "Giant bugs?"

Indeed, they were giant winged insects and they — four in all — came charging like ticked-off rhinos. *Locustans,* Ramya gasped. She was seeing Locustans face-to-face.

"Dakrhaeth, rail guns," Ramya shouted.

"Yes, Mihaal."

"I'll keep it steady," Ross offered.

Ramya eased the flight stick, lined up the Stryker's gun array with the first two, and fired. They went out in a shower of blood and slush. Ramya was more than prepared when the next two came closer, ripping them apart with a shower of hot metal. She grinned happily to herself as the Locustans' remains scattered all over in an unholy mess.

"How do you like that?" she muttered. Her joy was awfully short-lived.

"I see something below. People running," Lefrasi shouted. Ramya tugged the flight stick and made the Stryker circle around. It didn't take her long to spot them. Two Mwandans, both clad in black, were running through the forest, chased by a giant Locustan. There was some distance between them, but the Locustan was catching up quickly.

"Bring up the torpedoes," Ramya said. That nasty pest was going to get a taste of her anger. She adjusted the Stryker's speed, calculating the perfect trajectory of the missile in her mind. But while she was ready, the torpedo launch button stayed dark.

"Dakrhaeth, the torpedoes," she said impatiently.

Ross had been looking intently at the chase. He now flashed a panicked look at Ramya. "It's catching up. Hurry!"

"Mihaal," Dakrhaeth called suddenly. His tone was sharp and taut, and it wasn't one Ramya had heard before. "We have to leave. Please turn around."

"Turn around?" For a second Ramya couldn't believe she heard it right. The image of the settlement was stuck on the monitor, and the picture of the two Mwandans being chased by that enormous Locustan burned in her memory. They had to help. They couldn't just leave.

"I sense something . . . not good," Dakrhaeth replied. His regular chirpy tone had all but disappeared. "Have to leave before it gets close."

Ross rolled his eyes and shook his head. "What is it you sense?"

"I'm not sure. But we *have* to leave."

Lefrasi had stayed quiet for a long time, but now he spoke. "We can leave, but let's help these people below. We saw survivors."

"I agree," Ramya declared. "Dakrhaeth, do you follow?"

There was a pause, a somewhat hopeful pause. "I'll have to take the controls back from you then," Dakrhaeth said in a cold, dejected voice.

Ramya stiffened, her fingers curling around the flight stick possessively. "You're doing no such thing, Dakrhaeth. That's an order. Dakrhaeth! You can't—"

She couldn't finish the sentence. The control panel went dark as if the life had been turned out of the Stryker. Ross flashed a panicked look, and Ramya knew her face was just as horror-stricken.

"Dakrhaeth, stop this," she yelled, punching randomly at the buttons, hoping one would work.

None did. No one listened. The Stryker turned with a terrifying suddenness, tipping on its right wing, then righted itself and zoomed up toward the clouds. Ramya fell back against the seat, exhausted. In the minute before, she was concerned about the fates of the hapless Mwandans, but now she was not so sure even about her own life.

"All right, so what do we do?" Lefrasi broke the stunned silence.

"There's nothing we can do," Ramya replied, the realization of their helpless situation dawning slowly but surely. There was no escape hatch, no eject button on the Stryker that she knew of. They were stuck. "There's no way out unless Dakrhaeth lets us out. We go wherever he takes us."

"Let's hope he takes us back to the *Endeavor*."

There . . . an idea. Even if Dakrhaeth didn't tell them where he was going, the *Endeavor* could track them. She tapped the button of the communicator on the console. It stayed silent.

"The stupid AI must've cut off the link," Ross said through gritted teeth.

"Or maybe not," Ramya said. "They were switching channels, remember? Trying to contact the Mwandan HQ?"

Lefrasi shook his head. "You still have faith in this creature?" he asked, his gaze morose.

"Why the hell is it slowing?" Ross blurted just as Ramya sensed the slowdown of the Stryker. "And what in the name of the stars is that?"

Ramya forgot to breathe, her thoughts wiped clear in a heartbeat. She kept seeing and yet her brain registered nothing.

24

Ramya blinked. Her eyes were glued on the spectacle in front of her, but she couldn't answer Ross's question if she tried.

An enormous ship—almost the size of the *Endeavor*, if not slightly bigger—was flickering into sight ahead of them as it dropped out of the layer of clouds. It was shaped like a four-pointed star and almost iridescent. She'd never seen his ship before or even heard of before. It had to be Locustan, but how could that be possible?

Ramya blinked again, squinting as familiarity dawned and punched the air out of her guts. Those lines, that angle, the nose . . . her eyes scanned the contours in a mad rush. She knew these all too well.

These were Strykers. No, they had been Strykers. Now the four Strykers were connected somehow by a web of almost-translucent beams and bars, forming a deadly, monstrous, four-headed beast that stared down at them.

"Dakrhaeth, please tell me it's not what I think it is," Ramya whispered, not even expecting a reply. The massive craft looming ahead was undoubtedly and unmistakably hostile seeing the way the Stryker stopped and cowered like cornered prey.

"It's the others, Mihaal," Dakrhaeth whispered back. His voice seemed to have aged years in the last few minutes and Ramya could detect a whiff of futility in it.

"The four missing Strykers?" Ross asked what Ramya already knew. Habardein had said the Strykers morphed. This was what they had morphed into—a megaship woven together from individual units, forming a collective of sorts. Along with their metamorphosed pilots, it was laying the groundwork for the next invasion, conquering the galaxy from within.

"I failed you, Mihaal," Dakrhaeth said. "I have to go."

"Dakrhaeth, what do you mean? Go where?" Ramya asked, panic rising fast inside her.

"Be part of them, Mihaal." He paused a second and added drily, "I told you we should leave. Too late now."

A strange, low hum hit Ramya's ears. It swept over her in a wave, making her spine tingle. The Stryker lurched forward, its gait almost reluctant. Then it started to move, at a snail's pace, toward the towering megaship.

"No, no, no, no!" Ramya yelled.

"I have to," Dakrhaeth said. "Don't you hear them call?"

Next to her, Ross's fingers danced over the levers and switches at a frantic pace, but nothing he did stopped the Stryker or slowed it.

This was it. They were all going to be dead soon, or rather turned into Locustan soldiers. A thought, a desperate one, took shape in Ramya's mind. She sat up stiffly, staring dead ahead, planning.

"Dakrhaeth," Ramya called. She had to make this work. She could die, but her death could not be in vain. "Dakrhaeth, do something for me?"

"I told you, Mihaal, I cannot turn back," Dakrhaeth replied, his voice cracking.

"Not asking you to. Just send the visual of this ship to the *Endeavor*. Can you do that?"

There was a moment of silence. "Done, Mihaal."

Captain Milos, whenever he got back to checking on their channel, would find that picture. He could show it to the Confederacy, convince them on how real and immediate the threat was.

The megaship loomed ahead, and the closer they went, the louder the hum grew. Sweat trickled down Ramya's forehead, her ears buzzing painfully, the sound rattling her to the core. Her vision had long blurred but Ramya still saw the belly of the megaship open.

It's going to swallow us.

The hum grew to fever pitch. Ross plugged his ears with his

fingers and fell back into his seat, Lefrasi sat down with a loud thud. Ramya closed her eyes and tried to shut the noise out.

"Mihaal, I know," Dakrhaeth's said, clearly laboring to get his words out. "I know when they're coming. I know what the fading star is."

She wanted to ask how he knew, she wanted to know what he knew, but there was no time left. Her head seemed to crack open, the pain raw at the edges. Heaving to fill her lungs, Ramya struggled to string together her instruction. "Send everything to the *Endeavor*, Dakrhaeth. Everything you know. Everything!"

"I'll try, Mihaal."

Dakrhaeth's words had just about faded when the radio crackled.

"Commander," the captain called, his voice rushed. "Do you copy? What's your position?"

Any other time hearing the captain's voice would've brought relief and a hope that his presence would somehow get them out of the direst circumstances. Not this time. They were mired too far in an unsalvageable situation.

"No idea, Captain," Ross replied, his words coming in broken spurts. "We're being sucked into a gigantic ship."

"Sucked in?" The vehement voice didn't belong to Captain Milos. It was Trysten Kiroff's. "What's stopping you from turning around? Have you forgotten to fly a spacecraft, Lady Ramya?"

Ramya's nose crinkled. That was what he had to say to his soon-to-be-dead daughter? What was her father doing in the *Endeavor's* COM anyway?

"Of course I remember. How do you think I got so far?" she snapped. "The Strykers seems to be in some sort of a trance. They're calling him. There's a loud hum that's driving us crazy. It's just—"

"Quiet!" His voice cut through the buzz in her ears and the ache in her head. For a second, the world around her cleared. "Listen to me carefully, Rami," her father said, his voice slow and deliberate. "There's a green button, sort of a plunger, on the left of the console that says "Muffler." Press that. Now!"

"What? Why?"

Her father drew a sharp breath. "It's something we used to keep them from talking to each other. It might work in disrupting their call."

"Just do it, Rami. Now!" The captain's order came like an impatient whip. Ramya's hand thudded against the round mushroom-shaped button that sat conspicuously on one side.

In the following second, nothing happened. Then the hum ebbed, and then it disappeared completely as if a magic wand had been waved. The Stryker slowed slightly, and with a sharp screech, it rolled over and turned completely around. A tremor passed under Ramya's feet and the engines roared. Like a meteor, the Stryker shot out from under the megaship's shadow.

"Yes!" Ross yelled. The radio had been holding its breath and now it erupted in wild cheer. Ross raised a triumphant fist and turned backward to look at the megaship. His raised arm sagged a little. "We have a good head start at least."

One look and Ramya knew. The megaship's belly was closing. It was preparing to chase them down. Ramya's eyes narrowed, her gaze impinging on the web-like structure that held the Strykers together.

Ramya's fists clenched, nails digging into her palms and rousing the fury coiling in her guts. She was not going to run away. She had to strike back. She had to try one last thing.

"Dakrhaeth," she called. "What do you think of a fly-by over that beast?"

"Rami, no," Ross said, shaking his head vehemently. "Let's just try to outrun them. Maybe we can —"

Ramya held his gaze and made her case. "We can outrun them, Ross. But then what? They'll move on to the next planet and harvest it."

"We can't fight this huge thing, Rami. We have no backup. And we can't risk drawing the *Endeavor* into this fight."

"We can't eradicate it, but we can slow it down."

Ross sighed. Then shrugged. "All right. What's the plan?"

"You're sure of what you're about to do?" Lefrasi asked.

"Not really, no," Ramya said truthfully. She didn't see it clearly through yet, but she was going to try. She looked askance at the silent radio and took a deep breath.

"See those spindly connectors? That's what holds the four Strykers together. I'm betting those are the weakest links in that structure. If we can tear one down it'd make the whole thing unstable—"

"You're correct, Mihaal," Dakrhaeth said. "Those beams are quite newly generated. Not as sturdy. We might have a chance."

"Torpedoes?"

This time, the launch button lit up almost instantly. A flick of her wrist swung the Stryker back and facing the monstrous megaship. Ramya pressed on the throttle.

"Attack from over it." The radio crackled with her father's voice. "That structure's too bulky to turn very quickly to launch a weapon at you."

"Understood," Ramya replied. She tugged lightly at the flight stick, making a slight change of her path but not as much as to make the plan evident. She had to swing up and away when she was close enough, but keeping her path straight meant she had to stay in the path of fire.

"They're preparing to fire torpedoes, Mihaal."

"Shields up?"

"Yes, Mihaal."

"Here we go." Ramya's forced her aching fingers to press the throttle as much as possible.

A pair of torpedoes streaked out of the megaship, leaving a smoky trail through the atmosphere. Ramya waited until they were fearfully close. Then she tugged at the flight stick with all her might. The Stryker shot upward and over the pair of screeching projectiles.

The projectiles streaked past. And then swerved and turned around. Ramya's fingers on the throttle ached, but she pressed on. She aimed for the webs.

"Come on, come on," Ross said.

Lefrasi was staring at the torpedoes behind them. They were close, and getting closer. "Faster, Rami," he said.

"I'm trying," Ramya said through gritted teeth.

They were close. A few more seconds and she could make it between two of the main bars that connected the foremost units of the megaship.

"Brace for impact," Dakrhaeth's calm voice came just as an impact threw Ramya forward. A ball of fire erupted behind them and swirled around. A thunderous sound deafened Ramya for a second. Her vision blurred. But she held on, pointing the Stryker's nose at the bars.

A shrill alarm pierced her fragile consciousness. "Shields down to 35% Mihaal."

The last torpedo had burned through the Stryker's shield. They couldn't sustain another direct hit.

"Turbo boost, Dakrhaeth," Ramya yelled. She wanted to keep the boost for later, but if they couldn't shake off this torpedo, there wouldn't be a later.

"Rami!" Ross yelled. The boost kicked in right then. The Stryker shot through the bars and the space behind them exploded in another spectacular fireball. The Stryker wobbled from the aftershock before Ramya steadied it. She pointed its nose up and away from the megaship and pressed on the throttle.

"Are we hit?" she asked. The shield was still flashing at 32% and she hadn't felt an impact. But she needed to hear they were all right.

"No. The torpedo hit the Locustan ship," Ross reassured, looking over his shoulder. "Not sure if it did any damage, but they sure didn't expect it."

"Good, Rami!" Lefrasi said, thumping Ramya's shoulder.

"We have some more work to do before we're done here, guys,"

Ramya said. She tugged on the flight stick and the Stryker spun around.

Ramya zoomed toward the megaship at breakneck speed. The goliath started to tilt upward also, but it was far too slow. The Stryker reached firing range long before its target could swivel around.

Nearing the top of the megaship, Ramya swooped, guns pointed at the shiny black beams that held up two adjacent units. They'd have shields, but if she could penetrate it, the hit would cause enough instability. Enough, at least, for the pest to give up chasing them, as well as delay its plans of moving on to pillage the next planet.

She zoomed in close, and just before pulling up the flight stick to straighten the Stryker, she pressed the torpedo launch button. The area at the middle of the web of beams exploded in a wave of fire and a deafening boom.

"A hit, Mihaal. But the shield deflected most of it."

"We'll do it again then," Ramya declared. Beneath her the megaship was still turning, desperate to point its weapons on the Stryker. She didn't have too long to make this work.

Spinning the Stryker around to face the beams, she steadied the craft. "Better work this time," she whispered, and fired their last torpedo. The projectile streaked across space and slammed into the beams, forming a fiery ball at its center.

"Yes!" Ramya shot a fist into the air. She pulled the Stryker up and away from the megaship, feeling the reverberations from the explosion sweep through her. She saw the web twisting. It could fall apart, and even if it didn't, that megaship was far too unstable to move on to the next planet right away. They'd bought themselves a few hours to get Bucifer P9 quarantined if the Confederacy chose to believe them.

"Dakrhaeth," she called. "Back to the *Endeavor*, please."

"Surely, Mihaal."

The radio crackled and the captain's voice drifted out. "Great flying, Rami," he said. There was no mistaking the pride in his voice.

"You cut it dangerously close though."

"No one threatens my ship and goes about unpunished, Captain."

The captain chuckled. Ross reached out to pat Ramya's shoulder. "Good job, you," he said, eyes shining with appreciation.

"We're not out of trouble yet, Commander," Dakrhaeth said, candid as ever. "They'll come. They'll get us."

"Could you contact the Mwandan HQ, Captain?" Ross asked.

The captain's reply was prompt and grim. "We got no response."

The joy of a moment ago ebbed away in a blink.

"Well, we've done what we could," Lefrasi broke the stifling silence. "We've got evidence at least. The Confederacy will believe us now."

The captain didn't reply. Ramya knew that Captain Milos still didn't have much hope on the Confederacy.

Fixing her gaze on the clouds, Ramya fought the sting in her eyes. They couldn't do this alone. The Locustans were not a bunch of small-time space pirates they could take on and win. Heck, they barely just escaped today.

The galaxy's fate was as good as sealed.

Lefrasi sighed behind her, obviously coming to a similar realization. Next to her, Ross fidgeted.

"We'll find a way, with or without the Confederacy. Or anyone else," he said in a steadfast voice.

They could try. They *would* try. But the truth remained, stark as ever. They were too small. Too powerless to matter.

"We're not alone, Commander," the captain's voice came like a gust of wind. "We have the Berkari with us, and I'm sure Chief Dal has been able to find an ally in his government."

Ramya looked askance at Ross and his dim and still hopeless face. The Mwandans were good allies, but they needed more. They needed weapons and ships. No, they needed an endless fleet of powerful ships.

"Lord Paramount Kiroff," the captain addressed her father,

making Ramya frown immediately. Did the captain have to waste his breath? Trysten Kiroff wasn't one who'd budge, especially if it meant publicly going back on his decisions. Yet the captain didn't mind asking. "Where do you stand, Lord Paramount?"

Ramya sucked in a lungful of air, all her senses focused on the radio, which had fallen silent after the captain's question.

"Didn't we discuss that already, Captain?" His voice was sharp with an air of finality, and even though it conveyed an intent Ramya had expected, hearing it was disappointing as hell. The breath she'd been holding made its way out in a tormenting wave.

"Ah! So we did," the captain replied in a lighthearted, almost teasing tone. "Doesn't mean we can't talk about it again. You saw things today that you hadn't seen before. Smart men like yourself are not afraid to reassess their positions."

Her father chuckled. "You're playing me, Captain. I'm smart enough to understand that also."

"No, Trysten, I'm *not* playing you." The captain's voice had turned dead serious. "I'm appealing to your good sense. If we don't prepare right now, it might be too late to save the galaxy."

"I know. That's why I've already ordered my factories to ramp up production." Trysten Kiroff paused. Ramya sat up. She almost pinched herself to make sure she was not in a dream. Her father continued in a casual way. "Every ship on the assembly lines is being stockpiled. Yours when you need then, Captain."

Ramya's mouth fell open and she sank back slowly into her seat. Could he really mean that? From the silence all around her and on the radio, it was clear that she was not the only one stunned.

Then Captain Milos broke the silence. "Abelei would be proud."

"I would be a fool to let an opportunity like this slip. Wars are when fortunes are made, Captain Milos. This one is no different."

It would be a lie to say his reply didn't bother Ramya in the slightest. But she didn't let it cloud her happiness. It didn't matter so much as why Trysten Kiroff chose to support Captain Milos, but the fact that he chose to be on the right side. Hope was very much alive.

Ramya placed her aching finger back on the throttle and pushed. She couldn't wait to get back. They couldn't save Chief Mifek and his people but they had done quite all right in the end, even her father. Smiling, she fixed her sight on the small speck in the sky — the *Endeavor*. It was still far, but it was growing steadily bigger as the Stryker zoomed homeward. Maybe not for long, but they were safe at least for the moment.

An Excerpt
The Final Resistance
(Dark Universe Series - Book 3)

The galaxy was as good as lost. Even as Ramya forcefully tightened the collar of her parka and prepared for the long trek into the Hinterlands, she had little hope within her heart. Or confidence. In barely fifteen days, the galaxy as she had known it was teetering. And that was even before the Hive arrived. Starbase Zeta was partially destroyed, and Locustan Shadowhives kept trickling in through the wormhole. Captain Milos was at Anomaly Point along with every Confederacy squadron that was available. But the allies were taking hits, one after the other, hardly able to contain the Locustan waves.

How long would they be able to hold off the invaders? Not very long, Ramya was certain. Unless they found a different way to thwart the pests. In other words, hope rested on finding some information the Unosi left behind. The Hinterland was home to the Unosi archives, Dakrhaeth had said. That was what his Locustan squadron was tasked to destroy, so there would be no known way of stopping them. They would come again. They'd come the first chance they got to slip past the defense Captain Milos had put up. If only Ramya and her team could reach the Unosi archives before they did.

"Ready, Kiroff?" Gael Arlington's voice, sharp and insistent, made her stir. He, his GSO compatriots, as well as Chief Dal and Lefrasi, were dressed like her, covered from head to foot in thick leathers and furs to protect themselves in the freezing climate of Kyo-Sedra-8. They were all heavily armed as well, just as she was with a Meson Cannon.

"Yes, let's go," she replied in a robust voice, turning the viewer of her HUD on. The cramped tunnel, rocks jutting out in strange and often grotesque shapes, flickered into view. The Hinterland was about a half hour's walk from the mouth of the underground cave network, and the group started off, alert and weapons drawn, along the main vein of the cave with Gael's chief point, Amireh, leading the way. Gael and Ramya walked side-by-side after him, and the rest of the team followed behind in units of two.

For a second Ramya missed Fenny and Ross. They were a unit; they fit together. She felt safe around them, even in the direst of circumstances. Being with the GSO, and particularly Gael Arlington, was different. But this had to be done. The captain couldn't spare his commander or his navigator for the mission, as they were needed to hold off the Locustan onslaught. Then they had to use the Stryker to bring them here, a task only Ramya could carry out. Her father, Trysten Kiroff, had asked for support from the GSO, and Ramya had to agree that strategically they were the best option. Still, it was hard totally trusting Gael and his people.

Ramya took a long and bracing breath, the cold air chilling the inside of her nose. Well, at least Chief Dal and Lefrasi were here.

The sauntered along, their feet crunching under the ground in silence. After some time, Gael shot a curious look at her, his blue eyes piercing. "You're awfully quiet," he whispered.

Ramya barely managed to suppress a terrible need to roll her eyes. They were on a critical mission and he expected her to be chatty? "I have nothing to talk about," she said in as quiet a voice as possible.

"Not happy your father put us together on a team?" he asked, clearly unable or unwilling to take the hint to shut up. He wasn't far from the truth though. It irked her endlessly that her father had suggested Gael accompany her even though it was likely Trysten Kiroff was not working the matchmaking angle at the moment. But Ramya couldn't shake off the idea or the discomfort entirely.

"Not happy that this may be our only chance of survival," she said, forcing her thoughts in a weightier direction. "I can't believe it got to this so quickly."

"Well, you should be proud that you were on the right side all along," he said with a shake of his head. "As a matter of fact, you sounded the alarm early. And that helped. The shame's not on you."

Wasn't it? They had all gotten too happy with the temporary peace, busy with frivolous festivities and petty squabbles to remember the immense threat that had never quite gone away. The shame was on all of them. There was no avoiding it.

Gael seemed to sense her thoughts. "All right, maybe we're all to blame for not paying attention. But—"

He stopped abruptly, raising a fisted hand to signal the party behind them to stop. About twenty paces ahead, Amireh had stopped near a bend in the tunnel, his fist raised. Ramya's fingers tightened around her weapon as they stepped closer to Amireh, her heart skipping a beat or two. Her breath hitched in her throat when she looked around the bend and she forgot to blink.

-End of excerpt-

GLOSSARY

The Characters:

Ramya Kiroff -- Protagonist of the Dark Universe. Seventeen-year-old Ramya has a life anyone in the galaxy would give anything to have. But only Ramya knows, it's far from perfect. Her father, Trysten Kiroff is the richest man in the galaxy and he has impossible expectations of her. All her life she tries to prove her worth to him, but fails. When she's taken to task for dishonorable conduct at CAWStrat, her father terminates her education. Furthermore, he threatens her with a marriage to benefit his business and the family. With no way to avoid her father's punishment, Ramya sneaks out of CAWStrat and hitches a ride on the Endeavor.

Captain Terenze Milos – Veteran of the Confederate Space Fleet, Captain Milos is the legendary hero of the Locusta-Vanga War. His stand against the Locustans during the first Locustan invasion brought the galaxy back from the brink of extinction. He offers Ramya the job of the medic's assistant when she rescues the Stryker's pilot on Nikoor. She doesn't reveal her true identity but it is revealed later that he knew she was Trysten Kiroff's daughter. Captain Milos also served with Abelei Kiroff, Ramya's grandfather and Trysten's father, while in the Space Fleet.

The *Endeavor* -- Battlecruiser-turned-freighter commanded by Captain Terenze Milos. Home to our protagonists, the ship is a Class II battleship, from before the Locusta-Vanga War. One of many battered battleships discarded by the Space Fleet after the Locusta-Vanga War, it was salvaged from a junkyard by Captain Milos and later repaired. The *Endeavor* is antiquated but has a sound frame and is well maintained. The crew of the *Endeavor* is fiercely loyal to the ship.

Commander Ross Pornell – Second-in-command of the *Endeavor*. He is at the helm when the *Endeavor* comes across the debris field of destroyed GSO spaceships. He changes course and orders the investigation of the beacon for help. Quiet but contentious at times, Ross wants to impress Captain Milos of his competence, more so because of his legendary stature and his newly hired status. Ross is snappish to Ramya and suspicious about her. However, he saves Ramya when a deadly Pterostrich chick attacks. He also accompanies her in the Stryker during the final showdown with Admiral Kanaa at Totori.

Fenny -- Navigator of the *Endeavor*. Foul-mouthed and opinionated, Ramya often describes Fenny as a pocket-sized powerhouse. She can navigate a spaceship, wield a cannon, or nurse a Pterostrich chick with equal ease. She befriends Ramya from the moment they meet, becoming more of a confidante to her as time passes.

Wiz -- Pilot of the *Endeavor*. He is a nervous sort of a person, easily worried over small matters.

Flux -- Engineer of the *Endeavor*. He is seldom seen outside his cave, the *Endeavor's* engineering bay. Although extremely skillful and smart, Flux is often overextended and has trouble keeping the old ship in top shape.

Sosa -- Norgoran medic of the *Endeavor*. Sosa is anything but ordinary. Eclectic to stir-crazy, she is fiercely loyal to Captain Milos, whom she has known for decades. She is also the only person on the ship who calls Captain Milos by his first name. Ramya addresses Sosa as Domina, which is a respectful title for a Norgoran of high birth, and what comes naturally to Ramya on seeing Sosa's regal bearing and age. Sosa is also the masterful maker and mixer of potent concoctions, particularly her signature "Pax."

Habardein -- Original pilot of the last Stryker. He is rescued when the *Endeavor's* crew salvages the Stryker from the debris field in Sector 22. He wants to report the incident at Sector 22 to his employer Trysten Kiroff which goes against the directive of the Space Command. When stopped, he sneaks out of the *Endeavor* and is beaten up by a pair of thugs until Ramya rescues him. His injuries are grievous and he soon slips into a coma. He regains consciousness for a bit and recognizes Ramya as Trysten Kiroff's daughter. He tells Ramya about the Stryker before his condition worsens again.

The *Stryker* — A space fighter designed by Kiroff Industries in Sector 22. It has imbedded Locustan technology, with a Locustan Viriskshi (AI) controlling the major components of the craft. The Stryker is paired with a pilot who is the only person allowed to control over the AI. Directives from the Kiroff family can override all other directives in a properly functional Stryker.

Dakrhaeth -- An AI aboard the last Stryker, or as Dakrhaeth likes to call himself, the soul of the ship. Dakrhaeth is smart as he is snarky. A Locustan Viriskshi whose craft had crashed into Kyo-Sedra-5 along with its squadron lay buried for years in the frozen planet until Kiroff Industries discovered and resuscitated them. He considers Trysten Kiroff his creator and mistakes Ramya to be her father during the initial genetic scan. He addresses Ramya as "Mihaal" which means creator in Locustan tongue. He allows Ramya access into the Stryker and bonds with her.

Trysten Kiroff – Ramya's father and the leader of House Kiroff is an enigma. During his time, House Kiroff has grown into a galactic powerhouse. He's shrewd, ruthless, and indomitable. Even though the Confederate Senate is the seat of power in the galaxy, it is said, real power is in Trysten Kiroff's hands. To Ramya he's always dismissive and cold. He holds her to impossibly high standards. Ramya believes that being a female firstborn, she has let down her father since the moment she was born.

Lynden Kiroff -- Lynden is the younger brother of Trysten and Ramya's uncle. He is currently serving in the Senate where Trysten Kiroff is said to have placed him.

Brynden Kiroff -- Brynden is the youngest brother of Trysten and Ramya's other uncle. He's the black sheep of the Kiroff family who left CAWStrat before graduating and vanished. He's supposed to have left for the Fringe to wrest the Kiroff family hearth from the usurper, Callen Moanu, and bring honor back to the family. However, he's not been heard of since. Ramya has fond memories of Uncle Bryn and when she leaves CAWStrat, she wants to follow Brynden's footsteps to the Fringe and complete his quest of regaining the Kiroff hearth.

Abelei Kiroff – Ramya's grandfather and Trysten's father. Abelei was a member of the Confederate Space Fleet and one of the first to face the Locustans during the first invasion and perish. Ramya's memory of her grandfather is faded, but she remembers him as courageous and upright. Captain Milos served with Abelei Kiroff during his time in the Space Fleet.

Sonya Kiroff – Ramya's mother and Trysten's socialite wife. She likes spending time with her galaxy-trotting friends more than with her family. To Ramya, Sonya's presence is like a specter, she's never really there, even when she's physically next her.

Armand Danukis -- Scion of House Danukis and a staunch enemy of House Kiroff and Ramya. He insults Ramya's mother after he's lost a duel to Ramya. This causes Ramya to lose her temper and she punches Armand in the face and draws blood. This is considered dishonorable conduct at the CAWStrat and Ramya is threatened to with expulsion from CAWStrat.

Istapol Maroni -- Trainer at CAWStrat who is present at the duel between Armand and Ramya. He is also a veteran of the Confederate Space Fleet.

Callen Moanu -- Usurper of the original Kiroff hearth. After losing the hearth to the Moanus, the Kiroffs were branded hearth-less vagrants as was custom during the time when the galaxy was settled. The mark has stayed on the family since, even though they are currently the richest and most powerful house in the galaxy. Over the centuries, many a Kiroff has tried to wrest the family hearth back from the Moanus but none have succeeded.

Leona Calibe -- Administrator at the CAWStrat. She's fond of taking Ramya to task for the smallest of issues. Ramya suspects she likes to show her power over Ramya to take shots at Trysten Kiroff who is otherwise unsurmountable. Leona's threat to send Ramya packing for punching an offensive classmate makes Trysten pull Ramya out of CAWStrat instead.

Isbet – Ramya's best friend at CAWStrat. She is one of the younger daughters of a lesser noble families with insignificant standing in the galaxy. Isbet's network of spies at CAWStrat ensures she's on top of every breaking news in the galaxy. She also holds her year's flying record, much to the annoyance of her male counterparts. Isbet has two dreams: join the GSO and marry Rownack, a handsome senior at CAWStrat.

CSA Stevan Helves/Lieutenant Gael Arlington -- Ramya bumps into a mysterious stranger in blue GSO uniform during her last gala at CAWStrat and dances the last Decosset with him. She lies about her identity and unknown to Ramya at the time, he does the same. Later, she finds out his real name, Gael Arlington. He belongs to one of House Kiroff's major competitors, House Arlington. Gael serves as a Lieutenant of the GSO and commands a state-of-the-art Cutlass but is allied with Trysten Kiroff. He tries to secure the last Stryker but Captain Milos outmaneuvers him and the *Endeavor* escapes.

Wultoph Aristide -- A lesser lord and ally of Trysten Kiroff. Wultoph is a known spokesperson for Trysten.

Admiral Kanaa -- Admiral of the Confederate Space Fleet. She wants to destroy the last Stryker and the *Endeavor* along with it. She has known Captain Milos from his days in the Space Fleet.

The Places

Sector 22 – A largely uninhabited sector where Kiroff Industries has a secret research center and factory for conducting experiments with Locustan technology. A large GSO fleet stationed in this sector is eviscerated by unknown forces with a lone survivor—the Stryker, a space fight imbedded with Locustan tech. This precipitates the event of the Dark Universe.

Kyo-Sedra-5 – The fifth planet of the Kyo-Sedra star system where the secret Kiroff factory is located. This is where a squadron of Locustan spacecrafts had crashed during the first invasion.

Nikoor – Home planet of the Kiroffs and the location of

CAWStrat. It is classified a prime planet because CAWStrat is situated on it.

Somenvaar – Home estate of House Kiroff.

The Fringe -- A group of quasi-autonomous star systems at the northern outskirts of Confederacy space.

Totori – Star system neighboring the system of Alameda, known for its mineral-rich asteroid belt.

Alameda -- A prime planet and the seat of the GSO. It is also home to the Kiroffs' staunchest rivals, the Arlingtons.

NAB -- Noxillian Asteroid Belt. It is a mineral-rich belt off the AP at Totori. Captain Milos plans to drop off the Stryker on one of the asteroids during the handover with Admiral Kanaa.

Kashiyap – Star system near Totori with one habitable planet, the Mwandan sanctuary Morris II.

Morris II – A planet in the Kashiyap system, a Mwandan sanctuary.

Anomaly Point -- Anomaly Point is the gateway to the Locustan world. It is a wormhole that closed at the end of the Locusta-Vanga war. It has stayed closed since, but the worry remained that it could open again someday. Not knowing why it had opened and how to stop it in case it did again, the Confederacy has since erected stationary defenses in the area and positioned several Confederacy fleets around it.

The Terms

COM – Core Operations Module. It is the command center of the *Endeavor*, a scaled-down version of a ship's bridge.

SLH – Super Luminal Highway. These are a network of wormholes discovered when the galaxy was settled that interconnects the various colonized systems. Spacecraft can move through it at faster-than-light speeds. It is not yet known who built them and when, but without the SLH, the Galactic Confederacy could not exist.

SL mode – Super Luminal mode, also known as Faster Than Light or FTL mode. This is the mode spacecraft switch to when entering the SLH. Outside the SLH network, spacecraft can use the ordinary mode.

AP – Access Point. A gate that allows entry into the SLH. There is usually one AP per star system.

Galactic Confederacy – An alliance of four races—human, Norgoran, Mwandan, and the Octus. They are bound by laws that are passed by the Galactic Senate.

Confederate Space Command -- The top leadership of the Confederate Space Fleet.

GSO -- Galactic Special Ops. It is the premiere defense agency of the Galactic Confederacy, where most students of the CAWStrat hope to score an internship. GSO recruits take a ten-year vow of celibacy when they "don the blue."

CAWStrat -- Commerce, Administration, and Warcraft Strategy Institute, or CAWStrat. A premier institute in the galaxy where the scions of every notable family trains before taking up a vocation of choice.

Norgoran – One of the allied races that form the Galactic Confederacy. They are green-skinned humanoids with long life spans.

Mwandan – One of the aboriginal races of the galaxy, and currently allied with the Confederacy.

The Events

Locusta-Vanga War – The Locusta-Vanga War began a decade before the events of Dark Universe. It started with the opening of a wormhole at Anomaly Point through which Locustan swarms arrived at the galaxy. The war almost pushed the galaxy to the brink of extinction and only ended when the wormhole closed. There have been no signs of the wormhole reopening. Regardless, the Confederacy has since erected stationary defenses in the area and positioned several Confederacy fleets around it.

About the Author

Alex Sheppard has always wanted to be an author. And even though that dream eluded Alex for a long time, now, finally, the ducks seem to have lined up. This is the second of Alex's space opera series.

When not obsessively guzzling books (mostly scifi), tinkering with gadgets and gizmos, and wrangling rambunctious little ones, Alex likes to write.

Want to follow Alex's adventures in the writing world? Check out https://thefarworlds.com.

www.ingramcontent.com/pod-product-compliance
Lightning Source LLC
Chambersburg PA
CBHW030918120626
46554CB00001B/198